Fire & Ice

T.L. Heinrich

Contents

Summer 1963

CHAPTER ONE

B ullets pinged against the rusty old car and the graffiti tagged tenement behind Colleen. She grit her teeth and hoped to god the people in the building had thought to close their windows when the bullets started flying.

It was sweltering in High Tide this summer, more than it had been when she'd left a month ago for a trip down the Great River of Red Rock. The turf war between her mother, Tina Knight and the mysterious crime boss known only as Von had been raging since the day she got back. Von had been content for over a decade to stay in his territory of Devil's Own, and he hadn't made a single demand before trying to kill Tina a month ago outside of Cherry's Restaurant so his reasons for starting this turf war were a mystery to everyone.

Right after that incident, Tina sent Colleen to rescue a powered child that was being transported on a steam boat down the Great River. While Colleen had been running from corporate thugs that wanted to control the powers of the child and government agents who wanted to kill them, Tina had tried to bring Von to the table to talk peace. Von absolutely refused to show, and now here they were, neck deep in a war that was finally starting to show signs of ending.

Colleen knew that she and Rick, her mother's right hand man, had worn the old man down over the past three weeks until his forces were bare bones. She had no idea why Von had decided to attack this part of High Tide now, when he was barely holding his organization together. There was nothing here but old apartment buildings and the occasional small corner market. Tina didn't own anything nearby so why were they here? She'd been patrolling when she'd heard the shots and tried to take control of the situation. Her fireballs had scared the men at first, then they'd laid down more gunfire, turning the whole thing into a standoff.

The only thing Colleen could think of was that this was Von at his most desperate, trying anything to get an upper hand.

And if he IS desperate, then that means we're close to winning.

Another barrage of bullets sent sparks flying from the rust bucket Colleen was taking shelter behind and she swore.

"Great job, Fahrenheit," Rick said a few feet away.

His dark eyes were hard as granite as he pierced her with his gaze.

"This is my fault?" she spat.

"We had this under control until you started throwing fire!"

More bullets pinged against the car.

"Yeah, I can see that."

Rick fired across the street and ducked back down to reload.

"We're running out of ammo."

"And so are they."

"So what, we're supposed to wait this out?"

Colleen knew that was a terrible idea before the words were out of Rick's mouth.

The police had been nothing if not attentive to High Tides' rising gang war, though they didn't really care who got caught in the cross fire of their solution to the problem.

If they waited too long to get all of this under control, the cops would show up and then she'd really have a mess on her hands.

Colleen surveyed the terrain across the street, peeking up just enough to see over the hood of the old car.

Garbage was strewn along the wall of the tenement across the street, but not much. There was a store on the corner, just barely out of the reach of the fight. She could see Von's men hiding behind their cars across the street just like Tina's men were.

"I'll lay down some fire," Colleen said, "you and the rest follow me out and cover me. It should be enough to keep them behind their barrier. Then we can out flank them. I go left, you go right."

Rick swore under his breath and nodded.

She knew he hated taking orders from her, but she also knew that he wasn't stupid enough to let his pride cost him, and his men, their lives.

And if he let me die, my mother would kill him.

The order was relayed down the line and once everyone was ready, Rick nodded to Colleen. She took a deep breath, and drew power up through her veins and into her palms. In seconds, it covered her hands like a glove and she could feel the heat through every pore of her body. The world turned bright, like an over exposed photograph. She grinned, feeling at home in the furnace of her powers, and jumped to her feet, a blazing beacon that would be easy to hit.

Just as Von's men jumped to their feet, she unleashed a line of fire at their cars. The men yelped and jumped back down, but not before a few bullets had made their way from the bastards' guns. Colleen heard one of Tina's men yell and fall, but she didn't flinch. This was the gig. If they wanted to be a hired gun, they took a chance at dying.

Colleen advanced and began lobbing fire balls, instead of continuing the steady stream of fire, which would've depleted her faster.

The men behind her were firing, catching the thugs that she didn't see right away and just keeping the rest down.

We could actually do this without losing one civilian.

That's when a stray bullet grazed her shoulder and Colleen lost her focus, crying out at the unexpected pain. Three of Von's men took the opportunity as Colleen was distracted to run from behind the cars and into the tenement building. She swore under her breath and ran after them.

"Fahrenheit!" Rick yelled.

"You've got this," she replied over her shoulder.

She wasn't about to let Von's men loose in a tenement where innocent people would be seen as acceptable collateral damage.

Colleen went through the creaking door, the small entry way dark, and glass crunched under her feet. The smell of fried foods and something that might've been old beer or urine stung her nostrils. She could hear footsteps above her and the sound of someone banging on a door. If Von's men got into an apartment, it would be near impossible not to hurt or kill someone trying to get them out.

A distant siren wailed and Colleen wondered if they were headed here or somewhere else in High Tide. Cops rarely cared to come to the tenements for an actual emergency, preferring instead to harass the residents for petty or imaginary infractions.

She raced up the stairs and was met with gun fire that landed a few inches from her feet on the stairs.

These places are fire traps so I have to be very careful.

When the bullets paused, Colleen took the stairs two at a time and came face to face with the gunman. He sneered at her and leveled his gun in her face. Colleen leapt to the side as he fired and closed her hands around the barrel. Pushing heat fast into her palm, she melted the metal enough to bend it down. The rush of power left her a little light headed but she ignored it.

Colleen punched the man across his stunned face as she pulled the gun out of his hand, then delivered a knee to his groin for good measure. He fell to the steps and groaned as another man came up behind her. He aimed straight for her head and she ducked down. The blast shredded the already crumbling plaster over her head, raining white particles down on her hair.

Her fiery gaze blazed hotter as fury coursed through her veins. The man's eyes widened as if realizing his mistake. He raised his weapon again but not before Colleen burnt the man's shirt front. He panicked, even as Colleen recalled the flames before they could do any real damage, and the gun went off again. This time, the bullets zinged past Colleen and she heard a wet gasp behind her. She looked back to see the man she'd hit in the groin clutching his chest, which was now a bloody mess.

The vigilante seized the sawed off shot gun and clocked the man across the head with it. He fell down the stairs and lay still at the bottom.

Colleen ran to the man who'd been shot, but his eyes were already blank. She closed them and heard someone a floor above trying to force his way into an apartment.

Taking the stairs two at a time, Colleen made it just as the goon had splintered the cheap wood of the door.

"Hey!" she yelled, her voice causing the man to jump and turn around. "Why don't you pick on someone your own size?"

"It wasn't supposed to go this way."

"Yeah? How was it supposed to go?"

"With you as a greasy smear on the pavement."

He raised the shot gun and fired. Colleen flung herself to the side, just barely dodging the bullets. Someone yelled and a baby started to wail in one of the apartments. The goon pushed his way through the open door, and a woman screamed in terror. Colleen scrambled to her feet and ran into the apartment where he was holding a young woman in front of him, a gun pressed to her temple. Tears fell down her cheeks as she sobbed.

"You back off bitch or I'll spray her brains all over this place!"

No word could make Colleen angrier than the one this man had just spat at her. Her vision went bright once again and molten heat filled her.

"I mean it!" he said, voice screeching in time to the woman's loud cries.

Colleen studied him for a moment. He was shaking, sweat coursing down his forehead that had little to do with the extreme heat of the night.

I think he's bluffing, that he's out of bullets. Or…he doesn't think I care and he's scared of me. Either way, can I get to him before he hurts the woman?

With her hands down by her sides, Colleen took a tiny bit of fire and rolled it into a marble shaped ball. She'd only just started practicing with small fire projectiles, and her aim had improved, but it wasn't perfect. And to make this work, to make sure she saved the woman, Colleen needed it to be perfect.

A month ago, she'd been in a similar standoff, with Karen's fiancé, David, holding a gun to the little powered girl named Judy's head. Colleen had been so scared that he'd kill the girl or Karen, that she had misjudged and ended up burning the man to a crisp, getting Karen severely injured in the process. The vigilante was determined that this time, things would be different.

Because if it isn't, the whole tenement goes up like dry tinder.

The seconds dragged on and Colleen had to make a decision.

"Let her go," the vigilante said, holding the marble between her middle finger and thumb. "You can have me."

The man snorted.

"You think I'm stupid?"

"No. I think you're scared. No sense taking it out on her, is there? And if you bring me in, maybe boss man gives you a big fat bonus or promotion."

The man's face was an open book, and Colleen could read the conflict clear as day. The moment his gun swung in her direction, Colleen flicked the marble at the man's face. It hit him on the cheek and he flinched, the shock causing him to squeeze the trigger. There was one bullet left in his gun and it just barely managed to miss Colleen.

She rushed him, tackling the man to the threadbare carpet in the apartment. With two quick punches to his face, the goon was out and Colleen turned her attention to the hostage.

The young woman sat huddled on the couch, sobbing into her hands. The vigilante wanted to hug her or touch her shoulder to let her know it was all over, but experience had taught Colleen that, even though people saw her as a hero in High Tide, they were also a little afraid of her. So she stood near the woman and knelt down, trying to catch the woman's eye.

"You're alright," she said. "It's over now."

"Th-thank you, Fahrenheit."

"You're welcome."

Sirens pierced the humid night. They were close and Colleen could see the lights approaching from the window of the living room.

"What do I tell them?" asked the woman.

Colleen took hold of the assailant's ankles and began dragging him out of the apartment.

"If they ask you, tell them the truth."

The woman nodded, her fear now a different thing. Sometimes the truth was not proof against the brutality of an officer who was determined to get what they wanted.

Colleen managed to drag the man to his partner at the foot of the stairs and dug some cable ties out of a pouch on her belt. She had never asked Tina where she'd gotten these, but she was very grateful that her mother had insisted that she take some. It was a matter of pride for her that Fahrenheit had never killed anyone in High Tide.

Wonder how long I can maintain this kind of streak. After all, I am my mother's daughter.

The thought left a sour taste in her mouth and the phantom memory of burning flesh from the small town of Haven, where she'd been just a month ago, in her mind. Men from a government agency called the Bulwark, who hunted powered people, raided the Haven searching for her and Judy, whose powers of sonic screams would make a powerful weapon. Though they'd tried to minimize the casualties, it had gotten out of control rather quickly, and Colleen had killed many of the agents. But not before they'd set fire to the town, forcing Colleen to absorb a huge amount of heat into her body. It had sent her into a coma, and when she'd awakened, Colleen's powers had become stronger, more volatile than before. And even though Karen had tried to tell her that the deaths of those men wasn't her fault, that she had been trying to protect innocent people, Colleen still had a hard time accepting that.

The sirens were out front by the time she managed to tie the man's wrist to one of his friends' ankles. She had to get out of here, and fast.

There was a back entrance below her on the first floor and Colleen took off down the rickety stairs, nearly falling on her face when she tripped on a broken step. The police barged in just as she reached the basement stairs.

"Halt, police!" someone ordered.

Shots rang out after her as Colleen raced through the dark basement hallway to the door. When she burst through, she found herself in a narrow alley with a chain link fence at the end where it let out to the next street over. The door banged closed behind her, alerting the police at the other end of the alley to her presence. More gunshots as feet pounded the broken concrete behind her. Colleen didn't even bother looking back, putting on more speed until she reached the tall fence. The men behind her slowed and Colleen knew that they thought she was cornered.

With a grin, she pushed heat into her hands and pressed them to the chain link. It melted in seconds and she slipped through, pushing more heat into the burnt edges of the fence. If the cops tried to come through that way, they'd risk some nasty burns.

Left or right made no difference, so Colleen continued across the street where more tenements sat with claustrophobic distance from one another. There was no space for alleys, so she ran alongside the buildings toward the next block. The police would be getting in their squad cars, some staying to take care of Von's men, but the rest would be trying to catch the vigilante that was making their harassment of the High Tide residents ten times harder than they'd like.

Her side was starting to hurt, but Colleen ignored it as she turned the corner, smack into a patrol car that had nothing to do with the group she'd just left.

An officer jumped out and drew his weapon.

"Stop!" he said, firing without giving her a chance.

She skidded to a stop and fell on her knee, cursing the pain that shot through her joint. The cop ran around his car, eyes wide as he trained the pistol on her.

Colleen threw a fire ball at his feet, not intending to hit him. It was enough to make the man stop in his tracks, shock and fear twisting his blocky features.

The vigilante sprang to her feet and ran as best she could with her knee throbbing. There was a small grocer half a block away that she'd helped two weeks ago and he'd told her that she could hide in his basement if she ever needed.

She jumped the fence behind his business and grunted when she landed, her knee protesting. Heart racing, Colleen felt along the wall for the loose brick the grocer had told her about.

Sirens were getting closer now, and Colleen wondered if her luck had simply run out when she found the key and unlocked the old, squeaky door to the basement.

It was cool and dark, her eyes adjusting slowly to the lack of light. She slid down the door and sat on the cool, cement floor as sirens careened past. She knew they'd keep looking for her all night, and that she'd have to wait a while before attempting to go back to her apartment but she was safe, and that's what mattered.

Once her heart slowed and her powers were a sleeping behemoth in her veins, the words of the last goon shot through her mind and Colleen frowned. She'd wondered why Von's men had been here, what purpose it would serve when he was so depleted.

"Maybe they were here for me…maybe it was a trap…huh. I guess I riled the old bastard more than I thought."

She grinned, knowing that she'd foiled what would likely be Von's last, desperate attempt to win this stupid turf war.

"Wait till I tell Tina."

It was well past midnight by the time Colleen made it back to her apartment over Wanda's Bar and Grill. Her door creaked as she opened it to reveal the studio apartment with its sparse furnishings. She remembered her previous apartment, the rich red and orange walls and rugs, her carefully tended houseplants and treasured prints of framed art work. Some of it had been salvaged by Tina and stored for her, but most of it had been trashed by Grandfather. One print by Lois Mailou Jones had survived, as did her collection of Zora Neale Hurston books. But everything else had been slashed and ripped up by her Grandfather when she'd refused to come back to the family business. That was before Tina had orchestrated her own father's death and taken over the family business, before Red Rock, and before this war.

Unopened paint cans stood against one wall in the living area with unused brushes stacked on top. Two small houseplants were trying to thrive near the largest of her two windows and a bright green afghan lay on her low bed. She hadn't been able to find the energy to paint the bare white walls, or get rugs for the worn hardwood floors, so her apartment looked much like a monk's quarters - sparse and functional.

Regardless, Colleen was grateful for a place in the center of High Tide where she could come and go at all hours without stirring too much suspicion. But it didn't feel like a home.

Not like it had when I worked with Marco. Or hell, even on the run with Karen and Judy.

Before rescuing Judy and reconnecting with Karen for that brief time last month, Colleen had worked for Marco as a secretary. That is, until a case had forced her to be honest about her powers and Marco to be honest about his. Together, they'd uncovered a secret lab under Lumis Chemical where powered children were experimented on and turned into living weapons. It was also where her brother, Andrew, had been held and enhanced, though he'd volunteered for it.

At the end of all they'd experienced, Marco had become her best friend. They'd planned to have a private investigator agency together. But then his old flame needed his help in Jet City, and Marco ended up staying there to make a life with the woman he loved.

She sank onto her bed and sat there, staring down at her hands. Her body felt like one big bruise, sweat trickling down the sides of her body and back. She had to do inventory downstairs and set up the bar for the lunch crowd before she could even think of sleeping. Yet Colleen couldn't seem to bring herself to move. The only thing she could do was let the hot tears run down her face and onto her open hands.

She had gotten used to not having Marco around, though she missed him terribly. But letting herself love Karen again, opening herself up to caring for Judy, it all meant that when she had to let them go, the space they had once occupied was now left hollow and painful.

"It's been a month. When will this just go away?" she asked, closing her eyes.

Indulging in pity had never been Colleen's way, but these feelings seemed to have a mind of their own and wouldn't take no for an answer when it came to spilling out.

So, she sat there, crying it all out until her eyes dried and the memory of Karen's lips against hers didn't make her chest feel like it was caving in. She couldn't contact the fiery red head, not since she'd decided to return to the Bulwark and try to change it from the inside out. But, there was one person she could call.

A glance at the telephone had her reaching for it before Colleen could stop herself. Judy's number at Marco's school for powered children, Champions Academy, had been memorized for weeks now but still she hesitated. It was late there, but that wasn't why Colleen couldn't bring herself to dial it.

If I call, she'll never move on…and neither will I.
The phone clattered when she dropped it back in its cradle and she buried her face in her hands.

"This is ridiculous!" she said after a few more minutes of crying. "We made our choices, and this life isn't so bad."

The words sounded empty and unconvincing to her ears but Colleen pushed all that aside. What was the point of crying over this? She couldn't get them back and didn't want them here in this mess anyway.

Best to be alone for now and focus on finishing all this than drag someone else into Tina's mess with me.
She stood to her feet and wiped the tears from her cheeks, nodding at the determination that straightened her shoulders.

"Nice cold shower then to work. That's what I need."
The sweat had cooled a bit on her skin, causing the Fahrenheit suit to stick to her. Peeling it off was damn uncomfortable and she winced at the smell.

"I'll have to ask Tina to get this cleaned," she said, hanging it up in the back of her closet. "Good thing she's making me a spare."

The cold water felt like pure heaven against her skin. Though her power was within her, it warmed her body to a higher degree than others. The heat wave that had captured High Tide was miserable for most, and down-right hell for Colleen. Steam rose from her skin for half the shower and when it stopped, Colleen was reluctant to leave. But water was expensive, and she couldn't stick Wanda with a high bill, not after she'd given Colleen an apartment on such short notice.

And a job, which I need to get to.

With a sigh, Colleen turned the water off. She stood there, naked and wet, letting the tiny breeze from her windows drift over her skin before drying off. The cool cotton of a sleeveless shirt and Bermuda shorts was perfect after the stickiness of the suit.

The whole thing took barely half an hour, but something reset in Colleen just the same and she ran down the stairs with a focused determination.

Until her knee gave a twinge, that is.

"Damn it! I don't have time for injuries."

Even though she healed at an incredibly fast pace, Colleen knew that to push her body was a bad idea. So she slowed down and stepped with care as she went through the back storage room and into the bar. The fans had been off for several hours and the air was stale and stifling. Clicking them on now in the storage room, Colleen got to work on inventory for the bar first before moving on to the restaurant. They didn't have a large menu, but what they did have was popular and Colleen knew by now what they were going to need just by looking at the end of the week stock.

Working at the bar wasn't what she wanted to be doing, that was for sure. She hated dealing with the men who grabbed her ass when she had to waitress or ejecting the drunks during happy hour. But there were parts she was starting to enjoy, like the quiet nights she spent doing inventory. It gave her over active mind time to wander and try to figure out Von's next move or a myriad of other things that nagged in the back of her head.

Like why some cop has been poking around asking to speak with Fahrenheit.

A few days ago she broke up a fight between one of the neighborhood's new gangs and a group of younger boys making their way home after a pick-up basketball game. The gang activity had started picking up steam as the turf war raged, word traveling fast that Tina was having trouble keeping control of things. In Grandfather's day, no gang would dare rise up without his permission. But this month alone, Colleen had counted three new ones springing up overnight.

This particular tussle was more brutal than most, and when she was done her upper arms were crisscrossed with knife slashes. After doing her best not to use her powers on the young men, she decided a good fireball to the chest of the leader, enough to burn a hole in his shirt, was the only way to stop the fight. Afterward, one of the boys she'd helped out told her to that there was a cop looking for her, asking about where she patrolled and if anyone knew how to contact her.

"Thanks kid, do you know a name?"

The boy shook his head but his buddy spoke up, voice shaking, "Walter Lyle. He said to give this to you."

A crumpled, sweaty card was shoved into her hands.

"He's been handing those out to everyone," said the first boy.

Colleen had escorted them back to their apartment building with strict instructions to finish games before dark and then left to do more patrolling. Since then, she felt that someone was following her, that there were eyes everywhere.

Sparks fell from her finger tips and onto the package of napkins she was putting away. She dropped it to the floor and held her breath, waiting for smoke to rise up.

"Thank god," she said when nothing happened. "I think I'm done here. Freezer should definitely be next."

She shook her head at the fact that she still had moments when her emotions would dictate the control of her powers. It was much less frequent than before, but still frustrating.

"Oh man, this feels good," she sighed the moment she stepped inside the walk in freezer.

After a few seconds of glorious indulgence just standing in the freezing air, Colleen started to check their stock of ice cream and meat while her mind tried to unravel the answer to this question: What did that cop want with her?

Most of the police she interacted with had very clear goals: shoot to kill or capture her.

But no cop had tried to speak to her, and certainly not in such a secretive way. What did he hope to gain by it? Did the department want to work with her?

She laughed out loud at that thought.

"Keep dreaming girl," she said, as she noted how much beef they had on the shelf.

After the giggles dissipated, the question of 'why' still hung in the air. It made Colleen uneasy.

The police weren't exactly the biggest fans of vigilantes, although the two white ones that had sprung up in Metro City within the last month hadn't garnered all that much vitriol. But the fact that she was black and defending the most densely populated black neighbor-hood, created the perfect recipe for the department to hate her.

Maybe he's trying to find a weak spot, to see if I favor someone or a group more than others...maybe he's looking for someone to threaten so I'll give myself up.

She grit her teeth at the thought of anyone using others to get to her and took a deep breath. Setting something on fire in the walk-in would be hard, but Colleen bet even money with her powers that she could make it happen.

I'm more grateful than ever that I haven't gotten close to anyone here. If this cop is looking for someone to threaten to get to me, he's going to be sorely disappointed.

After a few more seconds of deep, focused breaths, Colleen opened her eyes and gave a quick nod.

"Right, totally in control, and focused on the job at hand," she chuckled. "Which just so happens to be counting frozen chicken breasts."

CHAPTER TWO

The smell of fresh paint, new carpet and hard wood varnish was pungent on the cool air inside the Torch and Grier Theater. Tina hoped it wasn't too terrible; she'd gotten used it over the past month as the finishing renovations ramped up but Madame Capelli might be distracted by the odor and not take in all the work Tina had put into her pet project.

Nothing I can do about it now.

With an encouraging smile, Tina pointed up at the colorful fresco on the ceiling, pride swelling in her chest as she did.

"I searched for months for the perfect artist that could do justice to Aaron Douglas," she said.

Madame Camille Capelli, resplendent in a tailored cream and blue skirt suit, smiled at Tina, revealing tiny lines around her eyes that only made the dangerous woman that much more beautiful.

Ruling the oldest crime family in Metro City with an iron fist, Camille had been Tina's most virulent, if secret, champion for years. She'd given advice, help and a swift dose of reality when Tina had needed it most. She wouldn't be standing here, about to seize a long held dream, without Camille.

So when the older woman stared around at the opulent theater lobby and the expensive frescoes on the ceiling with an appreciative smile on her face, it meant more to Tina than the praise of all the society peacocks in Metro City.

"You've out done yourself Tina," Camille said, trailing her finger tips along the mahogany bar that had just been finished the day before. "When is the opening?"

"Two weeks," Tina replied, her heart jumping up into her throat.

She'd loved this theater since she was a child, and had dreamed for two decades of breathing new life into this part of High Tide. Beginning with the reopening of one of the most famous theaters in all of Metro City, the rich art and music community that had once thrived here would be given new life.

"I remember coming here to listen to jazz music with my father," Camille said, as she continued her slow pace through the lobby. "The owners were very good liquor customers and my father made sure this place was protected, even after prohibition lifted. I was devastated when it closed."

She wandered into the theater proper and stood, taking in the space while Tina held her breath.

The chairs in front had been removed to make room for a large dance floor that jutted up against the fully restored stage. Large, U shaped booths lined the outside, while smaller tables that seated two or four were ringed closer to the stage. The opera booths had been converted into two private rooms that would have their own waitresses and complimentary champagne. Tina had taken advice from some of the younger architects and club owners in Metro City to get the aesthetic right while still holding onto some of the original charm of the place.

"A dance floor?" Camille asked.

"It's what is expected," Tina said, her stomach flip flopping even as she kept her tone neutral.

Or at least she hoped she did. Camille had an unnerving ability to tell exactly what Tina was thinking. But if she detected anything other than confidence, the older woman didn't say anything as her blue eyes scanned the theater.

"You have invested much into this place."

Tina knew that Camille was talking about more than money.

Getting out of the crime syndicate that her father had been neck deep in at the time of his death was no mean feat. It was taking everything Tina had to pay off those that could be, and bury those that couldn't. The Torch and Grier was meant to be her debut into respectable society, the signal that new times had come to her family and to High Tide.

The one exception was Camille, whose protection was still too necessary to Tina's plans.

"Our agreement is still in place," Tina said, the words a bit sour in her mouth.

The older woman's smile twisted a little as her eyes slid to Tina.

"Then you're not really out, are you?"

"Where it matters I am."

"Hmmm, yes I suppose…" Camille let the rest hang in the air unsaid.

"I anticipate that everything with Von will be finished this week."

"Oh?"

"And I was wondering if you would be so kind as to make the arrangements for a meeting about ending the hostilities."

"You know as well as I do that no one has seen Von face to face for ten years, except his most trusted advisers. I do not believe he would come. But perhaps I can make arrangements with one of his men."

"Thank you," Tina said, nodding her head in deference.

"Of course. I will keep the other families away until this is settled, as agreed."

Tina knew full well that keeping even the smallest business arrangement with Camille was risky. It was a slippery slope that could have her right back where she'd started. Or worse, make her subservient to another boss.

Camille might be like a mother to Tina, but that didn't mean the woman wouldn't take advantage of the situation if the opportunity arose. Still, Tina had little choice in the matter. Getting out of all this was tricky, no less so because Von had decided to go against her. If the other families decided to do the same, Tina wouldn't stand a chance.

The feeling of walking on a blade's edge sank deep in Tina's gut and she swallowed to keep the bile down. She learned long ago to bury her feelings under a mask of stone. But somehow, Camille was always able to sniff them out.

"I hope you get what you want, Tina," Camille finally said, walking into the lobby once again. "I truly do."

"Thank you. That means more than you know."

Camille's answering smile told Tina that she did, actually know.

"Will you be coming to the opening?" Tina asked.

"I have not decided yet. So many people make me uncomfortable. Perhaps once the opening frenzy has calmed some."

Tina knew that the amount of people was not the issue. Camille wanted to see how successful Tina was at wooing the rich elite and if she was able to keep Von off her back long enough to pull it off.

I'll save you a booth Camille.

One of the cream and gold trimmed doors opened, letting in the bright afternoon sunshine and the hot air. A short, thin man in an impeccably tailored suit walked through, followed by a thin woman dressed all in black except for a metal mask in the shape of a round cheeked, smiling child covering her face. Two large bodyguards followed last, flanking the odd pair. The whole thing made Tina's entire body tense.

"I see you have another appointment," Camille glanced back at the man who had captured Tina's attention, a frown wrinkling the space above her nose. "Lunch soon?"

"Yes, after the opening, I should have more time."

"Of course."

Camille spared one last glance at the man standing just inside the lobby, his shark like gaze never wavering from them, then she walked out, leaving Tina to whatever was about to happen.

Once the door closed behind Camille, Tina charged forward, refusing to show the fear that churned in her gut.

"This is highly irregular," she said once she was near Mr. Price. "You and I have no further business. I will have to remove you if you do not leave immediately."

She'd done many necessary evils in order to get to where she was in life. Mr. Price was the one that she regretted the most.

When it had become apparent that her father's deteriorating health was also affecting his mental state, Tina made a deal with Mr. Price to get rid of the old man and smooth out any wrinkles with the other heads of the crime families as she took control. But the cost of that partnership was higher than Tina could've predicted.

Mr. Price had ordered her to safe guard human cargo that turned out to be a powered child and Tina decided, for the first time in her life, to go back on the deal. She didn't have very many lines she wouldn't cross, but the creepy man had found one of the few.

"You owe my employer for the lost cargo," Mr. Price said, his voice soft and nasal.

She shrugged.

"It's not my fault there were other interested parties. If I had been told everything, I could've ensured that there was additional help. You simply said you needed someone to watch it get delivered, that was all."

Mr. Price's thin lips twisted into a grin that sent a chill down Tina's spine.

"Ignorance is not a good look on you, Mrs. Knight. My employer feels that a payment for the lost property is in order."

"And what would that be?"

"Your daughter."

The words didn't register at first. When they did, she laughed, as much in terror as disbelief.

"You are insane," she said, advancing on him.

The figure with the metal mask, stepped in front of Mr. Price and the bodyguards put their hands into their coats, as if to reach for firearms, when a voice behind Tina stopped them.

"Hands, now," Rick said, the click of his gun loud in the sudden quiet.

Mr. Price looked at each of his men and nodded. The burly guards withdrew their hands slowly and glared at Rick. The woman remained for a few seconds more, the green eyes behind the mask shooting daggers at Tina.

Mr. Price put a hand on her arm and the masked woman stepped aside at last.

"Your daughter is the perfect payment, and I think you know that," Mr. Price continued, as if there had been no interruption. "Or we will also take payment in blood. Yours, the people here. It doesn't matter. But my employer will have compensation. Good day, Mrs. Knight."

With the same amount of nonchalance, Mr. Price walked through the door, followed by his guards. The metal faced woman was last, her silent gaze sending a clear warning.

The moment the door latched closed, Tina let out the breath she'd been holding and the world spun around her. Clutching the nearby bar, Tina pressed her head to her knuckles and closed her eyes.

She'd faced down powerful men and women in her day, had survived the constant barrage of threats and abuse from her father, and yet Mr. Price struck such fear in her soul that she found herself defenseless against him.

I know in my bones that he's a different breed. Dear god…what have I done?

A heavy hand squeezed her shoulder and Tina knew it was Rick, her constant rock in any storm.

"Are you alright?" he asked.

"No," she said against her better judgment.

"Do you want me to take care of him?"

"No, that'll only make this worse."

"Then-"

"Leave it for now. I need to think."

The door opened again and Tina was about to yell at the person to go the hell away when she looked up and saw Colleen walk in, bright scarf hiding her hair and wide sunglasses on her face.

Likely hiding a bruise or cut. I hope this is all over soon because Colleen needs to get out of here.

The thought made Tina's heart constrict. The only thing she'd ever wanted was her family together and whole. Getting out of the illegal business her family had built was supposed to be the first step toward that. But now, because she'd made one wrong move, Tina wondered if that could ever happen.

"Didn't we have an appointment at Rachel's?" Colleen asked.

"Yes, we did," Tina said, squaring her shoulders.

Colleen opened her mouth and then closed it, for which Tina was grateful.

"The car is waiting out front," Rick said.

Tina nodded and went to get her purse from behind the bar. If everything with Von was finally at an end, as Rick assured it probably was, then she'd talk with Colleen soon about leaving, having her own life.

Maybe she'd like to go back to Cambridge, far away from Mr. Price and his employer.

The tension was so thick that Colleen almost choked on it when she walked into the theater. Whatever had just happened, whoever was in the car that just pulled away, it had Tina wound tighter than a spring ready to pop.

As they drove to Rachel's salon, Colleen eyed her mother, trying to see what might be going on. Tina had never been a particularly joyful woman, but the last two weeks, as the days drew near for the opening of her theater, Colleen had seen a definite change. She was more relaxed, less apt to snap and there were even times when Colleen spied the beginning of a smile on her lips.

All of that suddenly washed away and Colleen wanted very much to know why.

When they pulled up to the salon, Rick opened Colleen's door first and whispered, "Mr. Price was there, something's wrong."

She stared at him, recognizing that name all too well. If Rick was revealing this to her, that meant it was indeed serious. The man barely spoke to Colleen except to snarl disapproval.

Colleen gave him a small nod and walked around to enter the salon a few steps ahead of her mother, who was just getting out of the car.

"I'm telling you it was her, sure as I'm sitting here!" said a short woman in the middle chair that Colleen recognized as Mrs. Bolt, the owner of Cherry's Diner. "Fahrenheit chased those robbers right off my property, barely left a scorch mark on the new sign."

"My Bernie said he saw her the other night, hands all ablaze!" the stylist at the furthest chair replied.

Colleen felt heat rise in her cheeks, and it had nothing to do with her powers. This wasn't the first time she'd walked into a business in High Tide and heard the customers and owners talking about her. It was fast becoming a very common occurrence. But it never ceased to make her very uncomfortable. Everyone was starting to see her as some kind of shining hero and Colleen worried that being on that pedestal would be impossible to maintain. One toe out of line and how many people would she be breaking faith with? How much hope would she shatter?

Rachel walked out from the back room and her eyes went immediately to Colleen and Tina. She gave them a smile, the expression lighting up her weathered face and waved them over for a quick hug. The older woman felt more frail in Colleen's arms than she liked and worry began to wiggle in the back of her mind.

The owner of Rachel's Place had been a rock of the community as far back as anyone could remember. One of the first female business owners in the neighborhood, Rachel had sunk every dime into her salon and had fast built a reputation for being one of the best in black women's hair care in all of Metro City. Women waited weeks for an appointment at Rachel's but somehow, she always had a chair open for Tina and Colleen.

Not to mention a smile and some—

"I've got some fresh cookies in the back if you want to take some home with you," Rachel offered. "I made way too many and the doctor says I have to cut back on the sweets."

Colleen smiled. "I'd like that."

Rachel pointed to one of the empty shampoo stations and before Colleen had settled herself in the chair, a young stylist named Natalie sprang into action, while Rachel attended to Tina personally. Though everyone knew what Colleen's family did, no one said a word. The salon was neutral ground, no business on the premises and no judgment. Just women talking about everything from recipes to political candidates to who was dating whose child.

"I wonder if there's other people like her around here," asked one of the patrons Colleen didn't recognize. "That could be interesting, don't ya think?"

Colleen felt her shoulders stiffen at the thought of anyone looking for powered people. That could be dangerous on many levels.

"If there are, they probably want to be left alone," Rachel said as she worked shampoo into Tina's scalp.

"But if there are, maybe we could have a whole team of heroes! Wouldn't that be something!" said the stylist washing Colleen's hair.

She gave the woman a weak smile and closed her eyes, trying to relax.

"It's nice to have someone watching over High Tide," Rachel agreed. "And I hope whoever she is, Fahrenheit knows how much it means to us all. She's putting her life on the line every night for us. That's no small thing."

"I wonder if there's anything we can do for her?" Mrs. Bolt mused as she admired her reflection in the mirror.

"Like what?"

"I don't know, maybe…give her something for her services?"

"No," Colleen said, before she could stop herself.

The salon went quiet and she felt everyone's eyes on her as she sat up from the rinse bowl.

"I mean…well, I don't think she does it for money. She probably just does it because it's right and there's usually danger when she's around and I don't think she'd want anyone getting hurt just to…to you know…give her money."

The longer the silence stretched on, the more Colleen's stomach twisted in fear that she'd just revealed herself.

"Natalie, get a towel on Miss Knight, she's dripping," Rachel said, breaking the silence, "and Colleen's right. We have no business out and about when High Tide's vigilante is doing her job. But, if we want to leave little things out for her…well, that might be nice."

Rachel's eyes slid to Colleen for just a half second, but it was enough to make her wonder if the old woman knew that Fahrenheit was sitting right there.

She looked away and let Natalie finish towel drying her hair, pushing the question to the back of her mind.

"I just want to know if she's single," said Natalie. "My brother could use a good woman like her."

Colleen couldn't help a chuckle. She'd grown up with Natalie's brother and was pretty sure that no woman alive would be his type.

The match making comment set off a side conversation that made Colleen breath a sigh of relief that none of them would have the chance to get Fahrenheit "good and settled".

She closed her eyes and let Natalie put the rich smelling oils in her hair. The young stylist was a grudging concession on Rachel's part to the ever growing popularity of the 'natural style'. Most of the women in the shop hated it, but Rachel made it clear that no customer leaves her shop dissatisfied with their hair. So, she helped pay for Natalie's training and hired her right out of night school. Colleen was forever grateful to the old woman. Never had she felt so beautiful as when Natalie was finished with her growing halo of natural curls.

The conversation turned to the upcoming theater opening and the spotlight had shifted from Fahrenheit to her mother. Tina patiently answered every question, indulged every dig for gossip about the guest list and even endured the ladies ribbing about who she might be taking to the opening night. When Colleen looked over at her mother, that spark was back in her eyes, but it was dimmed a little.

Mr. Price's visit must've shook her pretty bad.

The thought brought back all the questions that had been forgotten during Natalie's pampering, and Colleen was more than a little resentful that the sparse time she got to relax was now over.

By the time Rachel had wrapped up some cookies for Colleen and they'd paid and walked out the door, the question about Mr. Price was thick on Colleen's tongue.

The moment Tina and Colleen slid into the back seat, she wasted no time in getting right to the heart of things.

"What was Mr. Price doing there?"

Tina let out an angry sigh and glared at Rick, who pointedly ignored her.

"Tina, I have a right to know after what he tried to make you do...make me do, actually."

It was Mr. Price's order that made Tina send Colleen down to Red Rock to oversee the delivery of a powered child, which turned out to be Judy. Colleen never delivered the child, of course, and Tina said she'd worked it all out.

"Is he after Judy?" Colleen asked, heat building in her veins at the thought.

"No. As far as I know, Mr. Price doesn't know where the child is," Tina responded.

"So what then? He just shows up to posture and threaten?"

"Yes, now can we leave it at that?"

Colleen gaped at her mother.

"No, we can't. That man is dangerous, with deep connections—"

"That you won't tell me about for some reason."

Now it was Colleen's turn to clam up. Even with all of Tina's assurances that she was getting out of the illegal dealings and building a legitimate business empire, Colleen still couldn't trust her mother with the knowledge that Jason James, multi-millionaire and one of the most powerful men in the country, was pulling Mr. Price's strings.

If she thought it would help her aims, I don't think Tina could resist partnering with the bastard. And that...that would be very bad.

"You still don't trust me," Tina said, the kernel of hurt in her voice made Colleen's jaw clench against guilt. "I suppose I understand that. But please, *try* to when I tell you that Mr. Price is one man I want you to forget. I have him handled. Now, how about some lunch? I have a reservation at The Butterfly Club."

Colleen knew she wasn't dressed for the Butterfly club but the owners wouldn't bat an eye at Tina Knight's daughter coming in against dress code. She wanted to say no but a long, empty afternoon stretched before her and a stab of loneliness hit her in the chest.

So, she smiled at her mother and nodded.

"Good. On the way, tell me about last night."

Colleen quickly relayed the fight, including what the goon said in the apartment building and what she thought he may have meant.

Tina's forehead wrinkled at that and she stared out the window for a few minutes before answering.

"So you think Von wanted to capture you?" she finally asked, her voice halting.

"Maybe. Or at the very least eliminate me."

"If he is at the end of his resources, then why do this now? Why not earlier?"

"I don't know."

Tina shook her head and Colleen could see the wheels turning behind the worry in her eyes.

"What is it?" Colleen asked.

"Nothing."

Colleen studied her mother a little longer and then looked away. She should know by now, if Tina didn't want to tell her something then wild horses couldn't drag it out of her. Still, she couldn't shake the thought that there was something going on that she needed to know about before it was too late.

CHAPTER THREE

The next day, Colleen stood in the courtyard of the High Tide Youth Center, setting out the last hamburger buns for the free lunch Wanda served every Wednesday. The sun beat down on the kids playing and climbing on the old play set. The thump of basketballs hitting the cracked cement court, and the jangle of the netless hoop punctuated the laughter and happy screams from the other children. Horns blared a few blocks away and in the distance Colleen could hear the faint strains of music from someone's apartment. Sweat trickled down her back and side, even though she was under one of the few shady areas, and the sodas in the cooler were already tempting her.

Colleen found herself slipping into autopilot, unable to shake her conversation with Tina yesterday.

Or lack thereof.

She couldn't decide if she was angry with her mother's insistence that she had Mr. Price handled or worried. She had come to expect plans wrapped in riddles from her mother, who seemed to have contingencies for every imaginable outcome at the ready. This all usually came with a confidence that bordered on the cavalier, not fear as it had yesterday.

She's hiding something, which isn't new but…I get the sense that this time it's something different.

Her palms itched as fire stirred under her skin. What she really wanted to do was go find out what the hell Mr. Price was up to, but she had no idea where the man lived or worked. It would be like trying to find a needle in a haystack, and she had to stay in High Tide to be sure Von was indeed beaten.

Wanda's voice jolted her out of these thoughts and she almost dropped the buns she was stacking on the table

"Colleen! Girl, where's your head today? I called your name a couple times," Wanda said, striding toward her.

The bar owner folded her arms under her ample breasts, round dark brown face splitting into a wide grin that was infectious. Colleen had seen that smile diffuse many a bar fight or argument in a shop almost as often as she'd seen Wanda's scowl scare off anyone dumb enough to come up against the woman.

"Sorry just…tired I guess."

"Well, wake up! We're about to get a line of hungry little ones. Lunch time!"

In spite of herself, Colleen had to laugh at how fast the kids ceased whatever they were doing and ran toward the tables. She couldn't say she blamed them. The smell of pulled pork, hamburgers, and baked beans was mouthwatering.

The youth center director, Mr. Nichols, surveyed the line and asked Wanda something, a worried frown on his face. Colleen knew he was concerned that they'd run out of food and she could understand why.

Since they'd started handing out hot lunches once a week to the kids, the influx of children to the youth center had gone through the roof. The place was busy in the summer anyway with latchkey kids and children whose parents were just absent for various reasons, but the offer of a hot, free meal had brought children in who'd never darkened the door of the place. Even though that was the point of Wanda's kind gesture, the director hadn't been prepared for just how many had started showing up.

"Wanda, can I talk to you for a moment?" he asked.

Wanda frowned but stepped out of the line, which just left Colleen to manage the hungry children.

A little girl shyly let two bigger kids in front of her and Colleen waved her over.

"You hungry sweetie?" she asked.

The girl nodded, chewing on her forefinger.

"Well here, let's get you a sandwich."

She helped the girl get some food while Wanda spoke with the director, hands on her hips.

That's not good.

"Can I get the soda myself?" the little girl asked.

"Sure honey, you go on ahead."

"Thank you Miss Colleen," she whispered, giving Colleen a smile that showed a missing front tooth.

Colleen glanced over at Wanda, who was now shaking her head and gesturing to the kids. Mr. Nichols, seemingly unfazed by whatever Wanda said, simply shrugged and walked away. Wanda's gaze followed him, a stony expression on her face that fled the moment she turned back to the kids.

What was that all about?

Just as Wanda made it back to the line, some of the children started pointing toward the street, whispering to one another about what they saw. A few of the older ones gathered their plates and went inside the center instead of hanging out by the basketball court like they usually did. This all brought on a furious glare from Wanda, who swore under her breath.

When Colleen was able to follow Wanda's line of sight, she understood what was going on.

A police car had pulled up and two people were climbing out. One was an extremely tall, broad shouldered older man with a long, square jawed face and somewhat bulbous eyes. The other was a shorter black woman with strong curves and a beautiful smile on her face. She waved to someone, which turned out to the be director, and walked over with a bouncing step. The man with her, who had to be her partner, followed behind the short cop, a smile on his craggy features that did nothing to calm the tension that had settled over the sunny afternoon. Colleen couldn't tell if the woman was indeed as short as she seemed or if she only appeared that way next to her giant of a partner.

Mr. Nichols shook the woman's hand and then the man's. They talked for a few minutes and then walked over to the table of food with Mr. Nichols in the lead. The exuberant chatter ceased, even the little ones realizing that the best course of action was to be as invisible as possible.

Wanda, who was serving the pulled pork, muttered something under her breath and then plastered a smile on her face as the officers and Mr. Nichols walked over.

"Everyone," Mr. Nichols said, "this is officer Shay Reynolds and officer Walter Lyle, they're here to help serve lunch today."

The younger children waved and said hello, while the older kids hunched their shoulders and focused on their food or chose to leave altogether. Colleen felt her body tense with recognition, her face reflecting the shock she felt.

That's the man that's been asking around about Fahrenheit. Why is he here?

Every muscle in her body warmed with the heat of her powers, readying for action. She scanned the area to determine if a fight would be possible and where the fewest casualties would be. Her pulse quickened at the realization that the place was too densely populated with children. There was no way to use her powers without hurting them.

If he's here to catch me, then he picked his spot perfectly. I'll let him take me just to keep the kids safe. Of course, in the back of the car will be a different story.

"Hi everyone," Shay said, her smile as energetic as her voice, "I grew up around here and I am so excited to be back. Officer Lyle and I could smell that delicious food from blocks away! Wanda's a good cook!"

Some of the younger kids smiled and agreed enthusiastically while the older ones remained suspicious.

The officers took their place on the food line, Walter at the end handing out cold sodas and fruit while Shay helped with the hamburgers.

Colleen tried to relax, to paint a smile on her face like Wanda had but she just couldn't. Every instinct told her to run, to get the hell out of there before it was too late. But there was no way to excuse herself without raising suspicion. And besides, this was her neighborhood, these were the people she was committed to protecting. The one day a week she worked at the youth center was something Colleen looked forward to. It was a chance to just be herself and play with the kids, to feel like she was doing some good that had nothing to do with violence. And damned if she was going to let Walter Lyle ruin that.

Shay ended up being a chatty addition to the food line, complimenting the girls on their braids or sun dresses and asking the boys about their basketball skills, even offering to play a little with them. No one took her up on it, and the kids were shy to the point of silence in many cases, but that didn't seem to deter her in the least.

Colleen felt her gaze slide toward the woman throughout the food service and she couldn't help admiring the beauty of her dark skin or the strength in her arms. The officer was short, but not nearly as small as Colleen thought at first, coming up almost eye to eye with Colleen. She exuded a relaxed joy that made the vigilante wonder why she'd become a cop instead of a teacher or business owner. Anything but a profession that most in her home neighborhood would be frightened of.

At one point, Shay caught Colleen looking at her, and smiled. Heat rose to her cheeks and she turned back to the kids waiting for food and tried to keep her focus on the task at hand. But after that, her senses were acutely attuned to Shay and she was aware of every word or giggle she made.

Once every kid had been fed to near bursting, the adults could have their choice of whatever was left over. There usually wasn't much, but today Colleen noticed that the food containers had more than enough for them all. Her brow wrinkled in worry at who might be going home hungrier than usual.

"Don't worry," Wanda whispered next to her, "I put away some food for the older kids that didn't come back for seconds. No one leaves *my* table hungry."

Colleen smiled at the older woman, who was still obviously upset by the addition of the officers.

"Now, you go on and get some food. You look more tired than when you started."

She was happy to do just that as her stomach cramped uncomfortably. Ever since she'd absorbed all that fire in Haven a month ago, Colleen's powers had become super charged, causing her body to need twice as much food and liquids as before. If she let her powers deplete her too much she would faint, and that wasn't something she wanted happening in front of friends or when fighting any of Von's thugs. But, lately, keeping herself fed and hydrated enough was becoming a full time job as she used her powers more and more.

Colleen was so busy loading up her plate that she didn't notice that Shay had come to stand next to her until the woman spoke.

"Hi, I don't think we've met officially. I'm Shay," she extended her hand.

"Colleen," she shook it briefly, desperate to start devouring her food.

The cop nodded, her own plate full and gestured to a spot in the shade. Her partner was talking and laughing with Mr. Nichols, his own plate full but not as much as Colleen's. Walter glanced over at her and nodded, nothing but questions in his gaze. It made alarm bells go off in Colleen's head and she turned away.

"He looks intimidating but Walter is a big Teddy Bear," Shay said, sitting next to Colleen. "I'm lucky I got him for a partner. He's got a lot of experience and he cares about the neighborhood."

Colleen took a large bite of her hamburger instead of answering.

"The youth center hasn't changed much since I was a kid," Shay continued around a mouthful of food. "Still the same smells, though Mr. Nichols doesn't reek of old pomade the way Mr. Winters did, thank god."

The officer chuckled at that and something about it made Colleen's lips tick up just a little.

"Oh, she smiles," Shay says. "I wondered what it would take. Did you play here as a kid?"

Colleen shook her head. She was never allowed and in any case, after her first and only best friend was threatened by Grandfather, Colleen never got close to anyone as a kid ever again.

"Oh that's too bad. It was fun, especially in the summer. I remember Mr. Winter had a deal with the ice cream truck and at the end of the day we'd get left over popsicles and fudge bars. God I used to get the worst tummy ache! And then mamma would scold me for not eating my dinner, which wasn't too bad since…"

Shay's trailed off and her eyes slid to Colleen who was staring at her in surprise. She couldn't remember the last person who had spilled so many words so fast to someone they barely knew.

"Sorry," Shay said, ducking her head and taking a bite of food. "I…I'm nervous I guess. I haven't been back in a while and I just…well, I want to give back and I know how hard that will be with the uniform and everything but High Tide is going through something hard right now and I just want to…help."

"Why are you nervous around me?" Colleen asked before she could stop herself.

"Well I-I'm not exactly nervous around *you*, though I guess that's what it seems, that's what I said, I guess but I just…um, I guess I'm just nervous in general."

Colleen's face heated again and she wondered why the hell *she* was suddenly so nervous around this woman.

"Oh, I'm…glad you're not nervous around me."

And then she took another large bite to cover up the fact that she didn't know why in the world she'd say that.

"Oh good! I'm glad that you're glad," Shay said, her laugh carrying a nervous edge. "You know I, uh, I just moved back and…well, the uniform doesn't exactly inspire people to be comfortable around me. This is actually the first nice conversation I've had with anyone my age in High Tide. Not that I know your age, I just assume…Anyway, what I'm trying to say is that it would be nice to hang out sometime. Maybe get a drink or an ice cream if this heat doesn't let up."

Colleen looked into Shay's dark eyes. They were as bright as her grin and suddenly Colleen found herself nodding in agreement.

"Great!" Shay took a pad of paper out of a pocket in the front of her shirt and scribbled furiously on it. "Here's my number, what's yours?"

"Um…I don't really have a phone."

"Oh."

"But I live above Wanda's bar so…you can call there and they'll get me if I'm working or at home."

Shay brightened and handed her the pad of paper.

Colleen's mind screamed at her for agreeing to this while her fingers nimbly wrote the number on the pad and traded it for the slip of paper with Shay's number on it.

"I'll call you," the officer said, standing to her feet.

"Okay…yeah…good."

Okay yeah good? What…why did I do that?

But as the officer walked away, Colleen found it very hard to tear her gaze from the way Shay's hips swayed as she walked…

Oh no…no, no, no. I am not attracted to this woman, I just met her!

She ducked her head and shoved the remaining food into her mouth, feeling a sudden loneliness take the place of the vibrant energy Shay had bathed her in.

"Can you believe that?" Wanda hissed, hands on her hips again. "The gall of that man! I told him not to let those cops barge in here all benevolent like, told him it would scare the kids, make them feel less safe. But did he listen? And now look, the older kids are leaving and it's not even dinner time yet."

Colleen glanced up, surprised to realize that she hadn't noticed how unusually quiet it had gotten. The basketball court, which was normally packed at this time of the day, was practically empty. The younger kids played on, but Colleen could see fewer children than normal.

"Mark my words, those kids are going to find trouble now that this place doesn't feel safe."

"I hope you're wrong," she said, mind already running over where to patrol tonight so she could keep an eye on them.

"Me too," Wanda replied, clucking her tongue. "C'mon, I need your help loading the containers and we gotta get ready for the dinner crowd."

"Well that was fun!" Shay said, trying very hard to control her excitement.

She'd been back for months now, all the time wishing she could find a way to give back to the neighborhood that had raised her. But every time she asked her mother for advice about where to start, the older woman would shrug and tell her that no one wanted *her* kind of help.

Becoming a cop hadn't made anyone in Shay's family especially happy, even though her father had been an officer. But Shay always supposed her family's discomfort with her career choice had more to do with the fact that her father had been murdered by a fellow officer, though no one had ever been able to prove it. The day she'd gone into the academy, Shay's mother had cried and locked herself in her room. It took a while for her to thaw and now her mother no longer ignored Shay when she came over, but it was understood that she couldn't step through her mother's door while in uniform.

Today was the first time Shay felt like a part of High Tide again, and it sent zings of joy through her body to the point where she couldn't sit still, her leg bouncing in the car in time to the music on the radio.

Something about the song brought to mind the tall, young woman that had been with Wanda, and Shay's grin widened.

Colleen was…interesting

"You had a good time, rookie?" Walter asked.

"You know I've been in the department for over a year right?"

"Yeah."

Shay shook her head and looked out the window at the neighborhood she loved so much. Walter was a legend in the department, for both good and not so good reasons. A decorated officer and detective, Walter had been up for promotion to chief several times but always refused to accept it. Then, about two years ago, something happened. Shay couldn't get anything but scant truths wrapped in rumors, but from what she could tell, Walter refused to stop investigating a case that implicated a very powerful man. The result was a demotion to beat cop. Problem was, no one wanted to work with him and finally the chief had enough of Walter going off on his own and assigned him the one person who was desperate enough to be his partner: Shay.

She hadn't cared about any of this when the chief finally promoted her out of the basement records room. Top of her class at the academy, she'd broken two records in fire arms and endurance and still didn't rate even a desk job when she first went looking. In fact, she was refused employment at all but one of Metro City's precincts.

Walter tried to wave her off being his partner from the start.

"You deserve better than me rookie, might want to think about your future," he had said.

But Shay knew her future if she refused this: records room.

And that wasn't something she was willing to accept.

"I don't think they really appreciated me being there," Walter said, breaking Shay out of her thoughts.

It took her a moment to understand where he was talking about, and then she sighed.

He was right, of course. When Walter said he wanted to go with her, Shay knew it wasn't a good idea. Her being there in uniform was going to be a hard enough hurdle, but Walter?

Putting aside the fact that he towered over just about everyone, Walter had a natural glower that still made Shay a little nervous at times.

But he tried. I even saw him smile. With teeth!

"Maybe not," she answered, "but you showed up without any expectations, just to help. That does mean something."

Walter shrugged.

"What were you and Mr. Nichols talking about? You guys were pretty chatty."

She could feel his eyes slide to her but kept her gaze straight ahead. It had been two months and still Walter was tight lipped with her about most things. He was suspicious of her, Shay knew that. And he had good reason.

The job came with one caveat from the captain, and it still left a bad taste in Shay's mouth. She was to watch Walter, and report to the captain if he did anything suspicious or strange. When Shay asked why, the captain was cagey and simply said that he needed to know.

Being a snitch wasn't something that cops were usually asked to be within their own precinct, at least not by their own captains. And Shay couldn't help feeling set up by it all. But she also didn't want to be stuck in the basement. So she'd agreed, telling herself that if Walter was a good cop then he had nothing to fear. And if he wasn't, well then he didn't deserve to be on the force, did he?

So far, Shay had seen nothing to give her pause.

But that doesn't mean that Walter doesn't suspect that I'm here to spy on him.

"I just asked how the youth center was doing with the escalation in the turf war," Walter said. "Ya know, if the vigilante had been a problem, if others were trying to copy her, stuff like that."

Shay nodded.

"From what I hear, the vigilante is turning into a kind of local hero."

"That's what he said, too. Not sure how I feel about that."

"Me, either."

Walter's eyebrow raised in surprise.

"She doesn't follow the law," Shay said, feeling more than a little defensive, "and I feel like she's made things worse. She fights in the turf war and it causes both sides to escalate. That's not going to end well."

"You surprise me."

"Why? Just because I'm from here doesn't mean I automatically agree with everything that goes on. I grew up with the threat of Grandfather Malone hanging all over this place. I remember what it was like to see young men recruited as hired guns and then go to their funerals months later."

She could feel herself harden at the memories of her friends crying at the graves of their brothers, the way her uncles had been hard pressed to pay the protection money some years and her cousins had been forced to go without basic necessities as a result. Even her father had tangled with one of Grandfather Malone's bagmen once, and the whole family had been sent to stay with her grandmother up state while it blew over.

"They say Tina Knight is dismantling the empire her father built," Walter said, his gravelly voice low.

Shay snorted.

"I'll believe it when I see it."

"You don't like the family?"

"Nope."

"Then why were you chatting up Tina's daughter today?"

Shay felt her stomach drop to her toes and then launch back up into her throat.

"That... Colleen? She's Tina Knight's daughter?"

"You didn't know that?"

"Well...no. I mean, I knew Tina had kids, everyone knew that but...no one ever really saw them."

The thought of that beautiful, quiet woman being in the middle of all that ugliness...

She was so normal, so nice and so damn attractive! She's working for Wanda and volunteering...why? What's the angle?

"You know, rookie," Walter's voice cut through her thoughts, "I've been doing this a few more years than you—"

Shay snorted again.

"—and I've learned that no one is really who you think they are at first glance. The good guys are usually not that good and the bad guys are usually not that bad. Everyone has shades of gray in them. Maybe don't judge this woman before you give her a chance."

She bit her lip and turned Walters words over in her mind, wanting desperately to do as he suggested.

But she did seem...different somehow...maybe...

Shay shoved it aside. It was too complicated, too strange. A cop and Tina Knight's daughter being friends?

More than friends if I'm right about her and…she is awfully pretty. Maybe she could be different than her family.

Dispatch crackled over the radio and Shay answered. A robbery two blocks away, and they were the closest car.

As she flipped on the siren and Walter gunned it, Shay was oddly relieved to have this to distract her from Colleen's gorgeous face.

CHAPTER FOUR

T he nightly symphony of sirens was surprisingly distant tonight as Colleen sat perched on a fire escape. She was keeping an eye on a business that had been getting harassed by some of Von's men lately, her mind wandering for the hundredth time to Shay.

It had been a few days since she met the cop, and Colleen couldn't seem to stop thinking about her. She'd picked up the phone in the back room of Wanda's bar half a dozen times to call but couldn't seem to make herself dial the number.

She's a cop and I shouldn't be having feelings like this for anyone so soon after Karen. Should I?

She shook her head to dislodge the whole internal conversation. It was pointless to let herself think about any of this, perhaps especially because Colleen had no idea if Shay was attracted to women or not.

Not like I can ask her though, is it?

Images of Shay's smooth dark skin and dancing eyes, her bow shaped lips and hips that were curved just right took free reign in her mind. What would it be like to put her hands on those hips and draw her body close, to brush her lips to Shay's?

Stop. It. Now!

She closed her eyes and took a deep breath, in through her nose and out through her mouth, trying to push the thoughts further away with each exhalation. After six deep breaths, Shay was still in the forefront of her thoughts.

With a frustrated grunt, Colleen stood to her feet and shook her hands out.

"I need to hit something."

At that moment, a yell echoed through the night and Colleen breathed a sigh of relief.

Saved by the bad guys.

She jumped from the fire escape and looked up and down the street just as a scream sounded to her left. Rounding the corner at the end of the street, she saw two men harassing a woman that Colleen had known her whole life.

What the hell is Rachel doing out here at this time of night?

She ran toward the three just as Rachel took her handbag and hit one of the attackers on the side of the head.

"You two should be ashamed of yourselves," she said. "I used to babysit the two of you and now you're—"

"Shut it, you old bat!" said the one she hadn't hit, as he drew his gun.

Rachel stared slack jawed at him just as Colleen got within striking distance and clocked him. The man stumbled back, while his partner seized Rachel's purse and took off.

"No!" she screamed.

Colleen lobbed a fireball in his path and he yelped in surprise.

"Now, I don't want to but I will set your pants on fire if you don't hand over the bag," Colleen said, holding the flames in front of him.

The young man tried to run around the barrier, but Colleen simply moved it over.

"You're not going to win, so you might as well—"

"Let him go or she gets some early retirement."

Colleen turned to see the one she'd hit holding a gun to Rachel's temple.

The vigilante clenched her teeth and called the fire back.

"Let her go."

"C'mon man I've got the bag!"

The one with the gun stood there, his face red where Colleen hit him, hatred shining in his brown eyes.

"You think you can run this town?" he asked. "You and the Knight family and the police? You think you can just grind us into the pavement?"

"No, I don't," Colleen said. "I think everything stinks and it feels like it's not going to get any better."

His eyebrows went up but he didn't lower the gun.

"You think this is going to make it better?" she asked, gesturing to the gun against Rachel's head.

"What do you know about anything? Probably live in a fucking palace while my brother and sister barely have enough to eat!"

"I'm gonna leave you here if you don't come on!" said the one with the purse.

"I know what it's like to need, and this way isn't going to fix it," the vigilante said.

The boy with the gun hesitated, his eyes filled with pain.

"Oh yeah?" he challenged. "You lose your father to some stray bullet? Your mama have to work two jobs? Nah, I don't think you understand anything."

His words put a lump in her throat. The police had never been particularly kind to High Tide, but in the last month their attentions had been anything but helpful to the residents there. Innocents getting caught in the crossfire had become more common and Colleen wondered if this boy's father had died during one of the shoot outs she'd been at.

Was it my fault?

She tucked the guilt away for later and held out her hand.

"Give me the gun, and I can help you. But if you do this, there's no going back. You'll leave your siblings alone and you'll go to jail, you want that?"

The other boy tried to run, and Colleen raised the wall of fire again.

"You leave the purse and you can go," she said to the kid in front of the fire.

He threw it on the ground.

"It's not worth getting killed over."

Colleen recalled the flames as the boy with the gun let Rachel go.

"You come to the Wanda's tomorrow. I'll make sure she has a job for you," Colleen said.

"Yeah sure," said the one with the bag. "You can't trust her, she's a freak."

"I might be, but I'm no liar."

The one who had the gun glared at her.

"What's the catch?"

"You stop robbing little old ladies like some kind of idiot."

"Whatever. Maybe I will, maybe I won't."

And with that the two boys ran off into the night.

It wasn't until they were around the corner that Rachel spoke.

"I hate what this neighborhood is becoming."

Colleen felt the words like a blow and couldn't meet Rachel's eyes.

She's right, this place…I was supposed to save it and the people are less safe now than when I first got back.

"Can I walk you somewhere, ma'am?" Colleen asked.

Rachel's eyes twinkled as she gave Fahrenheit a grin.

"You've got nice manners, don't see that too much nowadays. 'Course, I'd expect nothing less from you."

She looked away, eyes wide. Did Rachel know who she was?

"You can walk me to the end of the block," Rachel said. "The last bus is about to arrive."

Colleen was grateful that Rachel didn't say anything as they walked to the bus stop. Her mind was racing, trying to figure out how Rachel could know and if that was a bad thing or not. The bus pulled up to the curb just as they got to the stop.

"You're a good girl, don't ever doubt that," Rachel said, grasping Colleen's hand and giving it a squeeze.

"I…thank you, ma'am."

With one last pat on her arm, Rachel got on the bus. Colleen's mind reeled with suspicions and worry that Rachel knowing her real identity would put her in danger somehow. She was so distracted by this that it wasn't until someone gave a cat call that Colleen realized she'd been standing there too long.

"It's Fahrenheit!" someone yelled from the bus.

She gave the gawking passengers a halfhearted wave and began to walk away.

"You look good girl!" a man hanging out of the window yelled.

"You can set me on fire anytime!" another said.

"She's too hot for you to handle," said a woman.

The vigilante stifled a laugh and took off in the opposite direction, as catcalls and shouts for her to come back faded into the night.

Her eyes scanned the alleyways and listened for any sign of trouble but found nothing for two blocks, which left her mind ample room to worry.

It was easy to believe that she was helping night after night, even when she couldn't stop someone from being killed or their property destroyed. She'd gotten good at filing those things away behind the mantra that it would be worse if she wasn't there. But seeing the grief and anger on that young man's face tonight, hearing the desperation in his voice made her feel like she wasn't doing enough.

And because I attract too much attention. I know the police are here half the time just to try and find me. Maybe after all this I should leave…

Her thoughts were interrupted by the sound of breaking glass ahead and she hated the fact that she was actually relieved to have something to distract her.

The street lamps on half the block had been shattered, so the squat, square shop was shrouded in shadows. A ghostly fog hung on the ground around the building and out onto the sidewalk, making it look as if the place sat in an otherworldly fairyland. Her senses prickled and the hair on her arms stood up as a cold wind brushed over her body.

Cold wind? It's at least eighty degrees tonight.

She walked to the front of the shop with cautious steps, fire at the ready just beneath her skin. When she saw the sign above the door, her breath caught in her throat.

"The Sweet Spot," she whispered.

Memories as thick as cotton candy invaded her mind.

She and Andrew used to spend their allowance on bags of jawbreakers and gum balls, their hands sticky with licorice and lollipops. They'd wiled away hours in the back reading comics and trying to figure out how to convince the owner to give them the copies that didn't sell. It had been their sanctuary, a corner of the world that Grandfather had never invaded.

Andrew is…he's probably dead…

They'd never seen a body, never received one. Despite that, Tina acted like Andrew was in a grave and Colleen simply followed suit, even though she'd suspected he was out there, somewhere. It used to keep her up at night, thinking of him hurt and alone with only his fury to feed and care for him. Of course, that was the good scenario.

The one that woke her in a cold sweat even now was the thought that the monsters from Lumis had captured him again and he was being tortured.

He tries to kill me and all I can do is worry about him. I guess I should be grateful Grandfather was never able to beat my love for Andrew out of me.

The scar where he'd stabbed her with a knife of pure ice began to ache with memories of him and she grit her teeth against it. She had to know if he was in there, if he was alive, no matter what he might do to her or who he had become.

Heart pounding, she tried the handle on the candy store door and hissed.

It wasn't just cold, it was covered in a thin, crystalline layer of ice that burned her hand.

She pressed heat into her palms and thawed the door enough to open. The shop was exactly the same, as if someone had preserved it in a time capsule.

Rows of canisters filled with candies of all colors and textures lined the walls to her left, ending in a carousel display of comic books. The cash register was still the old kind, with brass buttons and a pull lever to open, though next to it was a more modern version. New posters graced the walls, in gaudy pinks and greens.

Yes, it really would've been like stepping back in time if not for the layer of frost that covered every square inch of the place.

She shivered, and a sick feeling began to spread in her gut.

"Andrew?" she whispered.

Something cracked under her foot and she looked down to see a frozen comic book. It was odd, not just for the fact that it was covered in a thicker layer of ice than everything else, but that it was the only thing out of place in an otherwise pristine shop.

She picked it up and felt her whole world spin.

It was a silly little comic that used to be her favorite, about a young woman who was a fashion designer by day and crime fighter by night. Andrew used to sneak her copies out of her room but she never minded as long as he let her read his Black Cat comic.

But when Grandfather saw him with it, Andrew was beaten for being a sissy…and I stood up for him, earning a beating of my own.

There was only one person who would know what this silly comic would mean to her. And only one person who could freeze it solid.

"I guess you took that comic to heart, didn't you?"

Andrew's voice hit her like a gut punch, forcing Colleen's breath out of her lungs in a thick cloud.

Slowly, as if she were half frozen, Colleen looked up into eyes that were at once so familiar and completely alien. Andrew stood in front of her, his head now bald, a webbed patchwork of scars stretched from under his dress shirt collar, over his jaw and ear to where his hairline should be. His broad body was clothed in a dark blue three-piece suit and tie, brown eyes now white like twin marbles of ice. His skin sparkled in the faint light and Colleen could only assume it was from a layer of ice.

That scar…I had left him in the building and it exploded. Oh god! He did get caught in it! How could I have left him there like that?

"The suit is a nice touch," he continued, interrupting her thoughts. "And no one would suspect Tina's daughter of being the hero of High Tide I suppose."

She stared at him, all the words of a thousand apologies, a thousand angry tirades stuck in the back of her throat.

He nodded, as if completely understanding.

"It must be a shock to see me. After all, you did leave me for dead."

"How?" she managed to say, her voice rough.

"The cold running through me saved my life, as best as we can tell anyway."

"We?"

"Yeah, you see, after that fiasco with Lumis, I was reassigned to another lab and got a kind of promotion. I was still an experiment, but at least I didn't have to stay in a cell and eat slop."

Colleen swallowed, her throat tightening at the memory of those small cages with metal cots and no windows.

"Andrew, I—"

"If you're going to apologize, save it. I don't need your apology. You see, I've had time to think, and I have to admit that I can hardly blame you for what you did."

Her eyes widened.

"What?"

"What choice did I give you?" he asked, pacing back and forth. "Really, I would've been disappointed if you hadn't done it."

"No, you don't mean that."

He laughed, a deep, crackling chuckle that sounded like shifting ice caps.

"Still trying to believe that I'm that little boy that used to step on the backs of your shoes? Oh sister...you need to grow up."

And without warning, a stream of ice hit her, knocking Colleen off her feet. She hit the frozen ground hard and winced at the impact across her shoulder blades.

"I have," he continued, throwing a solid ball of ice at her.

Colleen rolled just before it hit where she lay, shards of ice hissing against her skin. She tried to spring up onto her feet, but the ground under her was slick and she slid onto her knees instead.

"You want to kill me now, is that it?" she asked.

He stopped, hand raised with another ball of ice at the ready, his cold face had a wounded expression.

"What? No! I just want to get all this out of the way that's all. All the fighting and the testing each other's strengths so we can talk."

She stared at him, sure that the fall to the ice had somehow damaged her hearing.

"I...what? I don't want to fight you!"

"No? The hero of High Tide—"

"Stop calling me that!"

"—doesn't want to defend her territory against an intruder? What kind of defender are you?"

She stopped and really took in his words, heart pounding against her ribs.

"Wait," she said, rising slowly to her feet, "you...you're not here to just kill me?"

He snorted.

"Your arrogance knows no bounds. No, sister, not everything is about you."

"Then...why are you here?"

"To do what you haven't been able to. I want to save High Tide from Von."

"Von is beaten. He's barely limping along."

Andrew's face hardened and he shook his head.

"You have no idea what's coming, sis. Get out. Take Tina, and get out. I'll watch over this place I swear. But if you stay I'm not responsible for what's going to happen."

His words froze her blood and she could barely draw a breath to ask, "What's coming?"

"Me."

As a fresh blast of ice hit her, Colleen's mind exploded with the meaning behind his words. She toppled backwards over a counter of candies, the glass crashing around her and cutting her skin. Stars burst in her vision, the cold all around her biting and vicious.

By the time Colleen staggered to her feet, fire coursing through her veins and melting the ice around her, Andrew was gone.

CHAPTER FIVE

T ina took a sip from her crystal tumbler of forty-year-old scotch and sighed as the liquid seeped through her veins.

The office she'd kept in the renovated theater had always been her sanctuary. She could relax here with her dreams, safely tucked away in a corner of the world where no one would suspect what she was really thinking.

During the day, the theater sang with workmen rushing to put the finishing touches on her masterpiece. The chaos of sound and smell was like a shot of adrenaline to her every day because she knew that each nail hammered, each piece of crown molding installed was one step closer to the dream she'd nurtured for 20 years. But the last few days since Mr. Price's visit had tainted the blissful energy that Tina was at last letting herself indulge in.

I should've known not to let my guard down. There is always another shoe that can drop.

Shaking the thoughts away, Tina took another sip of her scotch and returned to the work at hand.

She picked up a pencil and scanned next week's schedule for the fifth time. The carpeting in the private suites would be finished tomorrow and a replacement bar would be installed by the end of the week. Then, the final set of sound equipment would be delivered and inspected.

Her fingers itched to check off the items.

Lists had always been a favorite thing of hers. The ability to write out things to be done and then cross them off one by one gave Tina a particular thrill of accomplishment that no one but her seemed to understand.

That's not true. Andrew…he used to copy me and…

She stopped herself with a sharp mental rebuke and opened a file containing a delivery schedule for the final air conditioner.

"I should double check that tomorrow…then call the employment service to make sure they are hiring extra wait staff from High Tide…"

She made a note and reached for her decanter of scotch to pour herself another glass. Usually she didn't drink this much but her nerves had been on high alert and she had to relax if she was going to keep the truth from Colleen.

"She doesn't need to know…she's free and I will be soon. I *will*."

She winced at the desperation in her voice.

So many years under her father's thumb, calculating every move, judging every relationship for the person's survivability and now here she was – about to start removing the last vestiges of the man's hold on her life when her one misstep decides to raise its ugly head.

Her mind drifted to the locked desk drawer to her left and she felt her chest give a familiar twinge. Photographs of her ex-husband, addresses that no one could know about and letters yellow with age, had been safely hidden away for the day when Tina had the courage to take them out and sift through the broken pieces of her life.

Her father had been dead now for over a year, and she still feared that the moment she opened the drawer. All of those memories would dissolve in front of her like the ephemeral dream she knew they were. Maybe it was best to simply keep it all locked away, and build something new?

Except it's all tangled up together, isn't it? I swore to Matthew that I'd tell Colleen and Andrew about him when it was safe. I just didn't think it would take so long and that everything would be so…broken.

The specter of her son rose up again in her mind and Tina suddenly felt too weak to push him away.

He'd been a sweet, quiet child, loving nothing more than to cuddle in her arms. She'd known early that Andrew would never survive Grandfather Malone's temper but also that there was no way to protect him fully from it. The only option had been to make sure the old man kept his focus on Colleen instead.

Tina flinched and drained her glass to sooth the guilt in her breast.

She knew it had been unfair to submit her daughter to that kind of fate, horribly so. But Colleen was strong, stubborn and Tina knew she could survive it.

But I miscalculated, didn't I? And lost Andrew anyway. Maybe…maybe I should've let Matthew take Andrew with him when he left.

She snorted and downed the rest of her scotch.

"Regrets are a distraction of a weak mind," she murmured.

A second later a chill ran up her arm and Tina frowned.

She had a fan in her office, but it barely kept the place from feeling like a stifling box much less produce truly cold air.

A creeping cold snaked up her legs and body. Tina's mouth went dry as a thought shot through her mind, producing both fear and hope.

No…he's dead. I'm just…I'm just hoping that…

The fact Tina had never seen the dead body of her youngest child was no hindrance to her belief that he'd perished in the fire at Lumis. It was easier than accepting that he was out there somewhere hurt and seething with hatred for her.

But…just in case.

Tina took a small pistol out of her desk drawer and confirmed that it was loaded. The air was getting colder now, a thin fog running along the floor like a trail of ghostly breadcrumbs.

She followed it out of her office and down the stairs, mouth dry, heart pounding. There were sparse lights along the stairs and the very back stage area, which was bare of the debris that had made it so claustrophobic for so long. Once off the staircase, Tina had a clear view of the stage, the ghost light shining its warm yellow light out onto the bare stage where a cold fog spun like a terrible apparition.

A tremble wracked Tina's body followed by an involuntary gasp from her throat. Everything narrowed to the man standing in front of her. There was nothing else in the world. Her arm lowered the gun clutched tight in her hand, in spite of the fact that old instincts were screaming at her to keep her guard up.

"Andrew," she whispered, her voice a croak.

He didn't turn around. Instead, he simply nodded.

She longed to move to him, put her arms around her son and try to make up for all the years she'd kept him at arm's length. But her limbs were stuck with the shock of it all and she could only stare.

"What…where have you been?" she managed to ask.

"Here and there," his voice was lower than she remembered, and harsher.

Tina licked her lips and at last made her legs obey. She walked slowly to where he stood, her eyes hungrily taking him in. His shoulders were much more broad and muscled than the last time she'd seen him, and he now towered above her. From a distance, his lack of hair had seemed odd, but now she could see spidery scars running over his scalp and down one side of his face. The same pattern repeated on his hands and neck.

The fire.

Finally, he turned and met her gaze, dark eyes replaced by crystalline ones that swirled like a snow storm. She bit back another gasp and forced herself to hold that gaze without flinching.

"Different than the last time you saw me, huh?"

Her hand ached to touch him, so she clenched it into a fist to keep herself in control.

"You survived the fire, how?"

In seconds his body was covered in a thin, glistening suit of ice. His cold visage grinned at her and then it disappeared. No puddle, no sign that it had ever happened.

"You're just like Colleen," she said, eyes wide.

"Well not just like, but similar I suppose. Maybe even better. Ice preserves after all, fire destroys."

"You're both exceptional, it's not a competition."

"Isn't it though? All our lives, that's been the rule. Compete, win," Andrew produced a large marble sized ball of ice and began rolling it up and down his fingers at a dizzying speed. "Of course, I wouldn't know anything about the latter, but Colleen would."

"It wasn't fair of him to make you try and win his…well, I won't say affection because he didn't have much."

"Approval."

"Yes, absolutely that. You were always enough," she said. "You never needed to prove yourself to me."

"No, that would mean you had to notice us."

The ice in his voice pierced Tina's heart and she could no longer restrain herself. She reached out and touched his cheek. The scars were rough under her palm and, just for a second, Andrew leaned in to her touch.

"I lived my life so afraid for you. I protected you the only way I knew how but that doesn't mean it was right. I'm sorry."

She felt a tremble in his cheek and thought she saw tears form in those strange eyes. But, as if realizing that he was letting his guard down, Andrew's jaw clenched and he turned away from her.

"I don't want your apologies," he growled.

"What do you want then?"

"High Tide."

If he'd asked for the moon, Tina wouldn't have been more stunned.

Her jaw dropped and a laugh escaped her, echoing in the vast, dark theater.

"If you haven't noticed there's a war going on. I can't exactly hand this place over to you."

"I know. I'm not asking you to."

Alarm bells began to ring in her head.

"Then, what?"

He turned back around, a grim set to his lips.

"I want you to retire, upstate to the summer home we never use. Take Colleen with you and get out of here while you still can."

"You know it's not that simple. Von is making a play for High Tide…but you would know that, wouldn't you?" Tina's eyes narrowed. "Why did you come to me, Andrew?"

His lips curled up into a wide grin.

"For my inheritance, of course! You didn't want it, even though you murdered the old man for it. And we both know Colleen could care less—"

"That's not true, she's been defending this place against that bastard for the past month."

"Oh I know, we had a nice chat about it. Though I don't think she really likes being a hero, if you want to know the truth."

Tina swallowed as nerves began to buzz all through her body.

"What did you do to her?"

"Why am I not surprised that you'd be more concerned for her than for anything else."

"That's not true and you know it! Now tell me, what did you—"

"Nothing, just a fight between siblings."

She studied him and tried to bring her growing panic to heel. Colleen could handle herself, she'd more than proven that over the last month. The situation before her needed her attention more than worries based on little information.

"So what, you're going to fight me and Von to…"

His smile widened and something awful fell into place.

"No. You…no," she gasped.

"Why do you think the old fool has been holding on? Mr. Price has been waiting until he's so desperate to win that he would do anything to save face. Even make a deal with him to hand High Tide over to me."

Tina's heart felt like it was going to pound right out of her chest and it was hard to breathe. She grabbed hold of the pole of the ghost light, hoping that it would hold her up somehow.

"You're working with Mr. Price? Do you have any idea who that man is, what he's threatening to do to Colleen?"

That took some of his bravado away and he stared at her.

"I know exactly who he is," Andrew said after a moment, forming a ball of snow in his hand. "He's one of the people who helped make me the man I am today."

Her eyes widened.

"He did this to you?"

"No, *mother*, I always had this in me. He and his friends just made it a little…more than it was before."

"Is he holding you prisoner then, is he making you do this? Please, let me help you."

"No!" His hand closed over the snow, face hardening. "Now for the last time Tina, go! Take Colleen and whoever else you want and leave!"

"Andrew, please don't do this."

"I don't know why you're so upset about it. You've been planning your escape for years. I'm giving you the perfect out."

"No," she shook her head, trying desperately to hold onto her hopes and plans. "You have no idea what you're doing! I—"

"Had a plan? What for exactly? Respectability? Approval?" He leaned toward her, venom dripping from his voice. "It's an illusion. I thought you would know that by now. They hold out this rule to us, this standard and even if we achieve it, we aren't good enough. Your plans, your theater? It doesn't matter, none of it. You could revive it all, the prestige of this neighborhood and this place. You could have them begging you to be seen here, and you'd still be the trashy daughter of a crime boss. One step up from a thug and a whore."

Something snapped in her as she heard her deepest fear flung in her face by the child she loved. Fury overwhelmed the panic that was building in her chest and Tina found herself pointing the gun at Andrew. In the back of her mind, a voice begged her to stop, to think, but she couldn't. Tina walked toward him, gun level with his chest.

"Get the hell out of here, and don't come back."

"I'll take that as a no then."

She pulled back the hammer of the gun and took one more step toward him, holding his gaze.

"See you around, Tina."

He took his time walking down the steps of the stage and out the red and gold doors, a trail of ice following him like a warning. She held the gun up for several minutes after he'd left, lowering it only because her knees buckled and she fell onto the still cold stage floor.

Years of hopes and plans, sacrifices and loss, ran through her mind. Tina usually held a tight leash on all of it, but Andrew had broken her control and it began to overwhelm her.

Tears would have been appropriate, she knew this. So would screaming. And both would've been a relief. But the only thing Tina could do was stare out into the dark, mind racing.

"Tina?" Rick's voice echoed through the theater.

Panic seized her and Tina sprang to her feet.

Oh god, if Andrew is still here…!

"Rick! Don't…stay there!"

"What? Tina where are you?'

She raced in the low light down the stage steps and sprinted to where Rick stood in the doorway between the lobby and the theater. Without thinking, Tina launched herself at him and threw her arms around his neck.

Rick caught her, saying nothing, though she knew that his mind must be spinning at this strange behavior.

"What happened?" he asked, his arms warm and firm around her.

Tina wanted to let him go and stand before him with all the strength and steel that she'd worn for the past twenty years. But she couldn't. It was as if Andrew had drained all of that from her in those few words.

"I...I don't want to talk about it," she finally said, her voice embarrassingly fragile.

"Okay," he said, holding her tight.

Sobs tried to claw their way up her throat, which was tightening by the second. Tina could barely hold them back.

Crying isn't going to fix this. But...what will?

The answer was clear, and something Tina couldn't bring herself to grab hold of. Instead, she took long, deep breaths, allowing herself to use Rick's strength to bolster her own until she could let him go and step back. When she did, Tina looked up into Rick's familiar face, so close to hers that she could feel the feather lightness of his breath on her cheeks. His dark eyes flicked down to her lips, sending a jolt of heat through Tina's body that both shocked and aroused her. She'd been feeling a pull toward him since the day she'd been shot outside of Cherry's Restaurant, the attraction building day by day. The fact that this younger, gorgeous man would be interested in her was ridiculous at first. Until she started catching him staring at her, the gaze unmistakably full of longing just before he'd look away.

Now, here she was, in his strong arms, his face so close. All she would have to do is lean in and...

No! You know how this all ends. He'll die because of you, or worse. You'll have to give him up like you did with Matthew.

Inch, by inch she pulled herself back until she was out of his arms and the distance between was no longer so fraught with danger.

"I'm fine," she said finally. "Just tired, there's a lot to do."

Rick eyed her with suspicion. He knew she was lying but god bless him, he didn't push her.

I don't deserve you.

"Can I get you anything?" he asked.

She still felt the heat from where his hands had been on her back, the warmth in his arms that drove away the chill left in Andrew's wake. Desire stirred within her again and she tamped it down with a firm hand.

"Could you please drive me home?"

"Sure."

He helped her lock up and then ushered her into the back of her car, eyes taking in every little movement she made. It grated on her as much as it also made her feel something she hadn't in a very long time: cared for.

Tears pricked her eyes as Rick drove the short distance to her brownstone. How long would she be able to keep doing this before she either broke or became so hardened that she drove everyone away?

CHAPTER SIX

Andrew sauntered into the Gothic style mansion, deep in the heart of Metro City, with far more bravado than he felt.

His mission had been theft of precious documents in Tina's safe, and that was all. Instead, Andrew paid a visit to his sister and mother, in hopes of getting them to leave. Such actions could be seen as insubordination, punishable by what Mr. Price and his associates called "tuning".

The thought of the procedure brought a sudden sinking feeling in his gut and he had to swallow hard to keep the bile down.

Calm down man! You know that he's way too close to getting what he wants to take you out of commission now. Keep a cool head, lie like only you can and you'll be fine...you'll be fine...

He made it two steps onto the wide stair case that led up to his rooms when a soft, lethal voice from the downstairs study stopped him cold.

"Come in here...now."

Andrew walked back down the stairs, taking the few seconds he had to get a grip on his emotions and school his features into a hardened mask.

When he stepped over the threshold and onto the thick Persian rug, Andrew's eyes went to the thin, pale man behind the massive oak desk.

Mr. Price was impeccably dressed, in spite of the hour. Papers were stacked in neat, alphabetical groups on the shining top of the desk, an even number of pens stood at attention in the onyx pen cup. The room was darkly appointed with black furniture and dark wood bookshelves stretching to the ceiling. Blood red drapes were closed for the night, not that they were open all that much during the day. Even the assorted drinks in their crystal decanters were a darker color than most.

Andrew always felt that it was all a bit much. Clearly, the man didn't have to work so hard to telegraph the fact that he was evil.

The ice wielder stood with his hands clasped in front of him before the desk, cold eyes meeting those of Mr. Price, who looked at him above thin fingers steepled in front of him.

"And where have you been, my cold little mouse?"

"Out getting things ready."

"You weren't told to do that."

"No, but I don't get all my orders from you, now do I?"

Mr. Price's smile turned even colder, if that was possible.

"Things are at a delicate tipping point. One wrong move and we lose our advantage. So, I'll ask you again. What were you doing tonight?"

"I sent a message to Tina and Colleen. One that will expedite this futile war."

"Do you really think that wise? After all, you might make someone think you were betraying us."

Andrew had been ready for this. He'd conjured up the perfect responses to every possible scenario that Mr.

Price might try. After working with him for six months, Andrew had gotten very good at predicting what the weasel would do. It wasn't a shock to hear this, even if it did send a stone of dread into Andrew's stomach.

"I have no reason to betray you, not if I get what I want," he replied. "Besides, even if they don't leave, seeing me has thrown them off balance. They'll be distracted by their feelings. Easier to topple."

Mr. Price paused, his eyes searching Andrew's as if looking for the truth behind his words.

"Just remember – as long as I am playing the role of Von, I hold your reigns," he finally said.

Andrew ground his teeth together at the reminder he didn't need.

The name Von had been a front for almost 20 years. Jason James needed someone who could be his representative to the criminal underworld of Metro City, but would also give him enough distance to never be implicated in anything. The original Von had been killed 10 years ago, though the rumor was that he was simply disfigured, no longer interested in seeing the world outside of his mansion. But the truth was that Jason simply replaced him with another. Andrew had no idea if that man was Mr. Price or if he'd recently been given the job. Whatever the circumstances, Mr. Price was the one who had been fighting Tina and was now determined to finish the job. Andrew had been waiting to get his shot at all this, trying to hide the fear that plagued him every day: the thought that Tina and Colleen would fall into the clutches of this man. Now he was here, so close to getting what he wanted but he had to walk a razor's edge to do it and also protect those he loved.

He swallowed the rage inside him at being this man's lap dog. There were more important battles to fight right now.

"Yes, sir, I understand."

"Good. Now, we must discuss how to use the information you stole from Tina."

"She'll have Colleen guarding the locations in the files."

"Yes, of course. Therefore, we must draw her out," Mr. Price leaned forward. "What do you think might draw her attention elsewhere, my cold friend?"

Andrew's heart beat faster in his chest, guilt and anger spiraling through him.

It was obvious what the odious man was driving at, and Andrew had expected such a request would come into play at some point. It was the reason he'd revealed himself, to hopefully convey to Colleen and Tina that he was beyond their help and that they should abandon him.

Everything would be so much easier if they would. But the way Colleen had looked at me...she will never give up.

"Me," he said, voice rough.

Mr. Price went back to the papers in front of him, and Andrew knew that he was dismissed.

The walk up the stairs to his sparsely decorated room wasn't all that long, but it gave Andrew sufficient time to let his anger boil to the surface.

He'd volunteered for the experiments at Lumis in order to better manage his powers. If successful, Andrew believed he would be able to wrestle control of the family business from Grandfather and bring some kind of peace to his family. But he'd sorely underestimated the toll that all of the experiments would take on his mind and body. The memories from his time in the lab at Lumis were patchy and dream like. Andrew had no idea what was real, and what was a hallucination from the weeks of blinding pain he'd had to endure.

Except for trying to kill Colleen.

Andrew winced at that memory and plopped down on his bed. Even now, there was an odd impulse in his mind urging him to finish the job. It had become quieter as the months had passed, but when he was especially tired, it would rise up like some ghoul to torment him. As it was, Andrew was haunted by the things he'd been forced to do by the men who controlled him. They had been very clear about the price of disobedience when Andrew had tried to break free after the lab at Lumis had been compromised. If Andrew wanted his mother to be safe, he'd play their game. If he didn't want Colleen strapped to a table and "enhanced" then he wouldn't step a toe out of line.

And then, when they decided they wanted High Tide for some reason, they'd dangled that in front of him, too.

Wasn't that what he'd wanted, to save his home?

"If you do as we say, you will have influence with us to protect your neighborhood," Mr. Price had promised.

Andrew wasn't a fool, he knew there would be many limitations and he'd planned for it. Every time he'd been let out of his comfy prison cell to do the bidding of Mr. Price, Andrew had listened and observed. Some of the men in charge didn't bother hiding who and what they were talking about in front of him, either because they thought him too stupid to understand or too loyal to betray. And he'd taken advantage of every moment, waiting for just the right mission, the right chance.

When this mission to High Tide had fallen in his lap, Andrew worked very hard to make his obvious glee show cold and cruel. Now, it was just a matter of waiting for the information he'd slipped to the cop to grow to fruition. It wouldn't be in time to save Tina and Colleen from being kicked out of High Tide, that was true.

But that doesn't matter. It will work. Mr. Price and the rest will all come tumbling down and I'll be there to drive a knife of ice straight into their rotten hearts.

CHAPTER SEVEN

C olleen watched the sun come up over the jagged rooftops, coffee steaming in the chipped mug in her hand. She'd swept every inch of High Tide after her confrontation with Andrew, looking for any sign of him and found nothing. She winced as her shoulder gave a twinge and looked over her arms where small nicks and bruises were already starting to heal.

She once thought she'd give anything to see Andrew again. But then she did, at Lumis Chemical's underground labs, and the brother she knew was gone, replaced by a powered man with a heart of ice.

"But I didn't exactly react well to that," she muttered, taking a scalding drink of coffee.

Andrews words came back to her, and Colleen winced.

He couldn't really mean that he was okay with her leaving him there to burn to death, could he?

"No," she said to herself, gritting her teeth, "I won't accept it. I can't. My brother is still in there, and I'll be damned if I'm going to just give up on him again."

Saying the words that had been swirling inside her head all night was a kind of release that eased all the tension in Colleen's body. This time she would do what she couldn't at Lumis. She would save her brother if it was the last thing she did.

Downing the rest of the overheated brew in her mug, Colleen went down to the bar kitchen to find some breakfast. Wanda never seemed to mind if a half dozen eggs were missing because Colleen needed groceries. Though the firestarter wondered if the bar owner might be docking her pay for it.

In a few minutes, Colleen had bacon frying and four eggs scrambled along with a fresh pot of coffee. Her stomach gave a loud growl and her body began to tingle. She'd gone too long without fuel.

"Maybe I should go to Jet City and talk to Marco after all this, see if he has any insights about how to manage needing to eat so much. If he has that same problem, that is."

She glanced at the phone on the wall, and realized that she really just wanted to talk to her old friend.

Shrugging off the impulse, she slid her food onto a plate and dug in. In a few minutes, she'd scrapped the plate clean and wished she'd made more.

Colleen took her time cleaning up, because what she had to do next wasn't something she was looking forward to.

Tina needed to be told that Andrew was back, that he was working with Von. And considering everything her mother had been planning the last few months, Colleen wasn't at all sure how Tina would react to the news.

I just need to convince her to let me handle this. Maybe she'll be so preoccupied with the theater that she won't care...
Colleen snorted at the unlikely chance.

She showered fast and slipped into a sleeveless green dress and sandals, wondering if Rick had stayed the night again. She knew that Tina hadn't started sleeping with the handsome young bodyguard, that he was only supposed to be there to keep watch. But she also knew the way Rick looked at her mother, and the way Tina had begun to look at him.

Not that I'm not happy for my mother but no kid wants to know their parent might be taking a lover. Ick!

Then Shay's face flashed through her mind, stopping Colleen cold with a rush of warmth that infused her limbs and stomach, bringing it with a jittery kind of energy that she hadn't felt in a very long time.

She laughed, nervous and disbelieving, as she walked out of her apartment.

"Get a grip! She's a cop and you don't even know her."

But the picture of Shay's glistening dark skin and eyes, her bow shaped mouth and small, yet muscular body stayed with Colleen for several blocks, providing a very welcome distraction to the conversation she was about to have.

The happy mood was broken as Colleen turned the corner where Tina's brownstone sat. Four black cars with armed men were positioned along the street, and two more were standing outside at the foot of the stoop. Her mother never had protection like this. Something was very wrong.

The men out front recognized her immediately and let her pass. As panic built in her chest, Colleen ran through the front door and rushed inside.

"Tina?" she called.

Two men who obviously didn't know her stood in the living room to her right and one more came through the arched way from the dining room. They had pistols drawn and at the ready. Her hands shot up as soon as she saw them, her stomach twisting. If Tina felt the need to hire new men, then the situation was worse than Colleen expected.

"I'm Tina's daughter. What is going on, where's my mother?" she asked the one in front of her.

"Let her through," Tina's voice was hard as it drifted from her office down the hall to the left.

Colleen made it down the hallway in a few quick strides to see a whirlwind of a mess inside Tina's usually immaculate home office. Papers were stacked haphazardly on leather chairs, broken crystal decanters glistened in the waste basket and a broken desk drawer sat against a disorganized book shelf.

"What happened?" she whispered, though she knew in her heart the answer to that question.

Tina's dark eyes shot up to her, shrewd and hard.

"Leave us," she commanded.

Everyone but Rick tromped out of the room and closed the door behind them.

"Andrew is back," Tina said, her voice hollow and firm.

Colleen knew that obviously, but the way her mother just threw it out there struck Colleen as strange. As if that wasn't the worst thing to happen last night. She looked around at the mess, not seeing any evidence of melted ice.

"So you think he did this?"

"Him or someone working with him. They tossed this room and stole some files from my locked drawer."

"What was in them?" Colleen asked, clutching the back of a chair in front of her.

"Locations of the last money laundering drops that I've been running for Madame Capelli."

Colleen choked.

"You're still doing that?"

"She's an old friend."

"She's the queen of the oldest crime family in Metro City!"

Tina threw her pen down and stared at Colleen, eyes narrowed.

"It was important to maintain the relationship up to the last."

Colleen nodded as understanding bloomed in her mind.

"An ace in the hole in case you needed back up."

"And protection from the other families. Now that's in jeopardy."

"More than that," Colleen said, holding her mother's gaze. "If Madame Capelli finds out her money is at risk—"

"She'll have no choice to but take me out. Yes, I know. But then again, your brother did warn me."

Colleen licked her lips, her mouth dry.

"Wh-What did he say last night?"

Tina's jaw tightened and Rick shifted uncomfortably where he stood off to the side.

"He's working with Von," Tina said, a slight hitch in her voice the only thing betraying that she felt something other than fury. "He told me to leave town and let him take over."

Colleen closed her eyes, and swore under her breath

So…I heard him right after all.

"You don't seem as shocked as I thought you would," Tina said.

"I'm not. He…he turned up at the Sweet Spot last night, and we had a walk down memory lane."

Tina's eyes flicked over Colleen's body, worry creasing her brow.

"I have a meeting with Madame Capelli tomorrow. I'm still in a position of strength compared to Von," Tina said, "I am hoping she will work with me to recover the information and bury him once and for all."

"And Andrew? What about him?"

Her mother hesitated and Colleen's stomach dropped.

"He's your son!"

"He's a reckless fool and he's going to get us and a lot of innocent people killed. I have no time for that."

"No time!"

"You promised to protect this place, and now, when it needs you most, you're going to become squeamish?"

"He's my brother!"

Tina shook her head.

"Not anymore and I think you know that."

"No, you're wrong. Andrew is still in there, I know it."

"Like you knew it at Lumis when he tried to kill you?"

Colleen's hand went involuntarily to the scar on her forearm.

"We failed him," she said, the words like ash in her mouth. "*I* failed him. And I'll be damned if I do it again."

"It's too late," Tina said, shaking her head. "He has to be stopped."

"That doesn't mean he has to be killed."

Tina put her hand on a small metallic box on her desk and nodded.

"No, it doesn't."

Dread coiled in her as Colleen realized what was in that box. The only thing she'd ever encountered that could render their powers gone, and make any powered person as weak as a kitten.

"You…you have—" she stuttered.

"A left over gift from your mission last month."

"Why in god's name are you keeping that poison?"

And then Colleen laughed, bitter and loud as the answer to her question burst in her mind.

"For me. In case I get out of hand maybe?"

"No, not exactly."

Colleen could feel fury rush through her and she let go of the chair, leaving scorch marks behind. She'd gotten much better at controlling her powers but the heat in her hands still managed to surprise her.

"You have the one thing that could leave me vulnerable to men that I've made enemies out of for *you*, for High Tide," Colleen's voice sounded like the hissing of hot meat on a grill, "and you're acting like it's nothing?"

Tina held her gaze but something was there that Colleen had never seen before.

Burning deep in her mother's dark eyes was real, stark fear.

Of me. She's afraid of me.

The thought was, at once, empowering and deeply sad.

But if she's really afraid of me, then I can use that to my advantage, god help me.

"You won't touch him with that stuff," she continued, a fire ball forming in her hand. "You will give me a chance to try and reach him."

Rick's hand went to the weapon at his hip, and Colleen spared him a quick glance to let him know that she saw it. He wouldn't be able to get a shot off before she threw the fire at him, and he knew it.

Still, he would die for Tina...and as much as I hate him, I don't want it to come to that. Can he tell I'm mostly bluffing?

"Or else what?" Tina asked.

"Don't make me," she responded, a waver in her voice. "I want a chance to reach him. You owe us both that much."

Tina's shoulders fell just a little and Colleen knew she'd hit her mother in one of her few weak spots.

"Fine, I will give you until the theater opening."

Colleen closed her hand over the fire ball and turned on her heel.

"In the meantime, I need you at the money laundering site tonight," Tina said, stopping her cold. "If Andrew tries to take it out before we've managed to move Madame Capelli's assets to a secure location, it will not be good."

She could feel a retort come alive on her tongue and looked over her shoulder at Tina.

"Do you really want another conflict in High Tide on top of this one?" her mother asked. "Besides, you can try to talk to your brother. You know, in between punches."

Colleen exhaled fast and angry, the hand on the door knob growing hot.

"Fine."

And she walked from the room without looking at anyone, head high and mind spinning.

She had gotten a small reprieve for Andrew, now she just had to figure out how the hell she was going to get through to her brother.

"Don't you think you should've told her about Mr. Price?" Rick asked once Colleen had left the room.

"No. Colleen would panic, try to find him or…god knows what kind of trouble she'd get herself into," Tina fell back into her chair, hand over her eyes.

She heard him move toward her, as if she had some kind of radar when it came to the man. When she opened her eyes, he was kneeling in front of her, adoration and worry shining in his gaze.

"Let me take care of this for you."

"How?"

"I can find out where Mr. Price is, where Andrew is and…take care of them."

She opened her mouth to answer and couldn't find the words.

Mr. Price was a whole other breed of man, and though Rick was tough, he wouldn't stand a chance against him. Tina could feel it. And as for Andrew, Tina may have shown a cold front to her daughter, but in truth she wanted her son home and safe. Rick would do what he could to provide that if she asked, and he'd end up dead.

Tina flinched at the thought and felt her stomach lurch in panic.

I can't lose him…dear god I might actually love him.

It took all her strength not to reach out and caress his cheek, to press a kiss to his waiting lips as a sudden need for him tried to take over.

"Just say the word," Rick said, voice soft, "and I will do whatever it is you need me to. I…I know you can take care of yourself, but you don't have to do it alone."

Tina jumped up from her chair and walked to the bar at the far end of the office before she gave in to the rising tide of desire within her. It was early for a drink and she didn't give a damn. She had to get control of these feelings before they controlled her.

Worst timing ever for a second chance at…this *to come around. What a cosmic joke!

She took a long pull from the glass of whiskey in her hand, breathed and took another drink. After nearly finishing it, Tina had her feelings contained with an iron hand and felt secure enough to turn around. Her mind snapped back to business, a welcome distraction.

"Mr. Price is a slippery bastard. He's already given me a warning," she said.

"You want to give him one right back?"

"Yes, but how? I have no idea where to strike him."

Rick nodded, brows drawing together as he thought about the problem.

"It seems like he has a stake in you losing to Von. Could be they're on the same side."

"Yes, but I thought that I'd nearly bankrupted the bastard. Now he's got reinforcements."

She took another sip from her drink while she turned over the problem.

"If we can keep Madame Capelli on our side," she said, everything taking shape as she spoke, "and reach out to the other families, we can isolate Von. A prolonged war isn't good for anyone's business. They were angry when Colleen started fighting for me, imagine how they will feel when Andrew is revealed to be on Von's side. All I have to do is hold on and protect Madame's assets, let Von stir up more trouble with Andrew. Then I'll ask for a meeting and strike with the backing of the other families."

"How long do you think?"

Tina shrugged.

"I don't know. First things first though. Protect the laundering sites and prove our strength. Maybe even reveal Andrew in the process. Then we'll see what we have to bargain with."

"There's an awful lot outside of our control."

"Yes, but do you have a better plan?"

"A final push into Devil's Own and a coordinated hit on all his businesses wouldn't hurt."

"And leave Madame's holdings unprotected? No, that's what they want, and I won't be that foolish."

Rick exhaled through his nose, furrowed brow screaming that he was uncomfortable with this. But, true to form, he wouldn't push Tina any more than he already had.

Sometimes, I wish he would.

"What do you want me to do now?" he asked instead.

"Get the boys over to those businesses if you haven't already, then have our spies in Devil's Own follow Mr. Price or Andrew to find out where they're hiding."

Rick nodded and left to do as she asked. When the door closed, Tina slumped against the wall, empty glass in hand. She wished someone would tell her if she was doing the right thing or not. Rick's unspoken doubts whispered in the back of her mind and Colleen's anger haunted her thoughts. This was all so precarious, one wrong move and everything would come tumbling down.

"Then I guess, I better not make a wrong move."

She sighed and poured another drink before returning to her desk.

CHAPTER EIGHT

C olleen had walked around High Tide all day, gone to every one of their old haunts, and never saw a sign of Andrew. Discouragement and fear tugged at her and she found herself turning over every word he'd spoken to her at Lumis and at the Sweet Spot.

What could she have done to save him? How did he get so hard and cold?

She chuckled at that and then winced.

"The two of us, fire and ice...damn ironic," she murmured, pulling on her Fahrenheit suit.

Tina hadn't budged in her determination to make Colleen guard the furniture store where Madam Capelli's money was being laundered. It more than grated on her that instead of being out in High Tide, protecting it and searching for Andrew, she was guarding a criminal's money.

She was just about to climb out the window and onto the fire escape when a knock sounded on her door.

"Colleen? Sorry for dropping by but...I was in the neighborhood," Shay's voice filtered through the door, the last words punctuated by a nervous chuckle.

Colleen's heart stopped.

What is she doing here?

"Umm…Wanda said you were home…I know this might be weird and…Oh my god, I'm sorry, you're probably feeling like I'm over stepping a boundary or something and I…I'm so sorry."

Panic seized Colleen. Much to her shock she realized that she didn't want Shay to leave.

Tearing the mask from her face, Colleen threw a robe over the suit and went to answer the door. She only opened it enough to peek around the corner and saw that Shay had turned and begun walking away.

"Wait," Colleen said, "I-I was in the shower, sorry."

Shay walked back, an embarrassed smile on her face.

"No, I'm sorry, I shouldn't have just stopped by like this but I…well, I called a few times and I wasn't sure you were getting my messages."

Colleen frowned.

"I wasn't, actually, so it's a good thing you came by."

Shay's smile lit up her face and Colleen found herself wanting to make her happy just so she could see it as much as possible.

Then she noticed Shay was in uniform and felt an instinctual tension rise up her spine.

"Just getting off work or going to it?" Colleen asked.

"About to go on patrol. I think Walter is frustrated I made him stop by, this isn't our beat for the night."

Colleen nodded, wondering what her beat was so she could avoid it as Fahrenheit.

"So I-I've been away for a while and it turns out that not everyone is keen on hanging out with a cop, go figure right?" her voice was too bright, too loud and Colleen found herself smiling at the adorable way this woman bounced up on her toes to emphasize certain syllables.

Is she nervous around me?

"And," Shay continued, "I know that you might not be too comfortable with it either, being Tina Knight's daughter and…"

The words stole the smile right off Colleen's face and she crossed her arms. She was such a fool for thinking, even for a moment, that Shay would be any different than anyone else that knew the reputation of her family.

Shay's eyes widened at the obvious change in Colleen.

"Oh my gosh, I did it, I made you feel even more uncomfortable, I'm sorry. I didn't mean anything by it—"

"You didn't mean that my mother is a criminal and I might be too or at least have that as an inclination and might not want to be around you in case I let something slip?"

The young cop's mouth hung open and then snapped shut. She took a deep breath and then began to speak again, the words slower, more deliberate but no less nervous.

"I'm sorry I said that. I don't know what I believe about your mom. I grew up hearing the same stories everyone else did but they were mainly about your grandfather and…well, to be honest the only stories about your family I hear now are that your mother is helping rebuild High Tide, create jobs for the people here. And there's nothing bad in that."

Colleen felt her shoulders relax just a little at those words.

"Alright then, what do you want to ask me?"

"Right, yeah, before I stuck my foot all the way into my mouth, I was going to ask if you'd like to go to a movie tomorrow night? There's a new one playing at The Tide Pool and I thought…well, it could be fun."

Colleen felt genuine emotional whiplash. One moment Shay is adorable, the next insulting and then a second later alluring. She wasn't at all sure what to think or feel about the request, especially after the way Shay had implied that her family were a bunch of criminals. But one thing was clear, despite all of the questions in her mind: she liked this fast talking, energetic woman. And if she was asking Colleen to go out, even as friends, she wanted to take the risk.

And why not? I haven't had a real friend since…well, since Karen. And I may never see her again, so…

"I would like that," Colleen said, a tiny smile turning up the edges of her mouth.

Shay let out a long breath and giggled.

"Oh good, wow! I was so nervous, especially after saying that about your family and…and I shouldn't bring that up again. Alright, I will meet you here at seven?"

Colleen couldn't help a chuckle of her own at the way Shay's mouth ran away with her.

"Yeah, that would be good."

"Good, okay… then I'll…I gotta go to work."

"I've got to go, too," she said, breaking the eye contact.

"Oh yeah, sure. Bye."

Shay waved and almost skipped from the door and down the narrow stairs.

Colleen stood there for a minute, staring after her and wondering if she had any right to feel this excited and hopeful about another woman, especially one that would likely arrest her without a second thought if she really knew what Colleen did with her nights.

The stake out across from the furniture store was beyond dull.

Colleen heard sirens every hour, echoing from places either near to High Tide or within the neighborhood itself. The portable police scanner she'd snuck up on the roof with her crackled with information, none of it anything that Colleen was really looking for. Although every report of something going on in High Tide made her grit her teeth and curse Tina's reliance on her criminal contacts. If she wasn't up here she could be out where it mattered, helping people.

Or looking for Andrew.

The only signs of activity were the occasional person leaving the back room, Colleen assumed to clear out the evidence.

After three hours of nothing, Colleen was ready to simply pack it in and tell Tina that she was paranoid. That's when the police scanner said the words she'd been waiting all night to hear.

"Ice, I repeat there's ice on the road. We spun out and now we're surrounded by men in masks. Send back up!"

The officer yelled their location, fear thick in his voice. It was on the far edge of where High Tide and the Devil's Own butted up against one another, the two neighborhoods sharing a tenuous border that Von and his goons had been defending for the past month.

She jumped to her feet and barreled down the fire escape. Colleen knew that she had promised Tina to guard the furniture store, to make sure that Andrew didn't do anything to it, but this was her chance. She had to get through to him before he did any more damage.

I'm not giving up on him, not this time.

The motorcycle that Marco had sent her as a present had been parked beside Wanda's bar unused for the past month because Colleen really didn't care for the machine. But, tonight, she'd taken it to the furniture store, just in case she needed to get out quick.

Not having ridden it much at all, Colleen was shaky on the damn thing, swearing as she swerved dangerously and almost crashed into several parked cars. By the time she'd gotten the hang of it enough to speed up, the police scanner was going crazy with reports of ice around the warehouse, making it impossible for the police to get into the building.

She stopped just shy of where the ice made a deadly sheet on the street and stowed the bike between two parked cars. Colleen peeked out from behind one of the cars to take in the situation.

Two police vehicles had spun out onto the sidewalk and were pinned down by Von's men firing from behind a barrier of ice, which was stationed in front of a small, squat building that could just barely be called a warehouse.

Her thoughts scrambled here and there, trying to come up with a plan to save the police and also draw Andrew out from wherever he was hiding.

The ice on the street first so the men can get out, then the barrier.

She put her hands on the ground and in minutes the street was clear of the thick ice. There was no need for flames, just a layer of heat that wavered in the air, on the cusp of revealing itself. Still, the cops noticed and pointed to the now clear road.

I hope to god they don't shoot me when they see me.

Darting out, Colleen flung fire at the ice barrier where the goons were hiding. Shouts echoed behind her followed by bullets. The police were shooting but was it at her or the men who were now vulnerable?

One of the goons went down and his four companions didn't hesitate to run for the cover of the building. The police ran from behind their vehicles and were stopped by gun fire that erupted in front of them from the broken windows. Sirens screamed nearby and Colleen knew that back up was seconds away.

If the police get here and start shooting, it's going to get ugly. I need to get to Andrew before they do and there's only one place he could be.

Doubt wiggled in the back of her mind, telling her that something was wrong. But she pushed it away, and ran around the building and to the back, grinning when she saw the back door. A quick flash of heat and the hinges melted, making it easy to simply push the door aside. Colleen stepped into a dark back room with a few boxes and the smell of old papers. The air was chilled and she knew that Andrew had to be inside.

She stepped out into the main room, where the goons were positioned at the few windows. With their backs to her, they were focused on the police outside so they didn't notice when she began to melt the fine sheet of ice in the room. Until it started dripping on them, that is.

They pivoted with a shout, one of them firing without really looking. The bullets hit the wall to her right, spraying her with plaster and left over ice shards.

She flinched and it was enough for them to charge her. A wall of controlled fire rose up in front of the men, their screams and cursing adding to the chaos of the moment. One goon fired his gun through the flames, the bullet grazing Colleen's arm. It broke her concentration for a second and the flames began to spread. She reigned them in, but now the men realized that they could still hurt her, even with the fire between them.

Men started shouting outside, and bullets smashed the little bit of glass remaining in the windows. At the same time, police broke through the door, yelling for the gunmen to get on the ground.

"She's here!" one of the police said, firing into the flames.

Colleen brought the fire back into her body as she ran toward a door to the left. Bullets followed her in a spray, bits of the floor hitting her calves as she ran.

The room she burst into was an office with a desk, filing cabinet and papers scattered around. It was obvious that it hadn't been used in months and Colleen swore.

Andrew wasn't here, that was obvious now. If he had been, there's no way he would've stayed out of the fight. And this place had been abandoned for a while at this point.

The police out in the main room were yelling, someone called for a search and Colleen knew she had seconds before they barged in. She shoved the desk against the door to buy herself precious time and looked around. There wasn't a door but there was one window, barely large enough for her to fit through. It would have to do. As Colleen stepped up to it, something crunched under her foot. Looking down, she saw a file encased in a sparkling layer of frost. Behind her, someone shoved on the door, the old desk scraping the bare floor.

Colleen snatched the file, which became damp at her touch, and blasted the glass out of the window. The small shards cut her hands and upper arms as she climbed through. The moment her feet touched the ground, a terribly familiar voice reached her ears.

"Stop, hands where I can see them!" Shay said.

The vigilante turned and looked the cop in the eye, knowing it was risky but not able to help herself. Shay's eyes narrowed, as if she were trying to place Colleen and then she raised her gun higher, taking a cautious step forward. Behind her, the mountainous body of her partner stepped around the corner.

"Good work, Reynolds," he said, his voice a low rumble. "I'll take care of this, you're needed out front."

Shay hesitated but stepped away, eyes glued to Colleen until the last minute.

Colleen's body tensed, ready to burn Walter just enough to scare him the moment he touched her. Instead, he put his gun away and raised his hands in a gesture of surrender.

"I don't have a lot of time," he said, "but I've been trying to contact you. I have questions about Lumis Chemical and what went on there."

She didn't say a word, just held his gaze, pushing a little fire into her eyes to make him see that she wasn't someone he could push around.

He swallowed and nodded, as if he got the message loud and clear.

"I want to find out what really happened. I'm on your side."

"How do I know that?" she asked.

Walter looked behind him, where the police were starting to cart Von's men out of the building.

"Fair enough. Look, call me, we can meet someplace and talk. That's all I want to do is talk. Now," he held out his hands, "make it look good."

Her eyes widened. Was he serious? He wanted her to assault him?

"I know it's not ideal, but if you don't there's going to be a lot of questions."

She shook her head.

"Not my problem."

She turned to go and Walter's huge hands seized her arm.

It was instinct, pure and simple. She let the heat out, grabbed a hold of his wrists and felt his skin burn.

He groaned in pain and cradled his hand.

Bastard!

"Walter? What's going on back there?" Shay said, coming around the corner.

Her eyes widened when she saw Walter bent over his hand and drew her weapon on Colleen. She could've melted the gun, shot some fire at her just to scare, but the last thing she wanted to do was hurt Shay. So Colleen made the only decision she could and ran, Shay's voice echoing behind her as she ordered her to stop.

Colleen had almost wrecked the motorcycle three times before making it back to her apartment over Wanda's. She leapt up the fire escape and ripped off her mask, heart hammering in her chest, adrenaline making her powers boil under her skin.

Shay almost shot her.

Walter wanted to talk about the place her brother had been experimented on, the place she'd left him to die in a fiery inferno.

And she had a sinking suspicion that Andrew had been at the furniture store while she was chasing a false lead.

She looked down at the file clutched in her hand. It was damp from the frost that had melted on it and the sweat from her palms. Andrew had frozen it specifically, she could feel it.

There was nothing else in that room, nothing in the entire building except this. Why would he leave it for me?
She sat down and flipped open the folder, her suit constricting in the sticky heat. She wanted a shower and a soft night dress, but the mystery of what her brother was trying to tell her captivated Colleen.

The first six pages were all shipping manifests with dates going back four years. Then, the one from the month when Tina took over Grandfather Malone's crime syndicate. Handwritten in red ink was *"Supplies no longer assured. Seek alternative supplier."*

Colleen read every letter on the shipping manifests, knowing she was missing something.

The containers were small and went over land to agricultural warehouses in the Midwest.

"What in the world would he be shipping there?"

The description was missing on every single one. She tried holding the papers up to the light to see if any impressions had been left, but there was nothing.

She turned over every possible connection between the illegal businesses Von ran to those that her grandfather oversaw. Only one overlapped and it was the first thing her mother had shut down.

Prostitution. But what would that have to do with shipping to these places? It could be a front but...I need more information.

Her eyes strayed to the card sitting on her bedside table.

He might know something from his years on the force but...

Colleen knew that if Walter had wanted to, he could've arrested her and turned her over right then and there. Instead, he'd let her go and asked for her help.

The faint strains of a song filtered through her window, carried on the warm night air and she smiled. Memories of Judy and her bouncy little grin as she listened to this song lifted Colleen's spirits. When Judy had first heard this melody in Haven, Colleen had seen the little girl dance as if the past was no longer haunting her, and because of that it had become a favorite of Colleen's.

I should find out when her birthday is so I can—
And that's when it hit her.

"Oh god," she whispered, staring at the file as if it were a viper. "That's what this is, that's what it *has* to be! They're smuggling *kids*! My grandfather...he and Von were..."

She felt bile push its way up her throat and she closed her eyes, taking deep breaths. Her grandfather had been an evil man, but this was something Colleen honestly never thought he would do.

"But it's the only thing that really makes sense. Tina would've stopped it when she took over, and Von would've been angry. And not just him, Jason James. He could be the one backing Von in this war, keeping it going."

She grabbed a pad of paper and began jotting down notes and possibilities. After an hour she had more questions than anything else, and no leads to answer them, save one.

She glanced at where Walters' card was stowed in the drawer of her bedside table and sighed.

I think I have to meet with this cop if I'm going to get to the bottom of this.

She placed her notes inside the file and stuffed it in between her mattresses. Even with all the unanswered questions, there was something that was very clear: Andrew was redeemable. He had left her this file because he wanted her to know what was really going on. The only thing she couldn't figure out was if this clue held a key to saving him from whatever Von had planned.

"I might have to sleep on that," she said and then grimaced when she caught a whiff of herself. "But first a shower, then bed."

CHAPTER NINE

The last customers left the tea room, the older couple giving Tina a smile as they passed her table. The small dining room was kept reasonably cool with the addition of fans scattered throughout. Sunlight was blocked at this time of the afternoon by the awning out front and some carefully placed blinds, but there still managed to be a glare from the small bar up front, where expensive brandies were displayed on the shelves.

The waiter hovering nearby poured more tea into her cup and she managed to give him a tight smile in thanks. She would've preferred coffee or something stronger, in spite of the fact that it was only noon. Sleep had been elusive even before she'd gotten the call from the lone person to survive the attack on the furniture store.

Tina had tried desperately to do some damage control when she discovered that the other two locations, small enough that she hadn't bothered telling Colleen about them, had also been hit.

Now, Tina fidgeted with the handle of her tea cup and tried her best to calm the pounding of her heart.

One thing. I asked Colleen for one thing and she couldn't even…

Anger flared hot and she clenched her jaw.

Tina understood Colleen's moral objections to keeping the relationship with Madame Capelli; in many ways, she shared it. But where Colleen had the luxury of seeing things as either wholly good or bad, Tina had to be more realistic than that.

The morning paper brought more bad news. The police commissioner, deciding that the addition of another vigilante in the turf war between High Tide and Devil's Own was just too much, had created a task force to hunt them down.

To hunt my children down.

Very little shook her at this point in her life, yet this was one of the few that made her stomach roil.

Before they'd pulled up to the tea room, Rick wanted to take the rest of the men and make sure Andrew couldn't do any more damage.

"A show of strength will prove—" he'd started.

"Nothing Rick, not now. We have to be smarter than them."

He'd been hard to restrain and even now he glowered from the front door where he stood guard.

Maybe he's right…maybe I should hit Von and Andrew with extreme prejudice. End it all with a show of strength.

But the thought was distasteful to her, if for no other reason than that she'd never forgive herself for killing her son. For the first time in a long while, Tina wondered if her father hadn't been right about personal connections after all.

She checked the delicate diamond and gold watch on her wrist and frowned.

Madame Capelli was never late, and yet, the set time for their lunch had passed ten minutes ago.

A heaviness of fear enveloped her as she looked around.

The place was empty, which wasn't necessarily strange on its own, except that her waiter had disappeared and the dim sounds from the kitchen had become silent. She met Rick's gaze, realizing what was happening a second before he dove for her and bullets sprayed the floor.

Rick dragged her under the table and pulled out his firearm. Tina reached under her skirt and found her tiny revolver. If she was going to die today, she would go out fighting.

The bullets came from two directions that had them hemmed in good and proper. And even though they might be able to hold out for a minute or so with the cover they had, Tina and Rick were laughably out gunned.

My men out front are dead, otherwise they'd be in here. And they've probably got both the front and back entrances covered. Which means…check mate.

She looked at Rick, the truth of the situation passing between them. Before she could do anything, Rick crushed his lips to hers. It was the kind of kiss you gave when you knew it would be your last and it made Tina's eyes burn with unshed tears.

"I love you," he said, voice gruff.

She opened her mouth to try and stop him from doing something selfless and stupid but Rick didn't wait for any of it. Instead, he flung himself out from under the table and fired at the assailants that had come in from the back of the tea room. His words and actions had shocked her enough that she sat there for half a second before turning the table on its side and firing from behind it.

The men backed up, taking cover behind the wall that separated the dining area from the kitchen. The body of two gunman lay on the floor, blood soaking into the rich carpet.

Rick ran to the other side of the small room to get a better look and fired again. A body fell to the floor and someone swore as they fired in Rick's direction. Tina took the opportunity and fired one well aimed bullet, wounding the gunman. But her revolver had a limited capacity and she was now empty. Looking at Rick across the room, she could tell that he was just about out, as well.

This was it, the end of all of her hopes and dreams just because she'd trusted one person in this lousy world to not desert her when the chips were down.

Madame Capelli's betrayal was like a stab through the heart. The woman couldn't even look Tina in the eye when she killed her.

The thought transformed her anger into something stubborn.

No…I'm not dying today because of this. I've waited too god damned long for my shot at the life I want.

The small candle that kept the tea pot warm on the table was somehow still lit and not causing a fire. Tina snatched it up and grabbed a napkin as she crawled to the brandies at the front of the tea room. Bullets sprayed the carpet and wood of the bar, splinters cutting her cheek. Tina ignored the pain and grabbed the first bottle she could. Ripping the napkin in half she stuffed one part into the brandy, ignited the fabric and threw it.

The Molotov cocktail exploded in the doorway between the dining room and the kitchen, a man's screams piercing the air. Rick ran to her just as Tina was igniting the second Molotov. They couldn't go out the front, there were too many places a gunman could hide. The only option was to run through the fire she'd started and get to the alley out back. Rick checked his gun and Tina saw two bullets left.

Between that and the bomb she held in her hand, it would have to be enough.

They ran, half jumping through the flames that licked her stockinged legs. She felt the telltale sting of burns but her adrenaline wouldn't let her stop. Instead, she threw the Molotov at the three men running toward them from the kitchen and realized a half second too late that they were standing next to the gas powered stove.

"Go!" she yelled at Rick, who seemed to understand her sudden panic.

They burst out the back door and kept running toward the next street over. The sound of the explosion from the kitchen was eerie and unnatural. It was something that should've been contained to a battlefield, not the middle of Little Italy on a sunny summer day. They slowed, and Tina looked back to see the roof of the place engulfed in flames, a hard look in her eye.

"We need to get off the streets," Rick said, grunting as he took a step.

She looked down and saw the blood on the calf of his trousers.

"You need to get that taken care of," she said.

"It'll keep. C'mon, I think I know a place where we can hide."

They couldn't go around and check on her men that were supposed to be guarding the front, and Tina's favorite car was likely a lost cause.

Small price to pay for surviving I suppose.

Rick led them two blocks away, keeping to alleyways as much as possible. When he stopped they were at the back door of a boxing gym. She raised a questioning eyebrow at him, but he just gave her a weak smile.

"Trust me."

The sweat on his face wasn't just about the heat, and he swayed a little on his feet. If this was a safe place where she could take a look at the wound, Tina didn't care if it was a filthy rat hole, she'd take it.

After knocking on the back door and waiting a few minutes, a short, barrel chested man opened the door. He took one look at them and swore under his breath.

"Colleen sent you?" he asked.

"Not exactly," Rick answered, "but this is her mother and we need a place to hide until she can get here."

The man shook his head, swearing again before opening the door wider.

"Up the stairs, first door on the left and keep the damn blinds closed. We just rebuilt this place from the last time you 'visited'."

Tina gave Rick a questioning look as they did as the man told them to.

"This is where Colleen was holed up when we were trying to get that person that your father wanted...remember?" Rick said.

It had been just before Christmas last year. Her father's mental state had degenerated into extreme paranoia and theories about special labs that created powered soldiers. He had been convinced that a woman had escaped and had knowledge of it all, knowledge that he was sure would give him an edge over all the other heads of families. The trouble was, Tina knew that it would point back to Colleen and Andrew, and she couldn't risk it. So, she'd sent Rick to take care of the woman, or capture her, whichever was easier. Colleen had felt betrayed, though that didn't stop her from breaking into Lumis and trying to save Andrew when Tina asked her to.

Tina opened the door they'd been directed to, revealing a small, neatly furnished apartment.

"How did you know he'd even let us in?" she asked

Rick fell onto the couch as Tina closed the blinds.

"Colleen visits this place, talks with the guy...I thought maybe she was...I don't know, but I hoped using her name might get us some help. It was the only thing I could think of."

"It was good thinking."

He winced as he pulled up his pants leg and Tina took a look at the bullet wound.

"Through and through," she said, relief flowing through her. "I'll see if there's a first aid kit here."

To her shock, there wasn't only a first aid kit, but it was outfitted with sutures and gauze. It made her wonder exactly what the hell happened here to warrant such a thing. When she walked back in and met Rick's gaze, Tina felt herself drawn to him in a way she hadn't let herself feel in a very long time.

The words Rick had spoken in the tea room and the passionate kiss hung in the air between them as she stitched him up and dressed the wound. She knew he wouldn't bring it up, giving her the space she needed to digest what it meant for them.

When she'd put the kit away and poured them both some cheap whiskey she found in a cupboard, Tina sat next to him, careful to keep some space between them. A choice sat before her. She could either ignore this, and let it be clear by her silence that she didn't feel the same way. Or she could admit to him that she cared for him, wanted him so much that it kept her awake some nights.

Both options sent her stomach lurching in fear, and neither felt wise with everything else going on.

She took a long pull from her glass and winced. The whiskey wasn't just cheap, it was foul. It was also exactly what she needed to snap her mind into focus.

When she had fallen in love with Matthew Knight, she had assumed her father wouldn't care that he wasn't interested in the family business. For a little while, the old man had let Tina believe that they could be happy, maybe that they could even leave and start a new life.

But then Grandfather Malone revealed his hand and Matthew had been woefully unprepared for the brutal choice before him: Accept his place in the business or leave and never come back.

Matthew may have come into our family without the stomach for things but I should have seen it all coming. I should have pushed him away, saved us both the heartache.

She took another drink as the memory of that last week with Matthew seared her mind. They had both tried to come up with a plan, tried to convince themselves that they could still have the life they wanted. And then Matthew's cousin was killed as a warning, signaling the death of their dreams. Matthew had left that night, kissing Colleen goodbye in her sleep and holding Andrew one last time. Tina had promised to find a way, that one day they'd turn up on his doorstep and they could be a family again.

Neither of them believed it, but it was a nice fantasy.

To her father, Matthew was dead to the family, a coward who didn't have the good grace to be the man he should've been. Tina, heartsick and now responsible for two small children, didn't have the strength to say any different, especially when the kids started asking questions about their father. Matthew could never come back, and Tina couldn't see a way out, so her husband might as well be dead.

But now, Grandfather was gone. The threat he posed to anyone she loved had been buried with him. And while there were plenty of other threats, as today's events attested to, Tina knew that Rick wasn't a thing like Matthew. Rick knew the risk and he accepted it every day.

And perhaps especially today. He was willing to die for me, but he didn't. We didn't because we worked together, because he's able to handle all of this.

She glanced over at him and let herself feel the desire that had simmered for so long inside of her. Rick's eyes slid over to hers and he looked away again.

"You alright?" he asked.

"No, I'm not but…when am I ever really alright?"

His hand twitched as if he wanted to touch her but he didn't.

"We should call Colleen," he said instead.

She nodded.

"But first I have something to say."

Rick downed his whiskey as Tina sat up to look him in the eye.

"Look, I know that you—" Rick began.

She stopped him with her lips on his. At first, there was no reaction. But then, his hand cupped the back of her head, his tongue exploring her mouth with slow strokes that made Tina's entire body suddenly ache with want. She'd held herself so removed and cold, for so long, afraid of giving her heart away again, that this small concession to her desires let loose a cascade of pent up need. In a moment, all her barriers were gone and Tina found herself on Rick's lap, straddling him as she ran her hands up his chest. When she pulled back enough to look him in the eyes, Rick stared back at her in shock.

"You've been by my side this whole time," she said, fingers tracing his cheek bones. "You've always believed in me, no matter the odds. I…I've never really had that and I didn't know how to accept it at first. But now…now, I want you with me through everything. Every day we might still have, every victory, every defeat."

Rick's breath became ragged, his eyes widening as her words hit him fully.

"I…I think I love you too, Rick. And I…I'm not good at showing it but I will try."

"You don't have to do anything. Just this, if it's all you can give, I'll take it. I just want to be with you, through whatever your life brings."

Tina hadn't cried in ages, yet tears slid down her face at his words. How long had it been since she'd had someone who saw her and still wanted to stand by her side?

Matthew was a very long time ago and he wasn't strong enough to stay, but Rick is.

Rick used his thumbs to wipe the tears away and that simple gesture undid her.

She crushed her lips to his and Rick moaned deep in his throat as if he were a starved man that, at last, was given sustenance. His hands tugged at her blouse and slid underneath to cup her breasts. Tina gasped as his thumbs circled her nipples sending jolts of pleasure straight between her legs. He pulled her blouse free and began kissing his way down her neck to her collar bone, paying special attention to that sensitive place on her neck. She reached back and unclasped her bra, yearning to feel his hands and lips on her.

But didn't make a move as he took her in, feasting on her body with his eyes, which only made Tina feel more aroused.

She pressed her hips down and felt him between her legs, hard and ready. Suddenly, all the years of loneliness, all the months they'd spent dancing around one another about how they felt came rushing in on her, and Tina felt ravenous for the man under her.

Their kisses became insistent, teeth and tongues clashing as they made short work of any remaining clothing. It was a fast, hot coupling without the finesse and seduction that Rick probably wanted to give her and Tina didn't care. They'd come too close to losing each other and she needed him in this moment like she needed air.

Afterward, they lay on the couch, breathing heavily and holding onto one another like lifelines.

Rick placed tiny kisses on her temple and she closed her eyes.

She'd have to get up in a minute, face what had happened, and try to figure out what her next move was going to be. But for this moment, Tina would indulge in being cherished and loved.

Colleen rushed through the back door of the boxing gym and found Dante on the phone in his office.

With one look from her the man got off the call with a hasty excuse.

"Where are they?" she asked.

"I put them in the spare apartment. The man was wounded. Haven't seen hide nor hair of 'em since."

"Thank you for taking them in."

Dante shrugged.

"We have an agreement and I owe you. If you hadn't talked to Marco, I would never have been able to come back here."

She turned to go but Dante put a hand on her arm.

"What's going on Colleen? I mean...you don't owe me an explanation but if I can help you—"

"You can't. I mean...I don't want to put you in harm's way. My family is tricky on the best of days. After today, I'll make sure they keep you out of it."

He nodded.

"Word from one of my cousins is that Madame Capelli is on a rampage. Just be careful."

She opened her mouth to ask how in the world he'd know anything about that and then realized that Dante wasn't stupid.

"Go on, tell them to stay until closing and then they can sneak out the back."

"What if Capelli finds out?" Colleen asked.

"She won't, half her gun men owe me favors, big ones."

Colleen didn't want to know why and left it at that.

A flood of memories hit her when she got to the door. Marco living across from her, cooking up a storm for her and his girl, Alice. Late nights of friendship that had started to feel like a family.

But my family is behind this door, whether I like it or not. She knocked.

"It's Colleen, open up."

A minute later, Tina opened the door. Her clothes were torn and looked as if she'd been in a fire. Though she'd managed to put her hair in order and wash her face, Colleen could smell the smoke on her.

Rick stood in the bedroom doorway, a gun hidden behind his back.

"Don't shoot," she said with a wry grin.

He snorted and limped to the couch.

The moment the door was closed, Colleen could feel the anger from their glares like a cold wind on her skin.

"You couldn't do this one thing for me? You couldn't follow the one direction I asked you to do!"

"I thought Andrew was elsewhere and I—"

"Stay with the operation, that was what I asked of you! Not to go traipsing around trying to get your brother!"

Colleen's blood boiled in seconds and her eyes sparked orange.

"Andrew—" Colleen began.

"Is your enemy!"

"No, he's not!"

"Because of your actions, you've not only caused the last safeguard for this family to be taken away, you've dug your own grave, too."

Tina turned and began to pace.

It might've been the heat coursing through her veins, or the fact that she had been wholly unprepared for the strength of her mother's anger, but it took several minutes for Tina's words to sink in.

"What are you talking about?" she asked. "How did I dig my own grave?"

"The police are creating a task force to hunt you and Andrew down," Rick said. "Now the police have an extra excuse to come in and start killing people."

Colleen's stomach sank and her power quieted as dread settled over her. She'd been able to staunch some of the collateral damage that the turf war was creating by being a distraction for the police. But now that strategy would only cause more innocent lives to be lost as the police indiscriminately targeted people living in High Tide just for looking like her.

"If I hadn't gone after him, the police might still be doing this task force," she said.

"Yes, but we'd at least be able to defend ourselves," Tina replied. "Maybe even to cut all this short so that the task force wouldn't have to be around for very long. But now?"

"Von will go all out, and that means Andrew will too."

Tina nodded.

"There might be a way to simply turn Andrew over to them," Rick said, "take out Von's most powerful asset."

Colleen stared at him, mouth open.

"You can't be serious?"

The fact that Tina didn't throw the idea out right away made Colleen that much more furious.

"I don't think he's fully on Von's side," she said, shooting daggers at Rick.

"What makes you say that?" Tina asked.

She told her about the file that had been left, all the while watching her mother for any sign of recognition.

"I think Andrew wanted me to find it. Why else leave it there like that when he knew I would be there?"

Rick shook his head.

"It could mean nothing, just something someone left there because it doesn't have anything useful in it."

"No," Tina said, her face pinched with frustration, "it's referring to child trafficking that my father was involved in. Specifically powered children, it was one of the first things I shut down…and then Von went to war with me."

"Did you know that was why?" Colleen asked.

"I suspected but…I had no idea he'd go this far because of it. If Andrew left that file it was specific, and it does raise some questions but…we don't have time to come up with a list of reasons. We need to end this, fast."

"I won't help you kill Andrew."

Tina stared at her.

"Who said anything about killing him?"

"You want him out of the way."

"Yes, but not dead."

"Then let me try and reach him, please. This proves that there's more going on with him than we know."

"You're still going to have the task force on your back," Rick said.

Colleen realized then that Walter would come in handy on many levels.

If he's telling me the truth…but I suppose I have to take the risk don't I?

"I might have a way to keep the task force off our backs, or at least avoid them," Colleen said.

"How?" Tina asked.

Colleen bit her lip as she considered how to explain this to her mother. If she had more time, she might be able to come up with a half-truth or a way to explain it away. Instead, Colleen gave Tina a quick breakdown of her interaction with Walter last night. At the end, her mother's face was hard, an angry glint in her eye.

"You can't trust him," Tina said.

"I've considered that but…what choice do we have?"

"Then I'll do it," Rick said.

"No, you weren't at Lumis."

Tina exhaled hard through her nose and shook her head.

"Fine, but be careful. There's probably an angle we're not seeing."

Colleen met her mother's gaze and felt a sharp stab of guilt as she took in the cuts on her mother's face and the burns on her legs.

"I'm sorry," she said, "what happened to you today was my fault."

If she hadn't known Tina so well, she would never have been able to see the imperceptible softening in her eyes.

"I should've known that sooner or later the sharks would smell blood in the water, even her."

"Still…"

"Okay, great," Rick said, his tone full of bitterness, "so glad you got that out of the way but the question remains, what now?"

Tina took a deep breath and let it out slowly.

"I have one ace card, but it's risky."

"Do I even want to know?" Colleen asked.

"Your grandfather was a controlling son of a bitch in nearly every way. He trusted no one. Going so far as to keep damning proof on most of the crime families in Metro City tucked away in a small safe."

"Including Madame Capelli?"

"I think so. In any case, it's our only chance."

"They could kill you," Rick said.

"Not if I arrange a parlay for tonight."

Colleen had only ever heard of these kinds of meetings, and as far as she knew, no one had been forced to ask for one in her lifetime. Until now.

"Be careful," she said, "we have no idea if Madame Capelli is playing a deeper game here."

Tina gave Colleen a weak smile.

"Don't worry, I'm tougher than I look."

CHAPTER TEN

The precinct was buzzing with activity, the main room crowded with officers on and off duty who were hoping to find a way to get themselves on the Powered Task Force. Phones from the dispatch pool on the other side of the wall were almost drowned out by the dozens of conversations going on, the sound a low, constant hum. Shay had almost gotten used to the ever present smell of stale coffee, cleaner and a hint of body odor from the drunk tank, but the it was the noise today that was really getting to her.

Normally, today she'd be grocery shopping and trying to find a way back into her mother's good graces, this being one of her few days off. But since news of the task force broke, Shay had been on high alert looking for a way to get into the special team. Today was the last day Captain Hill was taking requests, and there was no way she was going to let an opportunity like this pass her by.

Walter plopped down into his chair across from her and rubbed his eyes. She wondered if he'd gone home after the incident last night and if he was in any pain.

Shay eyed Walters bandaged wrists and grit her teeth. If she'd been there he wouldn't have gotten hurt and the vigilante would be in custody.

And my spot on the task force would be almost guaranteed.

"You should go home, rookie," he said, tired eyes crinkling at the edges as he grinned at her. "Why are you...oh, I see."

Her gaze had drifted to the door of the captain's office, which was resolutely closed as if to tell everyone to leave him the hell alone.

She was about to look away when her view was blocked by the bane of her existence, a tall, blond, boyish handsome officer by the name of Fisk. If he hadn't been one of the best cops on the force, Shay would've told him to go to hell a long time ago.

He winked at her as he passed by and she clenched her hand, itching to punch that smug look right off his face.

"You look a little tired today, Reynolds," he said. "Maybe you should take a little time off, or put in for a transfer to the dispatch pool."

"No thanks."

His grin widened and he looked at Walter.

"You've got a stubborn one on your hands. How you holding up, old man?"

Walter tensed just a little, but his grin never wavered.

"Fine, thanks for asking."

"You know," Fisk said, putting his hands on their desk and leaning down, "if I had been there we'd have that criminal in lock up right now. Maybe you're getting slow in your old age."

"Or maybe," Shay said, before she could stop herself, "she'd have burned you to a crisp."

"But not you?"

Shay leaned in.

"No, because I'm just that good."

Fisk's eyes flicked down to her lips and Shay sat back, realizing too late the position she'd put herself in.

"Yeah, I bet you are."

The office door opened, and out strode a bullish looking man with a deep scowl etched into his face. He turned back to say something to Captain Hill, who looked like a controlled explosion just waiting for permission to blow.

Fisk quieted down and they both leaned forward a little as if it would help them hear better.

"...don't need The Bulwark mucking things up here!" Hill said, his face getting redder by the second.

"...in over your head you damn stubborn—!"

"Out! Get out right now!"

This was said at a volume so loud that Shay would have to be deaf not to hear.

The bullish man glared at the captain and stalked from the room, fury rolling off him in waves.

The captain's eyes scanned the room, everyone ducking their heads to at least put up the pretense of working. When his eyes settled near Shay, her stomach plummeted to her toes.

"Fisk, in my office now!" the captain barked.

She watched him walk away and began to turn over all the possibilities of the conversation they must be having.

After a minute or two she turned to Walter, who was concentrating on the open file in front of him.

"What is the Bulwark?"

He shrugged. "Some government agency probably."

"But...why are they—Oh! The vigilantes, that has to be it."

"Most likely."

"You're not the least bit curious about all this?"

"Well, I know you are so you'll probably do enough thinking about it for both of us."

"I want to know what's happening so I can find the best angle to get on that Task Force. That's a career making opportunity and I'm the only one around here who knows High Tide like the back of their hand."

He finally looked up, eyes hooded under a deep frown.

"Why would you put yourself through all that? It's going to be full of men like Fisk, and most won't be half as good a cop as he is."

"You wouldn't understand," she said, turning away to finish up a report.

"Why, because I flushed my career down the toilet?"

Shay's eyes widened and she sat back, guilt spreading heavy over her.

"I didn't—I mean I—"

He waved her words away.

"It's fine, really. I get it, I used to be young and ambitious once too."

"So you're not anymore?"

His grin turned sardonic.

"Does it look like I'm on the upward career track?"

Shay sighed.

"God, I'm putting my foot in my mouth a lot right now."

"Go home, get some sleep."

She looked over at the captain's office again and bit her bottom lip. Would it really make that much of a difference if she stayed or left?

If I don't at least try, I'll always regret it.

"Seriously though, why put yourself at the mercy of Fisk and his cronies?" Walter asked again. "You know what it's going to be like for High Tide when they get out there, you really want to see that?"

"Yes, that's one reason I want to be there. I might be able to stop one kid from getting caught in the cross fire, one woman or man from being shot just because they have the vigilante's skin color."

Walter nodded.

"And the track toward Detective is a bonus."

"You think I'm being mercenary? I don't exactly have a choice. No one is going to advocate for me. I learned a long time ago that I have to do that myself."

"I know that. And I also know that you're not just a good cop but someone who really truly wants to do the right thing," he said, voice carrying a weariness that had little to do with physical fatigue.

"You say that like it's a bad thing."

"No, not bad just…hard."

Shay studied him, the slump of his massive shoulders, the dark circles under his dull eyes. She thought about his past, what cost him his career and wondered if he regretted his decision.

When he spoke next, his voice was low, tinged with sadness.

"Just be careful what you stick your neck out for, rookie. Make sure it's worth sacrificing everything."

She opened her mouth to ask him the one thing she swore she never would when the captain's door opened and he barked out her name.

The dark cloud that was hovering over Walter dissipated as he grinned at her.

"Go get 'em, rookie."

"I will, old man."

When Fisk passed her, he gave her a wink and whispered, "I put in a word for you. You're welcome."

"I can make my own way, thanks."

The playful glint in his eye faded and Shay swore she saw his gaze become something more than flirtatious. His eyes narrowed, and his smile became questioning.

"Yeah," he said slowly, "I bet you can."

"Reynolds! Stop flirting with Fisk and get your ass in here!" Hill said.

Shay ground her teeth together at the implication and silently cursed Fisk. She would have a hard enough time making the captain take her seriously without him thinking she was a shameless flirt.

Even if Fisk was my type I'd like to think I'd have better taste than him.

"Take a seat," he said, stamping out his cigarette and giving her a hard look through the lingering smoke. "Don't you have the day off?"

"Yes sir, but there was some work I wanted to get done."

"I see. Well, I'm glad you came in, something I want to talk to you about."

A lump formed in the back of her throat and she sat up straighter. It couldn't be this easy could it? Would the captain simply ask her to be on the task force because he could see her talent, her drive?

"I want to ask you about Walter."

The words deflated her and Shay had to work hard not to swear in frustration.

"What about him, sir?" she asked instead.

"That location you went to last night was...well it has history for him, bad history. About six months before he was demoted, Walter found a group of kids there, half-starved and kept in the basement of the place. We found the piece of shit that kidnapped them but Walter...well, let's just say he had other opinions."

Shay's innate curiosity was stirred to the point of frenzy. This was as close as anyone had ever come to telling her exactly what happened to Walter's career and she held her breath for more information.

The captain lit another cigarette and puffed smoke across his desk.

"I want to know how he was last night, if you observed anything out of the ordinary then or today?"

"Such as?"

The question was a rather obvious dig for more information and also a deflection. Shay liked Walter and the thought of being a snitch made her skin crawl.

The captain's eyes narrowed.

"I get it Reynolds, you're loyal to your partner. That's good, that's how it should be. Unless," he leaned forward, "your partner is doing something that will expose this entire precinct to a shit storm we couldn't hope to survive. Now, I'm going to ask you one more time, did you see anything suspicious last night or today?"

One thing came to her mind immediately: Walter telling her to leave while he secured the vigilante. It was beyond strange that he'd want to arrest such a dangerous person on his own, and then to have her escape on top of it all.

In spite of the fact that this had been churning in the back of her mind all day, Shay's instincts screamed at her not to tell the captain.

"Always go with your gut", that's what Walter says...so here goes.

"I didn't notice anything, sir," she said, "besides the fact that he was injured and angry that the vigilante got away."

"Do you know why he wanted you to leave while he arrested the perp?"

"I think he was concerned for me, sir. Walter is a little...over protective."

The captain nodded as if this went without saying, much to Shay's frustration.

"Anything else?"

"No, sir."

"So, you just came in on your day off to get some extra paper work done?"

"No, I came in to apply for the task force."

The captain blinked and then chuckled as if she were making a joke. Shay felt her blood start to heat and clamped down on the anger that was a constant companion.

Easy, you know letting him have it may feel good but it will sink you.

"I'm very serious, sir," she said instead, her voice hard. "I feel that my knowledge of High Tide will be invaluable to the task force, as will my knowledge of the people there. I can direct the task force to locations that will bear fruit and away from those that will be a waste of time. I scored top of my class in—"

The captain held up his hand.

"I don't need your resume, Reynolds, I'm aware of your scores."

"Then you know that besides Fisk, I'm the best qualified to be on that task force."

He sat back, took a long drag off his cigarette and studied her. Shay bore the scrutiny with head held high and back straight. She should be used to it by now, but knew she never would be.

"Ok Reynolds, I'll put you in."

Shay's heart jumped and her eyes widened, half sure that she misheard him.

"But," he said, "you'll be working directly under Fisk, answering to him, understand? If you can't handle that—"

"I can, I will! Thank you, sir."

"And you'll still be on patrol with Walter so some days you might be pulling double shifts."

Shay knew that no other officers were being asked to do that and for her, it could easily mean that she'd mess up because of fatigue. He was giving her the harder road, as usual.

But she really didn't give a damn.

She jumped up and extended her hand, which he shook briefly before waving her out.

When she left the office, Fisk's eyes snapped up to hers as if he had radar attuned to her. She simply grinned at him and walked to her desk, bursting to tell Walter, who wasn't there.

But the file he'd been looking at was.

Something happened at that place, more than just some kidnapped kids. What was it?

She looked at the file folder. It was old and had coffee stains on the front. The tab had the address of the place they were at last night with a green sticker next to it, indicating that the case was closed.

Her fingers itched to open it but the moment she raised her hand, Walter came out of the break room, a steaming cup of coffee in his hand, and she backed off.

He set the cup down and crossed his arms.

"Questions, rookie?"

Yes, hundreds. But you're not going to answer them, are you?

"I got on the task force," she said instead, unable to help the wide grin.

His face relaxed and he gave her a smile that brightened his craggy features.

"Congratulations, we should celebrate. How about lunch?"

"It's almost five."

"Is it?" he asked, checking his watch. "Huh...I guess I lost track of time. Well, how about dinner then? I know a place that has the best burgers in Metro City, little hole in wall place that looks like a health code violation but—"

"I've actually got plans."

The way his face deflated had Shay kicking herself. She knew he was lonely, no wife, no kids, and next to no one would talk to him in the precinct except to give him a hard time.

"Tomorrow night?" she asked.

"Yeah, absolutely," he nodded, gently slapping her on the back. "I'm happy for you, seriously."

Her eyes strayed to the file on his desk, for just a second and he swept it up.

"You should go, get ready for your night," he said, holding the file just out of sight.

"You got a hot date, Reynolds?" Fisk asked as he walked by.

She looked him right in the eye and relished the disappointment that flared there when she said, "Yes, as a matter of fact, I do.

CHAPTER ELEVEN

C olleen dialed and hung up half a dozen times before letting the call go through to the precinct. The operator connected her to Walter, who, much to her amazement, was at his desk.

"Officer Lyle," his gruff voice crackled through the phone.

She looked around the back room of the bar, making sure that the door was closed securely before answering.

"It's Fahrenheit, I...I want to meet."

The pause on the other end seemed to stretch on forever before he answered.

"When and where?"

"Before I answer that, I need to know if you're on the task force that's going to be hunting me down."

"No, I'm not involved with that."

She looked down, doing her best to hide the sudden disappointment. How would she be able to use this connection to get the task force to back off, or at least not attack innocent people?

Her brain started spinning options, things she could offer Walter in exchange for his influence with someone on the force when he spoke something that stopped her cold.

"But my partner is, and I can get you information on it that way if that's what you want."

The disappointment twisted into something else, something that ached. Shay was on the task force.

"Hello?" Walter said.

"Why are you so desperate to help me?" The words came out harsher than she'd intended.

He sighed on the other end and she could almost see him rubbing a hand over his face.

"Because I don't think you're trying to make things worse. And because…I think you can help me stop some very bad men that are hurting people like you."

If he'd said he wanted to give her diamonds and cash, Walter couldn't have shocked Colleen more.

"What do you know about that?" she asked, her mouth dry.

"Enough. Look, I can't talk here. Meet me and I'll tell you everything but only if you agree to tell me what happened at Lumis Chemical."

She licked her lips, turning it all over in her mind. If his intention was to hurt her, he could've done that last night. But if he's really trying to expose Mr. Price and Jason James…

That could be the key to getting all of us out from under Mr. Price and getting on with our lives.

"Alright," she said, "I'll meet you."

Walter let out a rush of air that sounded very much like a sigh of relief.

"Thank you. Can you meet tonight?"

Voices drifted to Colleen through the door, Wanda calling her name and someone else asking a question she couldn't hear.

"Colleen?" Wanda asked, her voice harsh. "You here? That cop is here to see you."

Colleen took a sharp intake of breath.

Crap! I forgot that we were going to the movies tonight!

The knowledge that Shay was now a member of the group that was hunting her down did give her pause but something else quieted the doubts.

She wanted to see Shay again, wanted to get to know her. Maybe she could be reasoned with, maybe she could be an ally.

Or something else…?

"I can't tonight," she said into the phone. "Tomorrow night."

"Alright, meet me at the old canning factory on the pier, Midtown Fish. Eleven o'clock."

"Got it."

She hung up as Wanda's voice got louder and more upset. The last thing she wanted was for a fight to break out between the hot headed bar owner and the officer.

"I'm here, Wanda," Colleen said, coming out of the back room.

Wanda put her hands on her hips and glared at her.

"What the hell is that officer doing here? I've already lost two tables of customers because she's hanging around."

"We're going to the movies, she's actually quite nice."

"Uh-huh. Well, hurry up and get her out of here."

Wanda turned on her heel and barked an order at the line cook.

Colleen had wanted to look much nicer for her…whatever this was.

Maybe she'd be willing to wait in my apartment…did I put my suit away or is it airing out…? Oh hell!

She walked into the bar and stopped dead when she saw Shay sitting at the bar.

The officer was wearing a white and green mini dress with matching sandals, her dark skin gleaming in the low light.

"Hey there!" Shay said when she saw Colleen, a wide grin making her face shine.

Colleen tried desperately not to stare and knew that she had to say something.

"You look great," she breathed and then immediately felt her stomach drop.

Shay's smile softened and she ducked her head.

"Thanks. You do, too."

Colleen looked down at her Bermuda shorts and sleeveless shirt and cringed.

"I'm so sorry, I got caught up in work and I haven't changed, but if you want to wait I can get cleaned up real quick."

"I think you look fine, but if it would make you feel better, I can wait here."

Colleen glanced over at Wanda, who shot daggers at them and realized that there was no way she could leave Shay here a second longer.

"Actually, if it doesn't bother you I'm good. Why don't you get a cab while I grab my purse?"

Shay nodded and left the bar.

"How could you ask her to come here? As if things aren't tense enough," Wanda hissed when she walked past on her way to the back stairs.

"We're friends going out. If it bothers you this much I'll ask her not to come back," the words came out sharp and annoyed and Wanda's face hardened even more.

"You just watch yourself," she finally said. "She's acting all chummy with everyone but never forget who she is."

Wanda turned away, the words hanging in the air. As Colleen ran up the stairs and snagged her purse from the kitchen counter, she felt those words stick in her mind.

The fact that even being friends with Shay was fraught with risk was something that should make Colleen call everything off. And in the back of her mind, she knew that the excuses, the hope that she was using to make herself feel better was a lie that had some very bad consequences.

As she paused in her doorway, Colleen closed her eyes. Shay's face, her words, her scent rose up like a siren's call and Colleen realized that she wanted one thing in her life that wasn't controlled by being a vigilante, or Tina Knight's daughter or any of the other things that made up who she was. She wanted to simply be Colleen, a woman. And she wanted to see if some of that, maybe just a little, could be with Shay.

Straightening her shoulders, Colleen shoved all the doubts, all the good reasons why she should say no, to the back of her mind.

She deserved one good thing, didn't she?

And Shay could be that thing.

Shay's stomach was bouncing around like a maniacal bunny as she sat next to Colleen in the cab. The tall woman was quiet, like she had been at the youth center, a nervous energy emanating from her that reminded Shay of a creature waiting for danger around every bend.

The way Colleen's eyes took in everything in seconds, Shay could almost see her evaluating her environment for threats.

Her childhood must've made her extremely cautious.

Sympathy flowed through her at the thought of what it would've been like to grow up in a family like Colleen's. Shay realized that Colleen was probably not used to having a friend.

Because people would judge her the second they found out about her family...like I almost did. Well, I can change that, starting now.

Shay turned to look at Colleen, who gave her a wary glance out of the corner of her eye.

"So, how long have you worked for Wanda?" Shay asked.

"Um...a little over a month."

"She bought that place from old man Setter right?"

Colleen nodded.

"She's done a good job getting it in shape," Shay continued. "Last time I was there when he owned it, the place was a total dive. Not that there's anything wrong with that, some of my favorite restaurants are dives but it's nice to see people investing in High Tide."

Colleen nodded again.

Shay's mind worked at lightning speed, searching for something to talk about. There was nothing more nerve wracking for her than uncomfortable silence.

"So, you grew up in High Tide then?"

Colleen's face tensed around her eyes and she looked down at where her hands were clenched in her lap.

"Yeah."

Shay waited, and when nothing else was forth coming she decided to just dive in.

"Me, too. My mom lived in High Tide until I went to the academy, then she moved in with her sister in Sparrow Heights. I visit when I can but the precinct keeps me busy. In fact, I just got a promotion."

That tense look around Colleen's eyes spread to her lips and shoulders, until she was radiating stress like a furnace.

Or maybe that's just the hot evening...good lord it's a sauna in here!

Shay rolled her window down, though the air wasn't exactly cool.

"Congratulations," Colleen said, her voice low.

"Thanks! I really do want to make detective soon, and this a step toward that."

Colleen cleared her throat.

"Will your partner be going with you to this promotion?"

Shay's muscles relaxed at the question. Finally! The woman starts to talk!

"No, he's pretty...well, I wouldn't say happy where he is but his career goals are different from mine."

"He used to be a detective right?"

"Yeah, how did you know that?"

Colleen's eyes widened just a little.

"Wanda mentioned it."

Shay nodded, ignoring the suspicion that wiggled in her mind.

"So, he doesn't want to be a detective again?" Colleen asked.

"I don't know actually. Walter keeps things pretty close to the chest."

She thought of that file, the locked drawer in his desk that no one but him had a key for and how she never saw him open it.

What does *Walter want?

The thought spun in her mind, distracting her from the beautiful woman next to her until the cab driver stopped at the theater.

Colleen tried to pay him but Shay waved her off.

"I've got it. You get the tickets."

Colleen gave her a small, wonderful smile and nodded.

Shay took a deep breath, trying to calm the nerves still racing through her. It had been a long time since she'd met a woman she wanted to get to know as much as she did right now with Colleen. She watched her walk a few steps ahead, the sway of her hips, the way she held herself with such confidence.

When Colleen turned around to hand Shay her ticket their fingers brushed and the cop felt a spark zing through her hand. She jumped and Colleen's eyes widened as if she felt it, too.

"Do you want popcorn?" Colleen asked, her voice shaking a little.

"Sure."

The smell of buttery popcorn and chocolate hung in the stuffy air of the theater, ancient fans doing very little to bring any relief from the summer heat.

They got their treats and found the correct room for their movie, the floor under Shay's shoes sticky from previous patrons. The seats squeaked as they sat down and the lights dimmed.

Colleen had gotten them one popcorn to share and Shay couldn't help feeling like she was in high school again. Dates had been mine fields before she had accepted who she was. After that, she'd been much better at sticking to her boundaries. Though it had been lonely when everyone else was pairing up and she wasn't.

She glanced at Colleen, her face lit up by the projections on the screen.

I could get used to being by her side I think.

The movie progressed in a series of ridiculous scenes and soon Colleen had relaxed enough to laugh right along with everyone else. The sound was deep, throaty and rich. Shay loved the way carefree look on Colleen's face, as if she knew that there was nothing required of her for the next hour or so. Shay felt like she was seeing the real Colleen without her protective barriers for the first time.

And she's stunning.

Desire stirred in her and Shay longed to wind her fingers through Colleen's, to run a finger up the woman's warm brown skin and see if she shivered from the sensation.

Shay's lips parted and her breath picked up as the daydream progressed.

She forgot that she should be looking at the screen but Colleen must've felt Shay's eyes on her because she looked over.

At first she was surprised and then something shifted in Colleen's gaze, a recognition. Fear gripped Shay's heart, what if she was disgusted by this? What if…?

But Colleen didn't turn away or try to distance herself from Shay. Instead, she gave Shay a soft, shy grin and, very slowly, raised her hand from her lap. Shay jumped when Colleen hooked her pinkie finger around her own. The woman stilled, her gaze checking in with Shay, who gave her a breathless nod.

Colleen tightened her finger around Shay's, who became lost in the bliss of the simple contact.

The rest of the movie, Shay found herself completely distracted by Colleen. She managed to laugh at the right moments, but her gaze kept drifting to the woman next to her. And, to her delight, Colleen was often looking at her, as well.

By the time they left the theater, the night had cooled to a more comfortable temperature, and they decided to walk back to Colleen's apartment. Shay was glad to have the extra time with her and decided to make every second count.

"I can raid the ice cream if you're hungry for something sweet," Colleen said, a relaxed smile on her face.

"I would love to."

Their hands kept brushing against one another as they walked, a subtle sign of affection that Shay longed to take further.

One day we'll be able to hold hands and no one will say a damn thing about it. Someday...

They walked along in peaceful quiet, the dull hum of cars and people talking on their front stoops the only real sounds. Every once in a while, music would drift out of an open car window or someone's apartment. Once, Shay picked up on a news report about the vigilantes, and snatches of a conversation in support of them.

It was the only thing that could dampen her mood; this knowledge that the people around her hailed the vigilantes as a hero and that she was trying to take them down.

But if there's not some kind of order, more people will get hurt. And besides, no one can take the law into their own hands, it's not right.

She snorted as the words sunk in.

I sound like a bad TV show!

"What's so funny?" Colleen asked.

Shay looked up at her, and felt this burden she carried lighten just a little.

"I was just thinking how much of a cliché I am sometimes."

Colleen tilted her head, her smile taking on a confused appearance.

"You're a black female police officer," she said, the last word containing a hint of bitterness, "I would venture to say that you're actually quite unique."

"No, that's not it. I mean the way I look at things...never mind. I was thinking about work, and what I should be doing is enjoying this nice walk with you."

She looked up at Colleen through her lashes and she bit her bottom lip, trying to contain the smile that spread across her features.

"I would ask if you're having a good time," Shay said, "but I've never seen you smile this much."

Colleen giggled.

"I don't usually smile this much and it feels good."

"I'm glad."

They walked along a bit more in silence, and although Shay mostly didn't mind, it was hard to keep quiet.

"Can I ask you about...well, you?" Shay asked at last.

Colleen gave her a wary look and shrugged.

"What did you do after high school? I mean, you act like you've been away for a while."

"I do?"

"Just a hunch but I'm guessing I'm right."

"You are," Colleen said, her voice guarded.

"Where were you? I mean...gosh that sounds like a cop asking, doesn't it?"

Shay bit the inside of her cheek and tried to think of how to say it better when Colleen started talking.

"I went to college at Cambridge actually."

Shay's eyes widened.

"England? That's amazing, what was it like?"

A wrinkle appeared above Colleen's nose and she was quiet for several minutes. Shay began to wonder if she'd over stepped a boundary she hadn't known existed when Colleen began to speak.

"It was...wonderful. The best time of my life. I was free from my family, free to be who I was. I...I met someone very important to me."

Her voice was so sad that Shay didn't need to ask what Colleen meant, it was written in every syllable.

"You lost them then?"

"Yes...in a matter of speaking. It's a very complicated story."

"And you don't have to tell it. I'm sorry, I didn't mean to drudge up bad memories."

Colleen laughed, but it was an empty, bitter thing.

"Ask me about any part of my childhood or past at all, and you risk stumbling into something terrible."

"It was that bad?"

Colleen hesitated before nodding.

"My mother sent me to Cambridge to get me away from my grandfather, who I'm sure you know all about. I was never supposed to come back actually but...well, as usual, the old man found a way to ruin that plan so..."

"Do you hate it here then? Is it...well, is it all bad?"

Again, she paused and Shay could practically see the wheels turning in her mind.

"No, not anymore. When he died, it freed this place for me...I know that doesn't make sense but it did. It took me a while to realize it though."

"It sounds like your mother isn't as bad as your grandfather was, if you're getting comfortable here again."

The change in Colleen was swift. Her gaze, which had been so open since the movie, became clouded, as if she had pulled a barrier between them. And Shay could guess why.

A cop asks the daughter of a well-known crime boss questions about her family. Well done officer!

"I'm sorry," she said, taking Colleen's hand and stopping her. "I shouldn't have pried."

"No, it's just...I know what everyone thinks of my family. I know what you must think and I just have no idea why you would want to be out with me."

"Well," Shay took a deep breath. This was a risk, on many levels, but she felt it in her bones that it was one worth taking. "I had thought that maybe I should walk away and let this go because why would you want to be seen with *me*. I'm not exactly a welcome sight in High Tide right now."

Colleen's face softened. She took Shay's hand and squeezed. It gave Shay the extra bit of boldness she needed.

Shay stepped closer to Colleen, the scent of her soap subtle and sweet.

"Why did you then?" Colleen asked, her voice becoming rough.

"Why did I ask you to the movies tonight? Because I thought that the risk of getting rejected was worth it to get to know one of the most beautiful women I've ever seen."

Colleen's eyes widened and she ducked her head.

"You need to get out more," she said, humor thick in her voice.

Shay playfully chucked her shoulder into Colleen's arm and continued to walk.

"Or you need a better mirror," the cop said.

"Well, whatever the reason, I'm very glad you did."

"Me, too. Now, is your promise of a sweet treat still good?"

Colleen's gaze took on something mischievous that sent heat zinging from Shay's face all the way to her toes.

"You bet it is."

Two bowls of rocky road, some hand holding and wonderfully easy conversation sped by in the blink of an eye. Before Colleen knew it, two hours had passed and she was resisting the urge to kiss Shay good-night. In the end, they both exchanged a long embrace and shy smiles. As she closed the back door of the bar, Colleen couldn't stop smiling. She felt light and giddy. Her giggle followed her up the stairs to her apartment. She couldn't remember the last time she felt like a regular girl doing regular things.

Maybe I never have...except for Cambridge.

The memory of Karen gave her pause as guilt tried to spread it's oily fingers through her heart.

"No," she whispered outside her apartment door. "It's time to let her go, we both agreed."

It hurt, there was no avoiding that. Karen had been the love of her life and Colleen would always, in some small corner of her soul, love that fiery redhead. But she had to try and live her own life, too.

The moment Colleen's hand closed over the door handle, she knew something was wrong. It was too cool to her touch and cold air hit her feet from under the space between the door and the floor.

Her mouth went dry and her heart sped up.

"Andrew..."

She let out a little heat in her veins, ready and waiting to be accessed just in case he came here to do more than talk.

When she opened the door, everything was normal, even if the temperature was unnaturally cold considering the heat of the night.

As she scanned her small apartment her eyes caught on something rectangular and frozen on her window sill.

When she picked it up, the ice melted into a cold puddle at her feet. In her hands was a comic book.

He wants to talk.

She threw the comic down and pulled her suit on. It was late, and the police would be patrolling but if Andrew had taken the trouble to reach out, she had to go.

It took twice as long to get there because Colleen had to go out of her way to hide from squad cars. More than once she had to intervene with an officer that was roughing a resident for no reason other than they were outside late at night.

She knew this would only exacerbate her position, but Colleen was finding it very hard to give a damn.

I can't just walk on by when I can do something about it.

By the time she got to the Sweet Spot, it was more than an hour since she'd discovered the comic and she worried that Andrew might have left.

But the moment she walked in it was obvious that she had nothing to worry about.

The air was deliciously cool, the scent of sugar heavy and tantalizing. Colleen walked around the counters and displays to find her brother sitting in the back corner munching on a bag of gummy candies and reading a comic.

She stood there for a second, taking in the sight of this tall, powerful man sitting cross legged on the floor of a candy shop like the luckiest kid in the world.

"You know, if you wanted candy you didn't need to leave a cryptic frozen comic in my apartment."

Her voice startled him and ice spread out underneath him in a thick sheet.

Colleen laughed.

"Did you just have the powered equivalent reaction of wetting yourself?"

He scowled at her and stood up.

"No."

"Uh-huh."

"Took you long enough," he said, stuffing the gummies in the pocket of his pants.

He wasn't dressed in a suit this time, but dark pants and a simple shirt. If not for the scars on the side of his face and the fact that his eyes were crystalline, Andrew would've been indistinguishable from any other man in High Tide.

She took that in, her heart aching for the lost time, the lost chance they had to be there for one another.

Andrew saw the hurt on her face and looked away.

"What's going on?" she asked.

He fidgeted with the comic in his hands.

"There's more going on here than you know, plans inside of plans. You need to stop."

"I can't, not while you're doing something that's going to get you killed, and not while High Tide is in danger. I think you know that."

"Do you have to play the hero all the time? Can't you just be a normal person and run when someone tells you to?"

"No, you should know that about me by now."

"You don't know these people Col, I do. You're in over your head!"

"So are you."

"I can do this, I have a plan and you're mucking it up! I can't keep protecting you or they'll know I'm not fully committed."

"Then stop protecting me! I can take care of myself. Or let me in on the plan so I can help you."

Andrew looked up to the ceiling, letting out a long breath.

"I'm taking over High Tide Col, and you know that can't happen while Tina is here. I don't want to hurt her but I will. So if you give a damn about her, or yourself, both of you need to get out of the city."

Colleen's mind turned everything over. The fact that he wasn't all in with whatever Von wanted to do, the drive he possessed to run High Tide and the way he kept trying to protect them.

I'm missing something…what is it?

"And stay away from that cop," Andrew said, heading for the door.

At first she thought he meant Shay and she opened her mouth to tell him to mind his own damn business when he cut her off.

"He's poking his nose into things that aren't his business and will get you killed, or worse. I won't be able to save you if that happens."

"Why did you leave the file for me to find if you want me to leave everything alone?"

Andrew paused at the door.

"It wasn't for you. It was for that cop."

"Why would you do that if you want him to leave it all alone?"

"Colleen, for Pete's sake! Let it go and trust me for once!"

"No," she advanced on him and took his hand in hers. "Let me help you! If you need me, just drop a comic off at my apartment, like you did tonight and if I want to meet with you, I'll turn the sign in the window for taffy upside down. You don't have to do this alone, Andrew."

He turned to look at her over his shoulder, those strange eyes so very sad.

"Yes, I do."

And with that, he shot ice into his hand. She hissed at the extreme cold and let go. Before she could stop him, her brother walked out into the night, alone.

CHAPTER TWELVE

Meetings like the one Tina was about to start were the makings of myths. People spoke about them in excited whispers, writing them into salacious stories and films with enough elaboration to make it laughable.

In reality, there was nothing glamorous or titillating about requesting parlay with a person who had just tried to gun you down.

The few men still loyal to Tina were scattered around the boxing gym, which Dante had generously offered up as a neutral location.

"No one would dare start anything here," he looked Rick over. "Well…no one from here that is."

Now, Rick shifted uneasily next to her, and she glanced down at his leg. He'd bled through the first bandage but had insisted on standing next to her for the meeting.

"You sure about this?" he asked. "We can get out of here now, hole up while we think of other ways to take care of her."

She glanced down at the empty briefcase and shook her head.

"I can do this. And really? There's no other option. We either do this, or we are as good as dead."

Rick exhaled through his nose and nodded.

Though her entire body felt like it was shaking, Tina knew that she wasn't showing the fear roiling through her.

The files her father had painstakingly kept were extensive on all but two bosses: Von and Madame Capelli. Whether he'd been unable or unwilling to gather dirt on them, the fact that the one thing she was counting on was missing made Tina's insides quake. Tina assumed that his business arrangement with Von was a kind of mutually assured destruction on its own. But why he wouldn't gather dirt on the Capelli family was beyond her.

Tina's only choice was to dig deep into that dank well of skills her father had taught her and put forth a strong, brave front. Having changed clothes, and cleaned up in the apartment, she at the very least looked every inch the picture of the brutal crime boss she needed to be.

At one minute to midnight, a car pulled up outside and Madam Capelli, dressed all in black, stepped out of her car.

She was on time, a good sign and it took some of the tension out of Tina's shoulders.

Madame stepped through the doors with six men behind her. Rick held up his hand to keep the men from coming any closer.

"Stay here," she said to the gunmen, walking toward Tina without so much as a body guard.

Tina turned to Rick and nodded. Though she knew he didn't like it, Rick stepped back, observing from a distance.

"I must applaud you, Tina," Madame said with a grim smile, "it isn't often someone escapes my men. Though

I am terribly disappointed that you destroyed one of my favorite tea houses."

"It was unfortunate that such a lovely establishment had to be collateral damage. There was no need for it really."

"I disagree. You broke faith and I had no choice."

"I suppose that's one way to look at it," Tina said, forcing her lips into a tiny smile, "but really, Camille, do you want another war between the families? Do the other families want that? I'm nearly done with this, after all."

"What is your proposal then?"

"A truce where we both walk away, calling it all even. You showed that no one can fail to keep their end of the bargain, and I will show that I am loyal by never throwing any resources behind another boss if someone moves against you."

Madame Capelli's eyes narrowed as she thought this through.

"I'm afraid not dear. You see, I have my own problems and letting someone who has jeopardized my business walk free would put me in a bad light."

Tina nodded. She'd expected that the first offer would likely be refused.

"Then I offer to compensate you, dollar for dollar, what you've lost and you cease all hostilities."

She laughed and shook her head.

"Tina, I taught you better than this! You have nothing with which to bargain, my dear. I only came here as a courtesy to you and to the tradition of the parlay. There is nothing that you have that will convince me."

Well then, here goes nothing.

Tina's smile hardened as she took a step toward Capelli, causing the crime madame's men to step forward. She waved them off, though a wary look began to blossom in her eyes.

Which emboldened Tina.

"I'm afraid that you did teach me better. In fact, I would say that I took every lesson to heart and that you have underestimated me and the lengths I will go to get what I want."

Madame's smile faltered.

"Oh really?"

She held her hand out to Rick and took the small briefcase from him.

"My father was a bastard, who held onto power with an iron fist. He also employed many spies in everyone's organization, except for Von unfortunately. He kept files on everyone, including you. Pieces of damning evidence that, if it were to come to light, would mean the destruction of everything you've built."

Madame's eyes flitted down to the briefcase and she shook her head, a nervous laugh escaping her lips.

"You're bluffing. I know you Tina, you don't have the stomach for this."

"Stomach for this…interesting turn of phrase. I seem to remember a string of brutal murders just before you took power where, and correct me if I'm wrong, the victims had their insides set outside their bodies. The killer was never found but you and I both know what those deaths gave you. It would be a shame if that missing piece of evidence to connect the mastermind of those crimes were to somehow find its way into the hands of the police. If I remember correctly, there is no statute of limitations on murder."

The woman paled, all bravado gone, as she took a step back from Tina.

"That's impossible…he couldn't…no one had any evidence that I had anything to do with that!"

Tina stepped toward her, using the skills she'd learned from a lifetime of surviving her father to mask her fear with a bitter strength that had made bigger men shake in their expensive shoes. She looked straight into Madame's eyes, holding her gaze with an intensity that made the older woman flinch.

"Shall we find out?" she whispered.

Madame said nothing, but a muscle in her cheek twitched, and her eyes began to take on a panicked gleam.

Tina simply stared at her, the empty briefcase clutched in her hand.

"No," Madame finally said, straightening her shoulders and putting on an expression of boredom. "I think the message has been heard regarding your unfortunate failure. There's no need to take it further."

"I am pleased to hear it."

Tina continued to look into her eyes, never wavering.

Just like the old man taught me.

"You know something, Tina? I was mistaken about you."

"Oh?"

"I used to think that you were so much weaker than your father. Now I see, it was all an act. You, my dear, are the truly dangerous one. Good luck with your new life."

The parting shot was well placed and Tina barely managed to keep from spewing her fury at the woman.

Madame Capelli left without another word, and it wasn't until Tina heard her car pulling away that she let out the breath she'd been holding. She could feel Rick's eyes on her, but didn't meet his gaze. Too much was coursing through her. Relief. Fear. Guilt.

She carried the empty brief case to the back and sat on the bottom stair, her body suddenly exhausted. The moment she let herself lean against the wall and close her eyes, the nerves in her stomach erupted and bile rose in the back of her throat. Tina swallowed and tried to pack away all her worries into neat little boxes in her mind. It was a habit she was well acquainted with and it usually worked.

But tonight, the things that haunted her would not be so easily ignored.

Everything hit her at once, the attempt on her life, the bluff, Andrew, Von, her father's disgusting business arrangement concerning kidnapped children.

Tina rushed for the back door and got outside just in time. She heaved until there was nothing left in her stomach, and then heaved some more. As the nausea passed, panic crested over her in wave after terrible wave, making her head spin. Sobs wracked her body, and she pressed a hand to her mouth to stifle the sounds. Through the fog, she felt a warm hand rubbing her back in circles and she didn't need to look up to know that it was Rick.

When the cry subsided, he handed her his kerchief to wipe her mouth and then he gathered her into his arms and held her until the shaking stopped.

It took Tina a long time to get to sleep, even longer because she asked Rick to let her be alone tonight. He'd hesitated, unspoken questions shining in his eyes. She'd tried to reassure him that it had nothing to do with what they'd done in the apartment, but he seemed more worried than usual.

"I'll be next door if you need anything," he'd said.

She'd tossed and turned for a good hour or more before drifting off to a fitful rest. Just as the morning sunrise was spreading soft light through her closed eyelids to tempt her to wakefulness, Tina felt something menacing in the room.

Instantly, her mind was alert and her senses were searching for the culprit. The sounds of a city beginning to wake up drifted to her, perhaps a stirring of air through the cracked window. Nothing out of place, but still her skin prickled with the hostility in her room.

Her hand went to the revolver under her pillow, slowly, with eyes still closed.

Once her hand was around the grip she bolted upright and pointed the gun at the corner by the window.

Sitting in her French style settee, shark like gaze on her, was Mr. Price.

"You sick son of a bitch," she hissed, cocking the revolver. "You have five seconds to get out of my house before I shoot you full of holes."

Mr. Price's lips twisted into a sarcastic grin.

"It's been quite an eventful twenty-four hours for you, hasn't it Mrs. Knight?"

Tina tried to press the trigger but found it stuck. She tried harder and still it didn't budge.

Mr. Price's smile widened, making him look like a cartoon villain.

That's when she saw movement out of the corner of her eye. The same rail thin woman that accompanied him before stood behind the door. Shrouded in black, with the exception of that metal mask, she resembled a round cheeked young woman with the barest hint of a smile. The sight made Tina's blood run cold, especially when she noticed that the woman's gloved hand was stretched out toward the revolver.

Tina felt the gun tug against her grip and before she could stop it, the revolver flew across the room and to the woman, who melted back into the shadows.

"Von will not back down as easily as Madame Capelli," Mr. Price said. "With my support behind him, he won't need to. Perhaps you should reconsider my offer."

Tina's heart stopped as his words sunk in.

Right after his appearance at the theater, Andrew showed up on Von's side as the one thing that could change the balance in the fight between them.

He warned me to leave, and if Colleen is right, Andrew had been experimented on so that…

She felt a fury rise up in her belly at the thought that her son had been subjected to the same treatment as the little girl Colleen had freed.

"If you think I'll trade my daughter just to hold onto High Tide, you're delusional."

"She will die—"

"Get out."

"She will die and so will you. Von will have High Tide, with my representative helping of course."

He leaned forward, forearms resting on his thighs, beady eyes glittering. It made Tina's skin crawl.

"I will get what I want with or without your help. If you change your mind, I can make all of this strife disappear. Von will leave High Tide alone. Your son will be lovingly by your side. Even the police will find better things to do than harass the good people of your neighborhood. All you need to do is pay your debt to me."

The door knob clicked, breaking Mr. Price's glower. Then the door itself moved, someone pushed against it.

"Tina, is everything alright?" Rick asked.

Her heart leapt into her throat. Who knew what Mr. Price and his powered lap dog would do to Rick if he came bursting in?

"I'm fine," she said, never taking her eyes from Mr. Price. "Just thinking out loud. Go get the coffee started and I'll be down in a minute."

Tina never thought out loud, Rick would know that, but she prayed he took the hint just the same.

There was thick silence as Tina held her breath, waiting, hoping. Finally, Rick said, "Alright."

"He's a very close associate, isn't he?" Mr. Price said. "It would be a shame for anyone else close to you to suffer for your obstinance."

The words broke her tenuous hold on the fury filling her veins. She launched herself out of bed, bare feet slapping against the cool floor. The masked goon started to move but Mr. Price held his hand out to stop her. Instead, he stood to his feet and sneered at Tina, as if he were untouchable.

Maybe it was that Tina was feeling bold after bluffing Madame Capelli so successfully. Maybe it was that she realized that the only reason Mr. Price would be there was because something had shifted, perhaps in her favor. Or maybe she was simply fed up.

Whatever the reason, Tina pulled back and slapped him across the face.

The masked woman came at her once again and again, Mr. Price waved her off. Though, that smile he'd been wearing with such glee was missing.

Good. Get used to disappointment you oily bastard.

"After I'm done with you and your precious High Tide, you're going to look back at this moment and weep for what you just did," Mr. Price said, his voice dripping venom.

"Oh, I highly doubt that. Now get out of my house."

Mr. Price stalked to her bedroom door with his head high, the left side of his face lit up with an angry red hand print.

Tina followed them out, wanting to avoid an altercation with Rick. The one thing she hadn't thought of were the men Rick had stationed outside her brownstone overnight.

They're likely dead now thanks to these two. Damn it! I'm losing too many good men in this fight!

Rick was in his bathrobe, gun at the ready as he came out of the kitchen. She held her hand up and shook her head.

"They were just leaving."

Mr. Price turned to glare at her one last time before walking out the door with the creepy young woman.

When the door closed, Tina's shoulders slouched and she closed her eyes.

"I was just about to come back up," he said. "The men I placed outside are dead. Precision work too, so whoever those two are...Tina maybe—"

"Don't you dare tell me to give up, Rick! Don't you dare!" Tina felt something snap in her, something profound and deep and she could no longer hold back the floodgates. "I've sacrificed, and played the villainous mother, and done awful things to get free, to get the life I wanted. And I'm not giving Von, or Capelli or Mr. Price one more square inch of my soul!"

Rick stared at her as Tina's chest heaved, her eyes wild. She knew she must look a little unhinged, and she couldn't care less.

At last his gaze relaxed and he nodded.

"Alright, Tina. I'm with you then, to the end."

Tina turned on her heel and walked into the dining room where Rick had laid out a coffee service and some of the small biscuits she loved. The food smelled heavenly, but she had no appetite.

She'd meant what she'd said to him, but she had no idea how she was going to succeed and not lose something precious in this war.

CHAPTER THIRTEEN

I t was impossible for Shay to wipe the smile off her face.

Hours of talking and holding hands last night had left her with the sensation of walking on air. She had no idea if this was going to become anything more, but if the way Colleen had looked at her was any indication, it could turn into something Shay hadn't had in a very long time.

"You look like the cat that ate the canary," Walter said, a grin splitting his craggy face.

She could feel heat rise to her cheeks and shrugged.

"I don't kiss and tell."

He nodded.

"Well, whoever it is, it's nice to see you smiling."

"I always smile. You're the one that needs a pick me up," she said.

Walter waved her words away.

"I tried that. After the third time you have to cut your losses and move on."

"You shouldn't give up, there could be someone out there for you."

"Rookie, I'm good on my own."

He was smiling but there was an edge to his words that made Shay's mind come to attention. Why did he distance himself so much, even from her? Was he hiding something? Did he truly believe that it was best that no one was around him?

"Enough about this sad old man," he said, plopping some papers in front of her. "It's your turn to do the paperwork."

She wrinkled her nose at him and was about to offer a trade when Fisk's voice rose above the din.

"Task force meeting in five. Don't be late."

Walter grunted and Shay looked up at him with a wide grin.

"I guess you're doing the paperwork?"

"This time. But next time you're not getting out of it."

Shay saluted in response and walked to the small meeting room with her notepad.

The place was crowded with a dozen officers, all of them taller and wider than her. The moment she walked through the door, every eye turned to her, a few muttered under their breath, others didn't even try to hid their displeasure at her presence.

"We need a secretary?" asked a dark haired officer by the name of Chris.

"Maybe she's here to take lunch orders," said the man next to him.

"Hey, sweetheart, go get me some coffee, two sugars."

The men around him laughed and tried to get their coffee orders in too when Fisk cut them off.

"Officer Reynolds is here as part of the team."

The laughter cut off and Shay felt even more on the spot. Especially when a few guffawed and shook their heads.

"What's next, one of them makes captain?" said someone to her left.

Her gaze found him, a man she didn't know by name but definitely by reputation for his brutality to young men in High Tide.

She pushed every bit of stubborn determination and confidence into her gaze until he looked away.

Remember, you earned this. You belong here.

"If everyone is finished?" Fisk said, lips pressed into a thin line. "Good, down to business. Now, we need a plan to draw the vigilante out and capture her. We know she stays mostly in High Tide, but we've also seen her in Devil's Own. Ideas?"

"Why don't we simply patrol the streets of High Tide?" asked Chris. "Show the vigilante that we're there. I'm betting she won't be able to resist."

"Why?" Shay asked. "She's not shown herself reckless, so simply showing up isn't going to make her appear."

"You have a better idea?" the cop to her left asked.

"Actually, yes."

"Okay," Fisk said, crossing his arms, "let's hear it."

Shay worked moisture into her mouth, mind scrambling to organize all the information she'd been gathering about the vigilante.

"Well, if you look at the reports about where she's been engaged by officers and also the reports of where she's been sighted, then put a marker on a map of High Tide for each location, we should be able to narrow things down to the area she's at the most. High Tide is a large neighborhood to cover, but if we eliminate the places she's least likely to show up it becomes manageable. Then, we can formulate a plan to draw her out."

"You want to waste time reading up on the criminal, be my guest, I'll be out there actually catching her," someone next to Chris said.

"Yeah, why don't you go home and curl up with a romance book and leave the work to us, huh sweetheart?" Chris said, chuckling.

"If you two think this is all a joke, maybe I should look for officers that will take this more seriously," Fisk said.

Shay's eyes widened.

Did...did Fisk just defend me?

"Do you think you can work something up?" he asked her.

"Yes, absolutely."

"Good, start working on that and come back when you've narrowed it down."

Shay nodded, doing her best not to smile. She knew better than to show any kind of pleasure when one of these guys got reprimanded, no matter how much they deserved it.

Her mind was already starting to come up with a picture based on the reports she'd read and the things she remembered from her own experiences.

I wonder if I could get some of the earlier reports...wasn't there a reference to a fire wielding vigilante in Little Italy around last Christmas?

By the time she'd walked down to the records room, Shay had quite a list of requests. The grumpy officer who smelled of rye whiskey and sweat complained under his breath for the full ten minutes it took him to find the first six files. Shay didn't feel like waiting in the stuffy basement for the rest so she told him she'd come back. He grumbled some more and went to search for the rest.

After three trips, Shay had all the files she could think of and stacked them on her side of the dual desk she and Walter shared.

"What's all this, rookie?" he asked, cup of coffee in hand.

"I'm triangulating a possible location to draw the vigilante out but I need to know where she's been sighted."

Walter picked up one of the files and took a long sip from his mug.

"Why are you going back so far?"

She looked at the file and frowned.

"I didn't request a file on...what's that name...Lumis? Wasn't that the chemical factory that went up in flames...why would he give me that?"

"He must have a hangover again. I'll take it back for you."

She frowned. There was something she was forgetting about...

"Maybe I should take a look at it," she said. "If it was mixed up in what I was asking for maybe there's something in there."

Walter didn't give it right back, despite fact that she was holding out her hand. When it was clear that he was going to hold onto it, Shay stepped closer to him.

"What is it?"

He took another drink from his mug and let out a throaty sigh.

"Lumis is a touchy subject around here, especially...well, let's just say that being my partner and asking about it will do you no favors. Let it go."

And with that, Walter turned away from her, file in hand and walked to the records room door.

Shay stared after him, mind spinning with the mystery he'd plopped down in front of her.

If that place has something to do with why he was demoted AND with the vigilante...

A thought struck her like a lightning bolt and she sat in her chair, stunned.

He should've had her that night, yet she escaped when he was alone with her. Could he have let her go?

She glanced at the locked drawer in his desk, at the spotless arrangement of notepads and pens. Walter never kept files on his desk when he wasn't right there. He even carried them with him to get coffee or he locked them in the drawer.

Why would he do that?

The phone on the desk rang and she picked it up.

"Officer Reynolds."

"Can you take a call for Officer Lyle?" the operator asked.

"Sure."

She waited as the call clicked over and then said, "This is Officer Reynolds, how can I help you?"

The line was silent, the only sound a quick intake of breath on the other line.

"Hello?"

One more second then the line clicked and went dead.

She looked at the phone, the suspicion she'd been nursing now fully taking charge.

Walter walked back from the records room and sat in his chair as she replaced the receiver.

"Everything alright?" he asked.

She frowned at him, and noticed the wary glint in his eye.

"Yeah," she said, forcing a smile. "Yeah, I just need some coffee."

As she stood the phone rang; Walter picked it up. He grunted a response and then took his pad out to take a note but stopped writing when he noticed her standing there, watching.

"Reynolds, you need something?"

"Nope. Not a thing."

Suspicion crawled over her skin as she walked away. She respected Walter, she liked him as a partner and he was a good cop. But he was also someone who had a mysterious past and a habit of holding onto cases that could sink her career.

I need more information.

By the time she'd come back to the desk, Walter had finished his call and stepped away. She saw that the pad of paper he was taking notes on was still there, though the note itself was gone.

She snatched the pad from his side and lightly shaded the blank top piece of paper with her pencil. After a few seconds, an address appeared. Shay tore the piece of paper off, stuffed it in her pocket and put the pad back just before Walter plopped down in his chair.

Sorry partner, but I need to know what you're doing.

Colleen hadn't been this nervous since she'd had to speak in front of her sixth grade class. Every sound or shadow put her on high alert, waiting for a task force member to jump out and shoot her.

When she'd called Walter to get the time and place he wanted to meet, and heard Shay's voice on the other end, everything that could go wrong crashed into her mind.

"I'm not sure this is a good idea," she'd told Walter. "It's too risky."

"I'll protect you, I swear it. I just need your help to put these guys away for good."

The possibility that anyone could bring charges against the men behind Lumis, much less Jason James himself, felt like a pipe dream. But Colleen wouldn't be able to live with herself if she let her fear keep her from helping.

So here I am, sweating in these leathers and hoping that the man can make good on his promises.

The old canning warehouse still stank of fish and machinery oil, a mixture that stung her nostrils something awful. It didn't escape her notice that Walter chose a location that was neither in Tina's territory nor Von's.

He doesn't want that conflict spilling over.

The sound of something metal falling to the cement floor echoed through the cavernous space and she spun around. Her gaze scanned the night, seeking any movement. When something did shuffle along in her vision, Colleen lobbed a fireball at it, and heard a rat squealing in rage or pain.

She winced at the sound and recalled the flames.

"If you've got a thing against rats, I should've chosen a different location," Walter said, walking into the room.

"I'm nervous."

"I can understand that, thank you for meeting me."

"What do you want?"

"I'll cut to the chase. I know you were at Lumis, along with another vigilante that bears an uncanny resemblance to Shadow Master in Jet City."

Colleen's fists clenched at the mention of Marco. Threats against her she could deal with, but if Walter thought bringing her best friend into this would make her talk, he had another thing coming.

"Shadow stays out of this or I walk."

Walter held up his hands.

"I'm not after either of you, and I can't even find out how to contact the man, so he's safe in any case. I need to know why you attacked it. What was going on there?"

Colleen hesitated. Those memories still woke her in a cold sweat in the middle of the night.

"Why do you want to know?"

"About a year before Lumis went up in flames, I had uncovered a kidnapping and child trafficking ring, right here in Metro City. The kidnappings were hard to track because they were orphans or kids in the foster system. Kids that could easily disappear and most wouldn't bat an eye. Looking closer at the kids I discovered that they were from two neighborhoods in particular: Devil's Own and High Tide."

Colleen's mouth went dry as the confirmation for her own theories were dangled in front of her.

"Did you...did you ever find out anything about an orphanage in Little Italy being one of the places kids disappeared from?" she asked.

"Yes, though it had shut down a few years before the pattern I was seeing started to appear."

"Was there a connection in the trafficking to either Reginald Von or Grandfather Malone?"

His eyes narrowed.

"Yes, actually. I believe that Malone was getting the kids to Von, who was then shipping them to labs in the Midwest."

Colleen's head spun. She had expected this, and even still hearing it confirmed that her grandfather was helping to sell children from High Tide filled her a sickening shock.

She leaned against a piece of dusty machinery and took deep draughts of air.

"Are you alright?"

"No...I have a file that someone left for you. It's got proof of what you're talking about, the names of the fronts for these labs."

He let out a relieved sigh.

"Thank god you've got it. I thought maybe one of the officers at that crime scene might have picked it up. Did you bring it?"

"No, it's hidden, safe. I'll get it to you."

"No, keep it. Probably safer with you at this point."

He stepped closer, cautious as if he wasn't at all sure what Colleen would do.

"Fahrenheit, I know you're trying to help the people here, and I know...I know that the kids that disappeared had a history of strange things happening around them or their siblings. I think they were being sold to a private company to experiment on. When Lumis went belly up and then was destroyed, I had already started to suspect that it was a front for this kind of sick business."

"So why are you pursuing all this in secret?"

Walter sighed.

"I underestimated the reach of the men I was accusing. They had half the department in their pocket and when I wouldn't let it go they killed my partner and I was demoted."

"I'm sorry."

"Yeah...he was a good man, he didn't deserve what happened to him. But up to the end he told me to keep going, he believed that this was right. I made a promise to him and myself that I'd bring these men to justice."

She nodded. Colleen understood a promise like that.

"What do you want to know?" she asked.

"What did you see there? Do you know who was in charge of it all?"

"I do, but the proof I have is less than nothing."

She told him about the lab, about the things she saw. He wrote it all down, scribbling as fast as he could. When he asked about the men in charge, Colleen hesitated.

If I tell him too much, will he make the connections and figure out who I am?

He held her gaze and smiled encouragingly.

"I swear, I'm not after you. Whatever you've done that you think I want to trap you for, I don't. My sources have always been protected."

She swallowed down the fear and nodded.

"Someone named Mr. Price is trying to get to Tina Knight, but he's not having much luck."

"Describe him?"

Colleen did and Walter swore under his breath.

"I know that bastard. Okay, anyone else?"

"Jason James."

His pen stopped dead, head whipping up to look at her.

"You have proof?"

"Nothing that you can use but I know it's him."

Walter exhaled through his nose.

"Everything points to him, but he and this other group...they cover their tracks really well."

"What other group?" Colleen asked, her frown deepening

"I don't know, but there's connections internationally. London, Leningrad, Tokyo, Egypt. I assume it's a group of them but I don't have proof."

"I'll keep my ears open."

"Speaking of that," he took a deep breath and Colleen braced for what he was about to say. "There's a warehouse in Von's territory that has been empty and dark for about a year. It's suddenly up and running, armed guards around the clock, and a few cops patrolling the area, protecting it I think. I can't get near it but I thought—"

"That I could go in there, fists ablaze and find out what's going on?"

"No, don't attack it. I need information to fill in the larger picture. Just see if you can find out anything, delivery schedules, and such."

Walter had the good grace to look grim as he asked her to ignore any potential crimes going on there.

If there are kids there, how can I leave them like that? Of course, if I play along I'll at least get the chance to make that decision for myself instead of just saying no and losing the chance.

"Alright, give me the address, I'll see what I can do."

He gave her a tired smile and handed her a slip of paper.

"Thank you."

She nodded.

"I should go, before anyone sees me."

"I know you took a risk meeting me," Walter said. "It means a lot that you trusted me."

"I don't trust you, not yet. But...I'm getting there."

"Fair enough. Now, let me give you some information. The task force is trying to figure out where to find you. I would stay away from your usual haunts for the next week unless you want to clash with them. They're going to get desperate to find you soon, some government agency called The Bulwark is threatening to come in and take over. That's the last thing any of them want, so be careful."

Colleen's heart jumped to her throat. The Bulwark was the agency Karen had worked at, the agency that hunted powered people and locked them up. Or worse.

They'll kill me on sight...and Andrew! I've got to get a message to him. I've got to...what? I can't contact Karen without endangering her. And The Bulwark won't care whether or not the police are able to catch us. Sooner or later, they'll be here.

She took two, deep breaths and forced herself to ignore the sick feeling in her gut.

"The agency is dangerous, stay away from them," she said once she could speak without terror leaching into her voice. "And thanks for the heads up."

"Sure thing. Contact me if you have any other information, tell the operator you're my sister."

She nodded, turned to leave and then paused.

"Jason was transporting a powered child on a steam boat down the Red Rock river a month ago. You might want to look into unconventional shipping methods, pleasure cruises or anything else he has that looks innocuous."

"Thank you."

"And leave the powered in Jet City alone, they have nothing to do with this."

"I promise."

Colleen wasn't sure she believed him. Walter struck her as the type that would break a promise like that if it led to a breakthrough in his case. But she had to hold onto the hope that he would at least hesitate long enough for her warn Marco.

"Oh," he said, taking a step toward her, "if I need to contact you how can I do that?"

"That's a tricky question."

"I know but if there's something you need to know…"

She felt like she was being baited, and in all likelihood, she was. Though she couldn't deny the sound logic of the suggestion, she had no idea where he could leave a message. No one but Tina knew who she was and anywhere else was sure to be suspicious of him.

But there is one place I can check in regularly without drawing suspicion, one place that always has the best gossip about High Tide. I'm sure to hear about a message as soon as I walk through the door.

"Rachel's Place, it's a salon. Leave a message there and it will get to me."

She went out into the night, careful to stick to the shadows and avoid her usual route back to High Tide all the time wondering if Shay was out there hunting her.

Shay felt as if she were seeing a Television show or a play as she watched her partner talking with the vigilante. There was just no way this could be what it looked like, could it?

But then she started to catch bits and pieces of their conversation. What she heard told her that Walter was working a case about Lumis and that Fahrenheit had something to do with it.

When the name "Jason James" came out of the vigilante's mouth, a chill ran up Shay's spine.

He was the most powerful man in Metro City, if not the entire country. His businesses spanned the gamut of weapons, pharmaceuticals, agriculture and apparently something having to do with powered people.

Shay wanted to believe that Walter was on the side of good, that he was doing something that was too important to simply walk away from. But the fact that he had let Fahrenheit go, he'd lied to her and thus put her career in jeopardy made her angry.

She'd scraped and worked up hill every day to get to where she was and all it would take was one wrong move and she'd be back in the basement.

Fahrenheit walked away, her eyes scanning the shadows where Shay hid. For a split second, the vigilante's eyes locked onto her spot and she stopped dead in her tracks. Shay ducked down, pulse racing.

After a few seconds Shay took a chance and looked over the broken window frame so she could see the main room where Walter and Fahrenheit had been.

She gave a yelp of shock when Walter appeared on the other side of the window, arms crossed and eyebrows drawn together.

"We need to talk," he said, his deep voice rumbling with disapproval.

"You're damn right we do! What the hell was that?"

"Something you should've kept your nose out of. But the minute you saw that Lumis file I knew I wouldn't be able to shake you."

"What is going on? You reveal to the vigilante exactly what I'm trying to do within the task force, not just undermining our ability to capture her but undermining me *personally!* Do you have any idea how hard it is to get an ounce of respect with those men? I started making headway with that idea and you cut my damn legs out from under me!"

Walter shook his head.

"Rookie—"

"No!" she came around the wall and stood toe to toe with him, craning her neck to look him in the eye.

"No more of that 'rookie' bull! I'm your partner Walter, your equal! And if you can't trust me and treat me like it, then…I'll find a new partner."

It was something that had never occurred to her until just this moment, but she meant it. Though the request would mean herculean efforts on her part, Shay couldn't work with a partner that she couldn't trust.

"You're a partner that was sent to spy on me and report to the captain," he said. "You want to talk about trust now?"

Shay took a step back and crossed her arms.

"I was asked to do that, yes. But I have never tattled on you, no matter what the captain said."

"I believe you. But I also know your kind—"

"My kind?"

"Yeah. The good cop kind that doesn't give up on a case when it means that good people are hurting and they can stop the bad guys. Even if it costs them everything."

"So you don't want a good cop on your side with whatever it is your doing?"

"I don't want to get another good cop killed. And trust me, you get mixed up in this with me, it will have consequences."

Shay weighed those words against what she'd seen and what her instincts were shouting at her. Everything was a jumble. On the one hand, she wanted to nail Walter to the wall for what he'd just done. On the other, she had seen enough of the old man to know that he was a good cop, if a little rough around the edges.

If I find out that what he's doing is wrong, then I'll tell the captain. But if it isn't, if he's really trying to help people…well then, I'll keep my mouth shut.

"Tell me what it is, and let me decide for myself."

Walter's hooded gaze studied her as Shay tried to keep eye contact and not look away. She wasn't naive, in spite of what he might think and if there was something she could do to help him solve his case, Shay wanted in.

"If I do," he finally said, "you'll have to accept associating with people the captain and commissioner view as criminals."

"But you don't?" she asked, her mind immediately going to Fahrenheit.

"Some of them, absolutely. Others? Well, I'm sorry to tell you this, but you're going to have to accept that most things aren't black or white, they're all in the gray. You'll find out things about people you might wish you hadn't. And you will probably also come to hate me for shattering a lot of your ideas about this job. So, please, think about it."

Shay felt like she was being put off, treated like a child that might not be ready to handle adult things. Her spine straightened out of habit as her ire was raised.

Walter saw it and gave her a grin.

"Oh kid, you've got a spine of steel don't you? I sure hope it doesn't get you killed one of these days."

"There's an all-night diner two blocks away," she said. "I'll buy you a cup of coffee and you tell me all about your case."

"You sure? I mean, really sure?"

"Yes."

He sighed.

"Alright then. But I want pie with my coffee."

Shay gave him a lopsided grin.

"Don't push it, old man."

CHAPTER FOURTEEN

C olleen swore she saw someone else in the abandoned warehouse where she met Walter. But as she stared into the darkness there was nothing there and she ended up shrugging it off.

The address he'd given her was deep into Devil's Own and she hadn't brought the bike with her since, the last time she rode it, she almost crashed it into the side of a building.

Looks like the only option is to run.

She did, dodging police cars and pedestrians out on their front stoop or couples holding hands. In High Tide, the sight of Fahrenheit would inspire shouts of support, but in Devil's Own she wasn't at all sure what her reception might be, so she stuck to the shadows and roof tops.

At last she was perched on a rooftop across the street from the warehouse Walter had told her about. Dim lights shone through the dirty windows, shadows sometimes walking in front. Men, who were barely bothering to hide their fire arms, were pacing in front of and on the sides of the building. After just ten minutes of watching, a patrol car crawled by, the officers stopping to chat for a moment with one of the guards. An envelope was exchanged before they drove off. Colleen's blood boiled.

I need to see inside that place, but how? I can't go in with fire balls and flames…can I? Colleen tried to think through the reasons why she shouldn't just barge in there. From what she could tell, there were four guards around the building, but an unknown number inside the warehouse. The smart thing would be to wait, find out when the next patrol car came by and then observe how many men came and went.

A large delivery truck with the words "Flemming's Fish" pulled up, a squad car following behind it. The delivery truck backed up close to the double doors of the warehouse, presumably to load or unload cargo.

Meanwhile, the cop car parked horizontally, effectively blocking the street. Its lights flashed and officers stood outside the car as if to make sure no one dared to come through their small barricade.

I need to know if they're dropping off or picking up.
She crawled over the rooftop, careful to make sure the police, who were scanning the night looking for trouble, didn't see her. At the far right corner of the roof, Colleen was able to get a good angle to see the truck's back. A ramp was in place from the truck to the warehouse, armed men on either side.

"C'mon move it! We haven't got all night!" one of them yelled, yanking on the painfully thin arm of a child coming down the ramp.

Colleen's vision went bright and sparks fell in sizzling flecks from her fingers. She was going to fry them all and leave their charred remains as warnings to anyone who dared to do this again.

"No quarter," she said, standing with a bold disregard for whether or not anyone saw her.

It wasn't until she'd reached the fire escape that reason began to pierce the fugue of fury she was swimming in.

Shay's face came to her mind, and Karen's and Judy's. Lastly, Marco and she felt some of the blind rage seep out of her.

He fights with himself every time he conjures the shadows. He and I…every time we give in we're left with nothing but regret.

She clenched her teeth, struggling against the desire to bathe all of them in flames.

It felt like hours but in reality, it was barely a minute until Colleen had calmed enough to realize that she could save the children. But she couldn't go in with the intent to destroy.

I'm not a killer. And besides, I might hurt one of the kids.

The world was still bright and power dripped from Colleen's fingertips as she stepped out from the building's shadow, but at least she wasn't being driven by unbridled anger.

One of the cops saw her first. He was able to point and say one syllable before Colleen shot a stream of fire that she twisted into a half circle between them and the warehouse.

Tying the flames off, she faced the first of the gunman to run at her.

Every fight she'd been in the last month, all the things she had practiced, discovered and even failed at, melded into battle instincts that felt as natural to her as breathing. Which was a good thing since half a dozen gunman were now about to attack her.

She launched fire in quick succession at the ones closest while a wall of bright flames leapt up in front of the ones who stood at a distance. The air was punctuated by the pop of bullets melting and exploding in her heat barriers.

The two men closest to her got to their feet and tried to fire at her, but Colleen simply pulled the flames over and wrapped it around their ankles. The men screamed, trying to beat the flames out with their hands but only managing to scorch themselves further.

Colleen pulled the fire back, grinning at the fear looking back at her in the goon's eyes.

This moment of glee cost her, however as the police had found a way around her barrier and started shooting at her.

A bullet pierced her upper arm and she cried out in pain as it ripped through. Her control over the flames around the men snapped and they began to crawl over the goons and the side of the warehouse.

The kids, they're in that building!

Horror propelled Colleen into action and she launched herself through the flames and into the warehouse. Fire was spreading fast and smoke was starting to fill the main room. Colleen reached up, wincing against the pain in her arm, and called enough of the flames to her so that the building wouldn't be consumed until she got the kids out.

She heard crying and men's voices just ahead and ran for it only to be met with a spray of bullets into the floor. The children screamed, the sound echoing in the space even as it was diminishing.

They're trying to get them out of the building by a back door!

Behind her, the men were rallying. Two walked through the charred doorway, guns at the ready. She was about to be penned in and then she would not only lose her chance to save the kids, but she'd probably die, too.

Colleen knew there was no good solution, so she chose the one that gave her the best chance at getting to the kids.

Letting go of her control of the fire that was still licking at the walls of the warehouse, the flames shot to life as if someone had just sprayed gasoline. In the same moment, Colleen shot fire balls blindly in the direction of the gunman in front of her as she took off at full speed toward where the back door had to be. Gun fire followed in her wake but she didn't look back. Instead, Colleen simply kept throwing the fire as quick as she could form it. When she was a foot from the door, she blasted it off its hinges and kept running.

She rounded the corner of the building just in time to see the delivery truck barreling away, a small face screaming at her from an opening in the back before being pulled into the darkness of the truck.

"No!" Colleen screamed, flames erupting from her hands.

Behind her, the warehouse was now fully ablaze and the remaining goons were fleeing the scene as sirens rose through the night.

She gulped air as furious sobs wracked her body and flames dripped from her clenched fists. Any minute, the entire block would be surrounded. She had to move and get to safety but her body wouldn't obey.

It wasn't until one of the police cars squealed around a corner that Colleen snapped out of it. But the moment she broke into a run, the full extent of her injuries became apparent. Not only was she shot in the arm, but she'd taken a bullet to her calf and there were stings of pain running up and down her back where she must've gotten grazed.

You've had worse. C'mon, keep going!

She healed fast, but not fast enough. Every step was a fresh wave of agony that she had no choice but to endure.

Colleen assumed that just getting away from the warehouse would be enough, but then she saw patrol cars driving slow down the streets, shining flashlights out of their windows. They were searching for her and obviously they weren't just sticking to where she'd torched the place.

She ducked into an alley and hid behind a garbage bin that stank of fish and onions. The car passed her hiding spot and she waited, counting the seconds until it would get to the end of the block. She was just about to stand up when she heard footsteps, and someone shouting orders.

They were on foot and in cars to probably cover more of the area thoroughly.

The vigilante looked up and saw a rickety old fire escape that had definitely seen better days. She used to laugh at Marco for preferring to swing over rooftops instead of simply running along the street. But now she was thinking that he had the right idea after all.

She gripped the metal and pulled the ladder down. It screeched something awful and she hissed at the excruciating pain in her shoulder.

Colleen closed her eyes and took a deep breath. The voices were coming closer, the footsteps slapping on the pavement. In less than a minute, they'd be here and the way she felt, controlling her powers would be tenuous, not to mention her wounds were starting to make her feel weak. She didn't have a lot of strength left, certainly not enough for a prolonged fight.

Gritting her teeth against the pain in her shoulder, Colleen swung herself up on to the fire escape and scaled it with the speed only a pursued person could access.

Soon, she was crouched up on the ledge of the roof among the clothes lines and ragged lawn chairs that signified summer in the city. It was even money the police suspected what she'd done, but at this point there was nothing she could do about that.

Colleen slid down the low wall that surrounded the edge of the roof and sat with a gulping sigh. Now that she could examine her shoulder, she saw that it was, indeed, a through and through. Her calf was more of a deep gash, as if the bullet had sliced the skin and tissue like a knife. It wasn't as deep as her shoulder and it was already clotting.

But her shoulder was another matter. It was still bleeding enough that her head was starting to getting fuzzy, as the adrenaline faded and her body was feeling the effects of the blood loss. She could heal quicker than any non-powered person, and maybe a few powered ones, too. But not fast enough.

"Only one thing then."

She clenched her jaw tight against the scream that clawed its way up her throat as she thrust her finger into the wound and cauterized it.

A sob burst from her lips and she clamped down on it. There wasn't time to let everything out, not when she was in Von's territory surrounded by police. She had to get to someplace she knew and trusted.

Problem was, it was also the one place the police would be sure to catch her.

No choice though. I can't stay up here and get caught in the daylight.

With a grunt of pure determination, Colleen got to her feet.

CHAPTER FIFTEEN

I t was easy to the point of making Colleen paranoid to get out of Von's territory and to the outskirts of her home. But that was when the obstacles raised their ugly head.

Patrol cars prowled, slow and menacing like a shark looking for chum. She found herself crouching behind more than one smelly garbage can and abandoned car to avoid detection. Several times, she had to stop herself from taking on cops who were harassing young men, their faces forced against the hoods of cars or the sides of buildings as the police searched them for god only knew what. Most she recognized from the youth center. She hoped to see them there again and not hear about how they were beaten for nothing more than looking at the cop wrong.

She was trying to circle toward Wanda's place and her comfy bed when she ran right into a squad car that didn't have any lights on.

The officers stared at her in shock, as Colleen stared back, before she sprang into action and took off down the street, her wounds sending shock waves of pain through her body.

They yelled for her stop, bullets pinging against the cars she ran past. She needed cover, and fast.

She found herself just outside of Rachel's salon and knew that the old woman's house wasn't far. Getting Rachel involved was the last thing she wanted, but there as an old root cellar in the back, a place she and Andrew used to run to when Grandfather was on the war path. If the old man knew about it he never let on and though it was a spider infested square in the ground, Colleen had always felt safe there.

One squad car had now become two and Colleen grunted as she put on extra speed to reach the hidey hole faster.

Pulling herself up and over the chain link fence at the back of Rachel's small yard caused a burning pain to course through her shoulder and Colleen cried out despite the fact that she'd expected it to hurt.

Colleen could hear the men yelling now, the lights from their car flashing red and blue against the pristine white of Rachel's house.

If they harass her, I'll have to come out. I can't let anything happen to Rachel.

Rose bushes had grown up around the rusty door of the cellar and if Colleen hadn't already known it was there, the cellar would've been invisible. Thorns pierced her skin and she hissed in pain but kept going, pushing them aside and darting through the thick leaves and cloying flowers. She could've singed a path through, but that would've made her presence obvious. So Colleen endured the hundreds of stinging cuts and got to the door.

She pressed her hand to the rusty bolt that Rachel had put on the door and felt the metal give easily. The entrance creaked so loudly, she was sure Rachel must've heard, especially since a light came on the moment before Colleen slipped down into the dark and shut the cellar door behind her.

It was pitch black and unbelievably cool. She let a little heat into her palm, just enough for a marble sized ball of fire and looked around. Cobwebs hung in thick strands from the low ceiling and Colleen swiped them away with a shudder. The musty smell was nearly overwhelming; she took several breaths to calm herself. Being underground, surrounded on all sides by walls that seemed to close in by the second, it was a fear of Colleen's that had been there as long as she could remember. She never hid here by choice as a child and once Rachel had mistakenly locked her in. Ever since, Colleen had been terrified of small, underground spaces. Even spacious basements made her skin crawl. Now, back here after so many years, Colleen had thought she'd be past this terror, but it clawed its way up her throat and threatened to blow the whole thing if she didn't get out and fast.

No, stop! You're fine… you're safe. You can get out any time because even if someone does lock the door…

An involuntary whimper escaped her lips.

…you can still get out. You are powerful, you are safe…you are safe…

She repeated this last part like a talisman that would banish the lingering fear.

After god only knew how long, Colleen heard the cellar door creak and braced herself for a rain of bullets from the officers.

"Well now, I wondered how long until you turned up on my doorstep," said a familiar voice.

Colleen turned around, eyes wide and heart pounding.

Standing there, purple robe closed tight in spite of the night time heat, was the beautifully weathered face of Rachel.

"Come on out of there," she said. "Those men are gone and I need to have a talk with you, young lady."

A different kind of nerves hit Colleen as she stepped inside Rachel's small, one story rambler. The older woman had turned on the light in the kitchen and was pouring two glasses of cold milk. She handed one to Colleen and went to the tidy kitchen table. The inside of the house was warm but not stifling, all the windows open to catch any cool air. The faintest smell of hair styling products hung in the air right alongside a sweeter scent that made Colleen think of a bakery. Crocheted afghans were scattered over the couch and arm chairs in the living room that Colleen spied just beyond the small dining area. She stood by the kitchen entry and looked at Rachel, who held her eye contact patiently as she waited at the table.

Finally, Colleen walked with leaden steps and sat down.

"Drink your milk," Rachel said.

"Yes ma'am," Colleen replied automatically.

It was hard to just turn off the manners and familiarity that was like an instinct to Colleen. Rachel had been like a grandmother to her, a safe haven that Grandfather would never have considered damaging. Her salon was sacrosanct, a neutral zone in the midst of everything.

The cool milk was creamy and Colleen found after the first sip that she was beyond thirsty. She drained the glass in one go and wiped the milk off her upper lip with the back of her hand.

Rachel's dark eyes twinkled at her in recognition and once again Colleen felt her stomach twist.

"You're a good girl, Colleen," she whispered. "But you're also reckless."

Colleen slumped in her chair, head in her hands.

"How did you know?"

Rachel snorted.

"I may be old but I'm not stupid."

"I...I never wanted to put the people I loved in danger."

"Do you see what's happening around here? I'm in danger every time I step outside my door. I'm not worried about it, and you shouldn't be either. What you should be focused on is thinking things through. You're reacting, not responding."

Colleen looked up, a frown creasing her brow.

Rachel took Colleen's hand, unafraid of the unnatural warmth in the vigilante's skin.

"You were always destined to lead us," Rachel continued, holding tight to Colleen's hand when she flinched at the words. "Now calm down, I don't mean in the way your grandfather tried to make you. I mean in this way, as a hero. But you're not going to last much longer if you don't start using your head as well as those powers you've been blessed with."

The words struck something deep in Colleen, opening up the wound of doubt and fear that she'd just started to really acknowledge. She could feel the wisdom in Rachel's words coupled with a helplessness that threatened to overwhelm her.

Tears welled up in her eyes and she shook her head.

"I did mess up. Big and I-I'm so angry!"

Rachel listened with patience as Colleen unloaded everything.

Andrew.

The mysterious Mr. Price.

Walter.

And the children that she couldn't save tonight.

At that last story, Colleen let the tears flow as all of it crashed in a terrible wave onto her.

"I made it worse, I know I did," she sobbed. "And I have no idea where they are now. That location won't be used again and if it is, they're going to have more security. Not to mention the fact that now the police have even more cause to come after me in High Tide. I've...Rachel, I failed."

"Poppycock," the old woman responded. "You didn't use your head, that's for certain. But I can't fault you for having a good heart and wanting to save those children. What I can fault you for is thinking you have to do all this by yourself."

Colleen took the hankie the old woman handed her and shook her head.

"You don't understand how dangerous it is. I can't—"

"Oh-ho! I don't understand, do I? Well, that might be true. I can't shoot fire from my hands, but I do know that God didn't make us to be alone. None of us. I know that if you just look around you, that there are people who could help you. And I know that it's easier to not ask for help, than it is to open yourself up to others just so they can hurt you. But honey, not everyone is like your Grandfather, not everyone will break your heart and trust and leave you with nothing. I promise you."

Colleen ducked her head in an effort to protect herself from what Rachel was saying. It hurt too much to be faced with it all, especially after tonight's failure.

Everyone who got mixed up with her and her family got hurt. Everyone. Even Judy and Karen. They might be safe, but the journey to get there was hell.

Andrew was so mixed up by what Grandfather did that he thought his actions were heroic.

Tina had plots within plots and Colleen had spent her whole life unable to trust that there wasn't something underneath every word her mother said.

The excuses she'd used a hundred times to protect herself from the very thing Rachel had zeroed in on began to run through her mind in a loop. It was usually soothing and in the past, she would find her equilibrium again in a few minutes. Tonight, it was a strain to access those thoughts, and it felt like a band aid over a gaping wound when she did.

"Alright then," Rachel said after a minute or so of silence, "I've said my peace, it's up to you if you listen or not. I hope you do because I believe in you, Colleen. Not because you're perfect, but because you are good."

That last word broke the vigilante and she dissolved into wracking sobs.

Rachel's arms came around her, holding her close and letting her cry on the older woman's breast.

When she was done, Colleen felt spent but relieved, too. She wasn't ready to trust her mother, or anyone else, though Rachel's words had lodged themselves pretty firmly in her mind.

No, it was the fact that if Rachel could believe in her, that she was good, that she could do this, then maybe it was true.

"Thank you," Colleen said, using the hankie again.

"Any time, any time. Now," Rachel walked to the back door where they'd come in and motioned for Colleen to follow her, "to get you home."

Colleen nodded. She started to consider what streets might be safe and where she might be able to hide when Rachel picked up an old shovel and shoved the rose bushes in front of the cellar aside.

"Would you mind opening the door for me?" she asked.

Colleen frowned, confused about what the old woman was doing but complying all the same. Rachel followed behind her into the cellar and clicked on a flash light that she pulled from the pocket of her robe.

The old woman led her to the back of the small, en-closed space and Colleen wondered if Rachel was going to tell her to sleep down there. She shuddered at the idea just before Rachel began feeling along the back wall.

"What are you looking for?"

Rachel grunted in frustration a moment before she murmured, "Ah, here it is."

As Colleen watched with wide eyes, Rachel pried loose a board that revealed a small door knob. She struggled to twist it but after a few seconds, the door gave a loud groan, swinging open to reveal a tunnel.

"What in the world?!" Colleen gasped.

"My first husband used to run moonshine during prohibition, before I met him, that is. After that, I would use this to help your mother and…your father when they were hiding from your grandfather."

Tina never talked about the man that she'd married and had children with, as if he had never existed at all. Colleen had one very fuzzy memory of the man before he'd died. When she'd been scared or lonely as a kid, Colleen would dig it out and imagine that her father would understand, that he'd take her away from Grandfather and all of his 'lessons'. But, of course, he never did. As she got older, Colleen wondered about what he looked like, what he did for a living and how in the world he'd convinced Tina to marry him. But mostly, she wondered if Grandfather had killed him.

"You knew my father?" she asked, the old hunger to know coming on strong.

Rachel gave her a sympathetic smile and a pat on the cheek.

"That's a story for another time. Now, I want you to use this for escaping or whatever you might need."

Colleen peered down the yawning, dark tunnel, feeling stale air on her face.

"Is it safe?"

"Should be. I have the son of the man that originally built it come check it every year. It runs under the foundation of my house so I can't have the thing collapsing. It lets out inside a back room in the Torch and Grier."

A small group of flames danced in Colleen's hand and she could see a little further. Some cobwebs hung down, but not nearly as many as the root cellar, and she could see how sturdy the walls and ceiling looked, some of the reinforced boards appeared new.

"Thank you," she said. "I...I don't know how to repay you."

"Just think about what I said, and don't be a stranger. Just because I don't work at the salon very much, doesn't mean you can't come around and see me."

Colleen smiled, embracing the old woman who had been the rock of her childhood.

"Go on," Rachel said, "I need my beauty sleep."

A chuckle echoed down the tunnel as Colleen stepped through and the door closed behind her. It took her several minutes to calm the pounding of her heart, to convince her mind that she was safe and that the sooner she moved, the sooner she'd be out of this underground passage.

CHAPTER SIXTEEN

A ndrew recalled the ice from his face so that it appeared like flesh before opening the door to the mansion and stepping through. He was tired after shaking down the dozens of business owners in Devil's Own and High Tide. Grunt work he was sure Mr. Price was using as a punishment for warning his mother and sister.

The moment he stepped over the threshold, Andrew was hit by the chaos. The usually quiet mansion was in an uproar. Three different phone lines were ringing nonstop, and Mr. Price actually had some color in his face, albeit an unhealthy one, as he went from call to call. The foyer was crowded with men, mostly hired guns, waiting to see what their orders might be. In a room behind the stairs, Andrew heard someone scream and realized that Mr. Price's prized pupil was trying to get information out of someone. Mr. Price usually had people questioned off site in one of the empty storage containers he kept at the docks. That this was happening in the mansion made every instinct in his body go on high alert.

He must want us all to hear this…it's a warning.

A man with singed clothing passed him, face pale as he was escorted to another room near where the screams came from.

"I don't know anything. I swear to god I don't," he whimpered.

The men pushed him along, faces impassable.

Andrew had gotten used to such scenes in his time with this organization. He'd seen plenty of people cry and plead in the labs, plenty more try to play along until an opportunity to escape presented itself. And a few even fought back over the long haul.

It never ended well for any of them.

His first thought was that Colleen had attacked a prime location and he felt a surge of pride well up inside of him. Followed by a firm smack down of such emotions. It would be suicide to even think such thoughts in his position.

For more than one of us. Damn it Col! You're going to ruin everything!

"What's going on?" Andrew asked a passing gunman.

"The warehouse in Devil's Own got hit, by Fahrenheit, and the cargo was almost taken," he answered.

There was only one warehouse that would cause this much of an uproar, only one that Colleen would hit like this. Andrew swore under his breath and the gunman next to him nodded.

"The police captain is calling, the men at the lab are calling. Even the Big Man called, that's who he's on with now."

They both looked back at Mr. Price standing behind his massive desk, talking quietly to Jason James. Andrew's stomach turned and the massive gunman next to him shivered at the thought.

"How the hell did she find it?" Andrew said, mostly to himself.

"Word is we have a mole."

The word hung in the air between them and Andrew clenched his jaw to keep from showing any emotion. He turned to go, not wanting to hang around and see if anyone put the pieces together, when Mr. Price called his name with that deadly quiet tone of his.

Eyes from those nearby searched Andrew's face then turned away, as if to look too long on him would somehow seal their fate. But Andrew didn't flinch, didn't show one ounce of the terror turning his insides to jelly. He kept his shoulders straight, head high and walked with the cool nonchalance that he'd perfected in the last six months.

"Close the door," Mr. Price said.

The heavy thump of the door closing cut off the scream that filtered from the interrogation rooms, much to Andrew's relief.

"I assume you've heard what happened tonight."

"Yes, sir."

"We've been ordered to plug the leak, immediately. Nothing can interfere with our plans, that includes your sister."

Andrew nodded. He knew that no matter how bad Mr. Price wanted to get his hands on Colleen for her abilities, he'd sacrifice her without a second thought if the Big Man ordered him to do so.

"We've had trouble with a few of the officers in the past, but this one," Mr. Price handed him a piece of paper and a photograph, "doesn't seem to want to back off. The captain should've taken care of the man, but was reluctant."

"And now?"

"He'll fall in line or lose his life, just like his predecessor."

Andrew looked at the photo and read the brief about the cop, even though he really didn't have to. It was the man he'd been feeding information to, the only one that Mr. Price was scared of.

*Stupid man! He just **had** to tell Colleen about the warehouse, and in her current state as resident hero, she went off half cocked. Damn it, Walter! You couldn't keep your mouth shut a little longer?*

"Do you want it done tonight?" Andrew asked.

"No. I want to know if he has an accomplice. The captain insists that his partner is too green and career obsessed to align herself with Officer Lyle's investigation, but I can't be sure. This man could have several people working with him, and I need to plug all the holes at once. Watch him for the next two days, find out who else he's working with."

"Isn't...what's her name finding that out now?" he asked, gesturing toward the interrogation rooms.

"Metal Maiden is doing her best, yes. But really, this is just for show, a little lesson for whoever leaked this information. And if the man just happens to end up in her chair, so much the better."

"And if there's no one else working with Officer Lyle?"

"Then he will meet with a dreadful accident at the hands of...what are you calling yourself again?"

Andrew's teeth ground. He didn't want to call himself anything, but Mr. Price insisted he come up with a stupid secret identity.

"Sub Zero."

Mr. Price chuckled.

"Ah yes, clever. There's a car waiting for you outside. Make sure you don't fail me. Or you'll be the one having a chat with Metal Maiden."

Andrew opened the door to see two of Mr. Price's favorite goons carrying a body bag between them. The men in the foyer, all of them experienced in bloody work, turned pale with fear. No one knew who would be next, who would accuse whom of what and it had everyone on edge.

A rail thin woman with a metal mask on her face, dressed in black leather and twirling a set of metal marbles between her fingers, stepped through the door of the interrogation room. If one looked closely, dark, wet spots dotted her chest and upper arms.

No one but Andrew had the stomach to look directly at her, not that he wanted to. She was a mysterious nightmare to the gunmen, and a fascination to him. He'd never really met anyone who'd survived the labs as an adult besides himself, though he supposed 'survived' should be used loosely where she was concerned.

The woman hardly ever spoke and never took off the mask. He'd seen her stand stock still for hours, and then spring into action with the reflexes of a vicious animal. Andrew wasn't even sure there was a person left in the shell of flesh the Maiden inhabited, and if there was, he pitied her.

As Metal Maiden walked past him she stopped and stared at him, as if she saw something in Andrew that required further study. He wanted to turn away like everyone else, but instead he grit his teeth and forced himself to stare into the two holes in the mask where green eyes looked intently at him.

Finally, she looked away and continued her deliberate, slow walk to Mr. Price's office. Just before she closed the door, Maiden looked at him again and Andrew heard his heart beat loud and fast in his ears.

The men she'd tortured and killed could tell her nothing about him, Andrew knew that. Still, it did nothing to make him relax.

Andrew let out a slow breath and walked out of mansion. Once at the car, feeling eyes on him, his looked over his shoulder and saw her glaring at him from the office window. The locks on the car door went up and then down, and the hub caps shuddered.

The driver swore under his breath and tore away from the house before Maiden could do anything else to the vehicle.

"Damned woman," the driver muttered. "Every time she's in a bad mood, the car gets picked apart."

Andrew kept his mouth shut, in case it was a test, and let the driver's words sink in instead.

If she's in a mood that means she's not getting what she wants from them. It means I'm safe. For now.

CHAPTER SEVENTEEN

The mood in the precinct was suffocating from the stress that rolled off everyone in waves. Shay tried to ignore it and find some equilibrium as she accepted a steaming cup of coffee from Walter. She hadn't slept more than a few hours when her phone rang and the captain had demanded that she come in early. Her stomach dropped to her toes, wondering if he had someone else watching Walter and had assumed that she was involved with the old man in his crusade.

She and Walter had spent a good three hours at the diner, drinking coffee and eating surprisingly good pie. When he was done spilling everything to her, Shay wasn't sure which way was up.

The fact that there were dirty cops didn't surprise her, every precinct had that problem. But that it was so widespread, that it was targeting her home and covering for one of the most powerful men in the country…now *that* made her stomach turn.

Shay could understand why he wanted to protect her. This case had cost him his career, and it would definitely bury hers before it had ever gotten started.

He also knew that once I heard about the kids I would never be able to walk away. I can't even be mad at him for telling me, though I sure as hell want to be.

It hadn't escaped her that the only hope High Tide had to stop the trafficking was the vigilante, and that she had just signed up with the task force to stop her.

What a mess...and I have a feeling it's about to get worse.

The captain stepped out of his office with an extreme-ly grim looking Fisk by his side.

"Last night, the vigilante known as Fahrenheit at-tacked a business in Devil's Own. Six officers were wounded; one is in critical condition from burns on his body when he tried to save the men working in the warehouse."

Beside her, Walter swore under his breath.

"This cannot stand. Good businesses are being de-stroyed and good cops are getting hurt. As of right now, I don't care what you've got going on, this takes precedence. The task force can tap any of you for help or back up. The commissioner and mayor have given us a deadline of five days to get this under control or they're calling in some government big shots called The Bulwark. I will not go down in history as the captain who had to have help from the god damn federal government! Do I make myself clear?"

Everyone nodded, most enthusiastically, although Shay couldn't help noticing a few who became distinct-ly uncomfortable.

Huh...now that's interesting.

"Officer Reynolds, a word," the Chief said from the doorway of his office.

Shay could feel the eyes of everyone zero in on her as she walked to the open office door. A warm flush rose to her cheeks and she tamped down on the panic.

Once the door was closed, the chief motioned to a seat and Shay gratefully took it.

"I can't get into specifics with you, but I need to know if you are aware of where Walter was last night."

Shay's throat became tight and it was everything she could do not to fidget with the loose thread on her pants.

"We met for coffee and pie, he'd sounded lonely so I thought I'd give him an ear to talk to. He mostly just reminisced about his years on the force and gave me some advice. After that, I assume he was at home or whatever he does when not working."

The captain's eyes narrowed and Shay drew on every resource she could to remain calm.

"The business that was hit, Walter has had a…well, let's just say "obsession" with some of the men connected to it. I just wanted to make sure that he wasn't involved with what happened somehow."

"Walter is a good cop, sir. I highly doubt he would associate with a vigilante who harms other officers."

The captain studied her for another moment and then smiled.

"You're probably right. Until the vigilante is captured or killed, I'm taking you off patrol. You'll be working exclusively with the task force."

"And Walter?"

"He'll be on his own. I think he likes it better that way."

There was something in the way the captain said it, the feral tilt of his lips as he smiled, that made alarm bells go off in Shay's mind.

"You're dismissed, Reynolds," he said, waving her away.

"Yes, sir."

The feeling blossomed as she stepped out of the office and saw the way Fisk and two others from the task force were looking at Walter.

"Everything alright?" Walter asked, a tight smile on his face.

"Captain wants me to work the task force exclusively until we catch the vigilante," she pitched her voice lower as she made a show of getting a few things together. "He also asked me where you were last night."

"And?"

"I told him we had coffee and pie, that I thought you were lonely and so I let you wax poetic about being on the force."

"The lonely old man story, thanks a lot."

Shay couldn't help a grin.

"It fits."

Walter snorted.

"Why do I get the feeling that I'm suddenly a suspect?"

"Because I think you are. Look, lay low about all of this, at least until I can figure out what to do about the vigilante."

"Be careful, Shay. You're walking an awful thin tight rope."

She stopped, noticing that he hadn't called her rookie or kid.

"Don't worry about me, old man. I've got this."

He turned away, his shoulders slumping and suddenly he looked very old and very tired.

She chucked him on the shoulder to snap him out of whatever melancholy he was sinking into. The last thing she wanted was to have Walter giving the captain any more reasons to suspect him. She got a weary grin out of him before walking toward where the rest of the task force was assembled.

Colleen was healing slower than usual and she wondered if it had anything to do with the fact that she was hungry and thirsty all the time today, in spite of how often she ate.

I'm going to have to keep better track of this…maybe keep a journal.

She cringed at the thought and pulled the tap to refill the beer glass in front of her. The bar was busy tonight and there was no way Colleen could get away to search Devil's Own for kids without drawing suspicion.

I'll have to do it after closing and hope that I find something.

Someone started a song on the jukebox and several people hooted in excitement. Immediately, people were out of their chairs, dancing to the music. It was the end of the week, and people were more than ready to blow off a little steam.

Colleen couldn't help smiling, the joy contagious.

Wanda shook her hips as she delivered orders of burgers and wings to a nearby table, one of the patrons giving her a twirl on her way back to the kitchen. She reached out to Colleen and spun her around behind the bar, causing the vigilante to bite back a hiss of pain from the injury in her shoulder. If Wanda noticed, she didn't say anything and went to collect another order.

Colleen just barely managed to heft the tray of drinks with only a small wince, dodging the dancers with reflexes that probably had more to do with her powers than mere practice.

The men at the table smiled at her, one of them eyeing her appreciatively, which she chose to ignore. As she turned back around, a beautiful, familiar face was waiting at the bar.

Colleen smiled, in spite of the pain and worry that occupied her mind, and sat down next to Shay, who was making short order of the peanuts in front of her.

"Hey there," she said, cringing internally.

Hey there? Seriously Colleen, what are you, fifteen?

But Shay gave her a weary smile anyway and bumped her knee up against Colleen's, the only affection they could share in front of everyone.

"You look tired, is everything alright?" Colleen asked.

"No, not really."

Colleen's mind immediately went to the meeting with Walter and the botched rescue attempt, wondering if Shay and Walter had somehow gotten blow back from it.

"You want to talk?" she asked.

Shay sighed, a heavy, exhausted sound.

"I wish I could. It's all so complicated and I just wish everything could be simpler. I mean, I'm not stupid, I know that not everything is completely good or bad, there's shades of gray, but I just didn't expect this many shades of gray, if that makes sense."

Colleen thought about Andrew, and the mixed up motivations he had, the feelings of guilt and anger and love he invoked in her. She thought of Tina and how she was probably trying to do good in her own way and how the legacy of their family was constantly muddying the waters. And then she thought of herself, of the men she'd killed while trying to get Judy to safety in Red Rock, of the times she'd lost control and how good it had felt.

"It does make sense," Colleen whispered, wishing she could unload all of it to Shay.

"I've never had trouble figuring out a way forward before, I've always followed my gut, no matter the obstacles, but now?" Shay shook her head. "I'm fighting with myself and I have no idea what to do."

Colleen took her hand and squeezed, Shay returning the gesture. After a moment, she smiled, the sight making Colleen's heart ache.

"How about we go do something fun, blow off some steam? I could use a late night movie or something."

Colleen opened her mouth to agree when the memory of those kids shot through her mind.

I have to find them. I have to make this right.

"I...can't. I'm working until close."

"Oh," Shay's face fell a little, "well, maybe tomorrow, dinner?"

"I'd like that."

"And then maybe when things calm down we can do something *really* fun, like dancing."

A spark hit Colleen - the perfect date, the one that would be the date to end all dates.

Tina had been on her case for weeks to get a plus one for the grand opening of the Torch and Grier Theater. It had been the last thing Colleen wanted to do, but now?

Seeing Shay in a fancy dress, dancing, laughing...not to mention that it's one of the most exclusive parties in High Tide.

"Would you like to go to the Torch and Grier opening with me?" Colleen asked before she could talk herself out of it.

Shay's eyes widened and she choked on a peanut.

Colleen reached over the bar and drew a glass of water. Shay guzzled it to clear the debris from her throat. When she was done, she laughed and nodded.

"That was a yes, in case you couldn't tell," she said, eyes watering.

"Oh, good."

They both giggled a bit more and held each other's gaze. Colleen wanted to reach out and trace the line of Shay's jaw, then her lips. She wondered if her skin felt as soft as it looked, and what her lips would taste like.

Colleen didn't realize that she was starting to lean in toward Shay until someone bumped into her on their way to get a refill on their drink. She snapped out of the daydream and sat back. Her body felt hot, her breathing fast and it had nothing to do with her powers.

"I better get back to it," she said, a little breathless.

"Yeah," Shay replied, her voice wistful. "See you tomorrow for dinner."

She watched Shay leave, longing to follow her out.

"She's hanging around a lot," Wanda said.

"We're friends."

Colleen could feel Wanda's eyes on her as she refilled the pitcher of beer and poured a shot of whiskey.

"Just be careful," Wanda whispered. "Her loyalty is to her fellow cops, not this neighborhood anymore."

"You don't know that."

Colleen spoke the words before she could stop herself and immediately regretted it. Wanda's face took on a hard expression and she stepped back from Colleen.

"Oh really? Well, if you get yourself in trouble, don't come crying to me."

Wanda turned away and barked an order at the cook, leaving Colleen feeling suddenly exposed and weary.

The thought entered her mind once again that Wanda could very well be right, that any relationship with Shay was not just risky, it was downright careless considering who Colleen really was.

But the need for connection, the feelings that were quickly building up for Shay were just too tempting.

I deserve this one thing, don't

CHAPTER EIGHTEEN

"Reynolds, get in here!" Fisk barked, his face pink as he leaned out of the meeting room.

She had just walked through the door, a half-eaten cherry danish sticking out of her mouth and her patrol uniform already clinging to her back from the heat of the morning. Without waiting for her to reply, Fisk ducked back into the meeting room, where the task force was already assembled, waiting on her. Shoving the rest of the pastry in her mouth, she gathered her notes and a map of High Tide, hoping that none of the sticky fruit ended up on the presentation.

"You're late," he said.

"I never got a call to come in early. What's going on?"

"Seriously, Reynolds?" asked Chris, around a bite of donut. "You been living under a rock?"

"Cut the chatter, we've got work to do," Fisk ordered. "Now, after last night's failure of a mission, we need a win. We need to bring the vigilante in *tonight* or those federal agent assholes are going to come in here and do the job for us."

Shay's eyes widened and she felt acid churning in her stomach.

They went out without me last night. They never bothered to call me in for this meeting. I'm being cut out...is it because I'm partners with Walter? Where is he anyway?

"Reynolds, did you have time to figure out where the vigilante was seen the most?"

She snapped out of her anger and worry, presenting a map with red ink circling each hot spot.

"These are the places she's frequented, with the dates of her sightings. The pattern is that she goes in a circuit, if you notice, there's an order to it. If we follow the pattern, we can determine in all likelihood where she will most likely be on any given day."

There were murmurs around her, most followed by snorts of disbelief. But when Shay looked into Fisk's eyes, she saw concentration, as if he were genuinely taking in her data and giving it serious thought.

"Good work," he said, his voice carrying a hint of surprise. "According to your findings, where would she be tonight?"

"Well, that's the problem, sir," she said, swallowing down the lump in her throat. "She broke her pattern a few nights back. She hasn't been seen in any of these locations or anywhere in High Tide for days."

"Could be a smoke screen," someone said.

"Or she just hasn't been caught," Chris said.

Fisk nodded and pointed at one of the pins on the map.

"According to your dates, she should be here tonight, right?"

"Yes but—"

"I heard you Reynolds, she's broken her pattern. So we make sure she keeps her pattern tonight. Ideas?"

"We need good bait if we're talking about setting a trap," an officer at the back said.

"She's always rescuing criminals in the neighbor-hood," said another. "What if we go rough up some thugs? That might draw her out."

Shay felt anger stir deep in her bones at the con-versation carrying on around her, but she schooled her features to show none of it. Who would listen anyway?

"No, that's not enough," Fisk said, rubbing his fore-head. "We need something bigger."

Everyone paused in thought, Shay included. She was not keen on the idea of setting a dangerous trap in civilian territory, but where else could they go?

Then it hit her.

"If she's broken her pattern, we need to find out why. Where has she gone instead?" she said, pulling out another map from her file.

This one was of Devil's Own and she had circled the attack that had caused such a ruckus a few nights back.

"She might still be around there; we just haven't seen her."

"You're telling me that dozens of cops, patrolling around that warehouse, haven't seen this costumed freak?" Chris asked.

"Not the warehouse specifically, but it could be that whatever she was after in that warehouse, she's still looking for. That's why she hasn't been in High Tide. If we do a sweep of the area, we might just find her."

"Might isn't good enough, Reynolds," Fisk said. "Un-less you have hard proof, we need to go with what we've got."

"I got it!" Chris said. "She obviously cares about the criminals hiding out in High Tide, right? And these spots are full of 'em. What if we pick a building near where she's supposed to be, and have a show of force, stir things up?"

Shay stared at him.

"You're talking about putting civilians in danger."

He snorted.

"C'mon, half those people are hiding from the law. We'd catch the vigilante and get other perps in the process."

"If you can find a target that doesn't have a high population…say one of the run down tenements, then I'll consider it. The key is minimal civilian casualties," Fisk replied.

"We can't do that," Shay said, the words pouring from her mouth before she could think. "Any civilian casualties should be too much. And you might think the tenements are half empty, but they're not! They're cheap housing for people who can't afford anything else. You'll be putting them all in the cross hairs."

"Whose side are you on anyway? Half of these people would as soon shoot you as look at you," Chris fumed.

"You with us or with them?" someone else asked.

She looked around at the hard glares, the tense set to lips and shoulders and could feel a spotlight of judgment on her. Most people in her position would have stewed silently and let the whole thing go. But Shay had never been one for that.

"We became cops to help people, to protect them. All of the people in our precinct deserve that. *All* of them. You do this, and you betray their trust. Do you really want the press getting wind of this? The commissioner?"

Fisk lost his cool. "Then what do you suggest, Reynolds, huh? We are out of options, and if we don't catch this vigilante then all those people you care so much about are going to be at risk, they will be in the cross hairs anyway. At least we'll care if any of them get hurt. Can you say the same for the vigilante and the crime families that have been tearing up High Tide all summer?"

Shay knew he was right. But she was, too.

She pursed her lips and held his gaze with a defiance her mother used to say was going to get her in trouble someday.

Fisk let out a long exhale and turned away.

"Fine," he said after a moment. "We'll evacuate the civilians to a nearby location before trying to draw the vigilante out. Does that sound good enough?"

He may have offered a compromise, but his tone held just enough contempt for Shay not to give a damn.

"Sure," she said.

"Great. Officer Page and Officer Demos, I need to talk with you. The rest of you can go."

Shay was the first one out the door, fury driving her so fast that she felt like she was going to fly out of her skin. The entire meeting played in a loop in her mind, each time adding fuel to the anger in her belly. She needed space, somewhere to calm down where they wouldn't see.

She practically ran to the women's bathroom and slammed the door. The cold water was bracing on her hands. She splashed it on her face until she felt like she wasn't going to beat every one of those idiots into a pulp. Though that didn't mean the anger was gone. Instead, it became a low simmer, ready to boil over again.

It's acceptable risk because it's High Tide. Maybe momma was right, maybe I have been a fool for thinking I could do anything about how we are treated by cops.

She looked up at her reflection in the small mirror, water dripping off her chin and nose, dark eyes full of determination and anger stared back at her. Being the only black cop in the precinct wasn't something she could forget; it was there every second of every day. But Shay was determined that it wouldn't stop her from her goals. She'd spent years telling herself that she would prove her mother – and all the others – wrong, that she could succeed here and she didn't have to give up who she was to do it.

But what if that's not possible?

The answer was clear, especially after today's meeting.

She steadied her jaw and shook her head at her reflection.

I won't become one of them. Even if...even if it means throwing it all away.

She dried her face and took some deep breaths. Those men would go on that mission tonight, and it was unlikely that she was on the roster now since she'd disagreed so fervently.

But I have to go too, because if something happens, I might be the only one who will protect those people.

Somewhere in the back of her mind, it occurred to Shay that maybe that was why Fahrenheit did what she did: to protect those that had no one else to do the job. It was unsettling to see something she had in common with the woman, and she wondered if maybe, just maybe, Fahrenheit was on the side of right after all.

Then she shook herself out of the thought, knowing that there was already plenty of trouble to be had without sympathizing with a wanted criminal.

She walked back to her desk with a fast stride, ready to bully her way onto that task force mission tonight, come hell or high water. What she saw when she rounded the corner blew all those thoughts straight out of her mind.

Walter was picking up a box full of papers and his few personal belongings. He met her eyes, a deep sadness in their hooded depths.

"What is going on?" she asked.

"I'm on administrative leave."

Fear settled in her throat like a burning lump.

"Why?"

"Guess," he set the box down and took her hand. "You have to be careful now, they'll be scrutinizing everything you do, looking to see if I corrupted you."

"I'm used to scrutiny."

"Not like this. You can't show one ounce of sympathy for me if I come up in conversation, not one word that you know anything that I was doing. Do you understand?"

His voice trembled and Shay saw a glimpse of tears in his eyes as he turned away from her and picked up his box.

"Wait, you can't just leave and not tell me what's going on. How do I help you?"

"You can't."

She opened her mouth to argue and he cut her off.

"Damn it, Shay, it's too late for me so, for once, listen to me, will you? It's not just your career I'm trying to protect. Forget everything, focus on the task force and stay the hell away from me. Got it? Take care of yourself, rookie."

Without another glance or word, he turned away from her and walked out of the precinct with a determination to get out of the place. Shay stared after him, mouth hanging open in disbelief as her mind reeled with questions.

Captain Hill must be in the pocket of whoever is behind all this, otherwise he wouldn't have put Walter on leave. And if that's the case, I really don't have many options to find out what's going on or help Walter. Not without being fired. But I can't let this stand!

She turned to follow Walter out when she saw Fisk walking with a fast, purposeful gait toward the captain's office. If she wanted to protect High Tide and get on the mission for tonight, then she couldn't go after Walter.

Damn it!

She jogged up to him and cut him off just before he reached the door.

"What is it, Reynolds?" he asked, voice thick with frustration.

"I want in on the mission tonight."

"The mission you were so critical of?"

"Yes."

His eyes narrowed, and he crossed his arms

"Why should I do that? How do I know you'd be an asset and not a hindrance?"

"Because you need me, that's why."

"Still not convinced. Why do I need you? You've already given me what you've got."

Her back straightened and she shook her head.

"Not hardly Fisk. That's *my* neighborhood. You want success there? You put me in."

"It's because it's *your* neighborhood that I can't do that."

He tried to go around her and she jumped in front of him.

"Damn it, Reynolds!"

"I'm not giving up on this. I want to be there. If you have to know the truth, I want to make sure no one does anything to an innocent civilian. They're all going to be itching to take someone down, what if it's a kid? Or an old woman?"

Shay knew that this had actually happened plenty of times, and no one blinked, no one reported on it. So she was taking a risk betting on the chance that Fisk actually had a heart beating his chest and would care if a negro was shot.

He exhaled through his nose and shook his head.

"Fine."

She smiled and whispered, "Yes!"

"But, you need to be on board with things, understand? I can't have someone out in the field going off half cocked and getting people hurt."

"Of course, absolutely."

"Mission briefing at nine. See the officer in the equipment room for your gear," he said, walking around her and reaching the door to the captain's office.

"Gear?"

He glanced at her over his shoulder.

"Yeah, vests, helmet, gun. What, did you think you'd be going in just your uniform with your side arm?"

That's exactly what she though, actually. She now felt more grateful than ever that she was going.

A group of cops in what sounds like military gear storming a tenement…dear god.

Suddenly, she remembered a certain tall, beautiful woman that she had a dinner date with tonight and cringed. Shay would have to cancel and she hoped Colleen would understand and not see it as a brush off.

Although she did ask me to be her date to the Torch and Grier in a few days so…

Shay found herself grinning at the thought of going to the fancy party as she dialed the number for Wanda's bar. A surly voice answered that could only be the owner.

"Is Colleen there?"

"Who's asking?"

"Shay Reynolds."

The line was quiet for a second.

"She's not here," Wanda said, voice curt.

Why don't I believe you?

"Well, can you tell her when you see her that I won't be able to go out tonight, I have to work?"

"Sure, whatever."

Before Shay could say another word, the line went dead.

I hope that battle ax gives Colleen the message, I don't want her to think I've stood her up.

CHAPTER NINETEEN

The phone in Andrew's grip sparkled with ice and he hid his face as best he could inside the phone booth. It was in neither Devil's Own nor High Tide, but instead, a busy area just outside the bustling center of Metro City. Walter had a dozen places where he'd met Andrew, many of them tiny holes in the wall that no one but a twenty-year cop would think of.

This phone booth wasn't one of them and that was why Andrew was here.

This morning he'd called Walter at the precinct and was told that he was on leave. The woman wanted to know if she could direct him to the captain and Andrew hung up.

The captain, not his former partner. That means he's being watched by the cops, so why does Price need me to do it?

There was only one answer: Price was watching him.

So he went to an innocuous phone booth, nowhere near where Walter lived and tried the man's home phone, which was sporting a continuous busy signal.

Either the line has been cut or it's off the hook because it's been knocked over.

Andrew hung up the receiver and walked out of the booth, eyes casually taking in the people on the street. Though it didn't give him the kind of sight that could see through walls, his powers did give him the ability to somehow notice things with sharper detail when he wanted to. There were two men standing too casually by a newspaper stand and Andrew recognized them as the gunman that usually stuck with Price on his excursions.

As a child, Andrew had loved games, any kind of games. But then the games became treacherous, full of blood and dire consequences for the losers. Now, Andrew hated games.

That's why as soon as he crossed the street, he walked right toward them.

"You have a message for me, Tommy?" Andrew asked, as if this were completely normal.

The man gave him a scowl.

"What makes you say that, Frosty?"

Andrew's hackles rose at the nickname and he let his powers out just enough to make the hair on the man's arms raise up.

"I'll ask you one more time, do you have a message for me or are you just following me for the fun of it?"

"Calm down or someone will think you're jumpy from a guilty conscience."

Tommy and the other man chuckled, but Andrew's expression remained as cold and furious as ever.

"Boss wants you to call in," Tommy said with an eye roll. "He's got something he needs to you to take care of for him."

Andrew stepped close to him, his cold breath making him shiver.

"Now, was that so hard?"

Tommy's smile was gone, replaced by a blue tinge to his skin.

"C'mon, let's get out of here before the freak does something to us," the other man said, pulling on Tommy's arm.

"One of these days, *Frosty*, you're going to step out of line, and I'm going to love watching the Maiden tear you apart."

"Until then."

Andrew's chilling gaze followed the two men as they got into a black car and drove off. Just to be sure he wasn't being followed by anyone else, he doubled back and went to a phone booth that stank of piss and beer.

"You wanted to talk to me," Andrew said when Price picked up.

"It's time to plug our leak," he said. "Go to his house, watch him for a few hours, see if he contacts anyone. If he goes out, follow him and see if he meets anyone. If he does, take them both out."

Andrew's stomach dropped. If Walter was working with Colleen and he didn't kill her, then Price would know Andrew wasn't on board fully.

"Sub Zero, what is it?" Price asked when Andrew didn't acknowledge the order.

"Nothing sir, I was just wondering why me? You've got others that could make it look like a hit—"

"To send a message in case anyone else is thinking of double crossing us, of course. Unless you would rather come back here and explain to me why you refuse to do your job."

The implication was clear as day and Andrew cringed at his misstep.

"No, sir. Of course I'll do it."

"Good to hear. I will be taking care of other concerns tonight that should ensure that we both get what we want at last. You should be happy."

"I am, sir, thank you."

Mr. Price hung up and Andrew slammed the receiver down into the cradle. He could feel all his finely tuned plans disintegrating into dust right before his eyes. He couldn't spy on whatever Price was doing tonight because if Walter lived until morning, it would be Andrew who was next. And he couldn't risk sparing the man and have him pop up later to try and take down Price and the Big Man.

Then there was also the fact that Colleen could be with Walter tonight, and if she escaped...

Andrew ran a hand over his face, a sudden fatigue slamming into him. He knew this would be hard, dangerous and needed a light hand to achieve. He just hadn't counted on so many variables outside of his control.

Nothing I can do now except try and make the best of it...I wonder if this is how Grandfather started. A sour compromise, not feeling like he ever had a choice and before he knew it, he was neck deep with no way out.

He indulged in another second or two of such melancholy thoughts before shaking himself out of it. No sense in feeling sorry for himself, what the hell would that accomplish?

Colleen was not thrilled at all with meeting Walter in High Tide. Anyone might come up and see them together, and who knows what kind of rumor would start.

She'd gotten a call earlier from Rachel, saying a very big white man had left a message for Fahrenheit. She'd taken it even though she told him she didn't know who was behind the mask.

"You in some kind of trouble?" Rachel had asked.

"No, it's complicated but it's alright. What was the message?"

"Said to meet you at the old soap factory on 20th and Gold."

The alarms in Colleen's mind went off loud and insistent but she didn't let on to Rachel. Just thanked her and hung up.

That was five hours ago, and now Colleen found herself at the old soap factory that smelled like cleaner and dust, the large windows all around making her feel exposed.

I really need a watch with this suit. I have no idea if he's late or I'm just really early.

She'd taken a detour into Devil's Own before coming here, hoping to track down the kids. After two nights, she'd come up with absolutely nothing except the delightful experience of being shot at and chased all over that neighborhood.

I think I know Devil's Own almost as well as High Tide by now.

The sound of a door opening echoed through the space and Colleen ducked down behind one of the long conveyer belts.

"It's just me," Walter said in his rumbling voice.

Colleen stood up, keeping her powers just on the edge of springing forth. She wanted to be prepared in case Walter had switched sides and this was a trap.

"What's going on?" she asked.

"I could ask you the same," he said, hooded eyes blazing with anger. "I told you to observe, damn it, not go in and light the place up!"

"I couldn't stand by and let those kids be taken and I think you know that."

"I hoped you'd have better sense! That you'd see that doing something like that would expose everything! Now, because of you, I'm fired and being watched.

It took me an hour to shake the cops that have been following me for the past two days."

"That must mean that the warehouse was incredibly important. They're probably scrambling to replace it which means they will make a mistake. What other locations do you know about, maybe they're using one of those to—"

"Stop it! You're in way over your head and you're only going to make everything worse."

Colleen stepped toward him, she could tell by the way he tensed that he could see the power swirling in her eyes, wild and dangerous.

"I will not sit by and wait for the law to do what's right. If I did that I'd be waiting forever and you know it, otherwise you wouldn't be doing this."

Walter exhaled through his nose, hands clenching into fists.

"I do know it. And I also know how skittish they are, how deep their reach goes, and you don't. I'm not doing nothing, I'm being careful because one wrong step and our entire case falls apart."

"I'm not interested in your 'case'."

"Well you should be! It's the only way these bastards get taken down."

Colleen held up her hand, flames dancing in her palm and grinned.

"Not the only way."

"You gonna burn down the world then? What will that accomplish?"

"You'd be surprised."

He paused, studying her and then nodded.

"I get it; I understand why you want to go full bore into it all."

"No, you don't. You don't understand, not really. You might be angered by it all, you might have a peripheral glimpse that rouses your compassion, but you don't understand."

"No," he said, his voice quiet, sad, "I guess I really don't. But will you at least believe that I want to help?"

Colleen extinguished the flames.

"I can believe that. And while I don't regret doing what I did, I'm sorry you were caught in the cross fire."

"Thanks."

"What now?"

"I don't know. I can barely sneeze without someone seeing it. My place has been ransacked twice already and—"

A long, sharp spear of ice sliced through Walter's back, lodging itself halfway through his body. Colleen stumbled back, gaping at the hole in Walter's chest. He seemed confused at first, looking at her and then down at the bloody ice jutting out from his body before collapsing to the ground with a groan. A second later, another spear of ice shot down, this one grazing Colleen's upper arm.

She looked up frantic to find her brother and get him to stop. The upper level office was dark but there was a flash of white just before two more spears of ice shot down and lodged into the conveyer belt.

"I'll be right back," she told Walter.

"No," he said, his voice wet with the blood that bubbled up onto his lips. "Take…this. Give it to…Shay…partner…my partner. Keep her…safe. Promise me."

He shoved a key into her hand, the chain it dangled from was slick with blood. She met his eyes, knowing this was it, there was no hope he would survive this.

"I promise and I'm so sorry," Colleen said, her heart aching like someone was squeezing it with an iron fist.

"Get…the bastards."

He coughed, the sound wet and garbled just before his eyes rolled back.

Colleen didn't really know him at all, but she did know that he didn't deserve to die with ice in his chest. Her eyes burned as she stood, the world turning bright and flames erupting in her hands.

Andrew sailed down from the upper office on a path of ice and stopped a few feet away.

"I know you won't believe me, but I didn't want to kill him."

Colleen sent a stream of fire straight at her brother. He dove out of the way as he thrust out his hands, ice flying in small knife-like shapes. The blades sliced her thigh and cheek, but she barely felt the cold pain.

"Damn it, stop!" he yelled. "I don't want to hurt you!"

"Then why are you here?"

"For him, and just him."

Sirens echoed outside and they both swore.

"Oh, is that all?" Colleen spat, shooting fireballs at him in quick succession.

Andrew intercepted each with a small shield of ice, batting them away and creating new shields as fast as she could throw the fire. After a minute, both were wet from the melted ice.

"I had no choice!" he cried.

"That's a coward's excuse!"

"Maybe, but it doesn't make it any less true."

She laid down a wall of fire, then pushed it toward him. Andrew countered by spraying ice at the floor in such volume that, for a moment, it looked like a bon fire in the middle of a snow storm.

Colleen focused and pushed her power harder, letting that bright inferno loose as anger took hold of her. How could he do it? How could Andrew kill a man like that?

On the other side of the wall of flames, Andrew let out a guttural scream and a blizzard erupted in front of her, halting the progress of her wall. No matter how much either of them pushed against the other, neither gained any ground.

When they both realized that they were at a standstill, Andrew and Colleen let go of their powers. Sweat dripped down Colleen's body and her chest heaved as she glared at her brother, whose skin sparkled with frost, as hers shone with sparks.

"Well, what do you know," Andrew said with the merest hint of a smile on his face, "we're evenly matched."

The sirens were getting closer and Colleen knew they'd soon be surrounded by cops, ready to shoot them both on sight. Trouble was, Colleen had to know something before she left.

"Why, Andrew? Are you so far gone that you don't see that this isn't right?"

His face hardened and he looked away from her.

"Am I so far gone...? That's a good question. I wish I had the answer."

She took a step toward him and he shot ice at her feet, freezing her in place.

"Good visit sis, but I have to go."

He tore off into the night, leaving Colleen next to the body of a dead cop.

She let loose her flames on the ice at her feet just as the sound of voices reached her from outside.

"C'mon!" she grunted, letting loose on the thick manacles at her ankles.

As the ice finally released her, Colleen heard the unmistakable ping of bullets hitting the machinery around her. Throwing fire behind her to distract the men,

Colleen ran through the closest door and didn't stop until she got to Wanda's.

As she climbed the fire escape to her apartment, however, something bright caught her attention. Colleen turned in horror to see flames reaching to the sky from the midst of High Tide.

That can't be me...that's not the soap factory that's...oh my god! That's one of the tenement blocks!

Tossing the bloody key and chain onto her bedside table, Colleen returned to her window, down the stairs of the fire escape and back out into a night thick with enemies.

CHAPTER TWENTY

The gear was too big for Shay but she made the best of it, pulling the straps of the vest and helmet as tight as they would go. The gun was a rifle with large rounds that made her incredibly nervous considering they were going into a residential area.

When she got to the van where the other task force officers were climbing in, she saw Fisk in his usual suit, talking with Chris.

"You not going?" she asked.

"No, I'll monitor from here. Captain wants me hanging back on this one," he replied, his voice tight.

Shay wanted to know what had caused the captain to make such an odd decision but from the look of frustration on Fisk's face, Shay thought it best to not ask.

"Chris will be in charge of this mission," Fisk continued and Shay's heart sank with the words. "Follow his lead. Understand, Reynolds?"

Shay nodded with far more nonchalance than she felt and tried to ignore the foreboding that was sinking into her gut.

The drive to the tenement was short, the roads relatively clear this late in the evening compared to how they were in the middle of the day. They parked down a nearby alley and climbed out as silently as half a dozen officers in riot gear could.

"Okay, here's the situation," Chris said in the center of the group. "We have residents on the third and fourth floor. According to the information we have, the building is only half full but as Reynolds brought up earlier, that might not be the reality. Alpha team," he said, pointing at Shay and two others, "you will go to the residents that we know about and evacuate them as quickly as possible to the abandoned building across the street. Beta team you're with me, we will clear the other apartments and set up the building to lure the vigilante. When that's done, Alpha team, take up positions across the street at each corner, Beta team you know what to do."

It was that last part that sent chills down Shay's spine, especially when she caught the grins of anticipation on Beta team's faces.

She wanted to switch teams, to ask what they were going to do and make Chris think it was so she didn't mess anything up. But her team was already running toward the tenement and she had to keep up or risk losing the scrap of respect she had with the men.

The front door was probably unlocked and looked like it was barely usable, still one of the officers kicked it in and Shay grit her teeth. They ran up the three flights until they reached the first apartment. The same officer was about to kick the door down and she shoved him out of the way.

"We're supposed to be evacuating them, not scaring the piss out of them," she said.

He rolled his eyes as she knocked on the door and waited.

"Go try the others, we haven't got all night," she said.

The men didn't want to obey, she could see it written in every tense inch of their faces, but they did anyway.

"What do you want?" said a booming voice from the other side of the door.

One of the officers raised his gun in her direction at the sound of the man's voice and she motioned for him to lower his weapon.

"Sir, it's the police. We need to evacuate this building. Get your family and come out in two minutes."

He swore, and Shay heard scrambling as if he were walking quickly through the apartment. The sharp cry of a baby pierced the night and in a minute the third floor was filled with civilians in various states of sleepiness.

When the door she was in front of opened, a tall man carrying a sleepy toddler stood in front of her.

"Sir, I'm sorry to do this, we have to ask you and the rest of the residents to go across the street to the abandoned building and wait for us to clear out the threat."

He looked her over, circles under his eyes and a weary sadness hanging on his shoulders.

"Bear bear," the toddler said in a sleepy voice. "Want bear bear."

The man shoved a tattered teddy bear into the child's hands and motioned for the frightened woman behind him to follow.

Even though Shay knew this was saving their lives, she still couldn't help feeling like she wasn't doing them any favors.

Within minutes, the third floor was cleared and Shay began to move up to the fourth when an explosion rocked the building.

She could hear screams through the ringing of her ears, smoke stung her eyes and the floor was tilted under her. When she could move, Shay pushed herself up, the muscles in her back seizing. With her face pinched in pain, she stood and looked around. The rest of Alpha team was getting to their feet, looking as perplexed as she was.

More screams reached her ears along with the distinct pop of gunfire.

"We need to get to the top floor and get those people out," she said.

"The stairs could be compromised," said one of the men.

"Up or down, they could be dangerous. But at the top we can get people out through the fire escape and follow them."

The two officers looked at each other and then nodded. Shay had no idea if one of them had been assigned as leader of this group or not, and right now she really didn't care.

She went first, testing the stairs as smoke began rising from below. They weren't exactly stable, but they also weren't falling apart. Shay knew it was as good as they could hope for. As she took the plunge and ran, Shay had a moment to wonder if that look Beta team had exchanged had anything to do with what was going on.

I swear, if they've hurt any of these people…

When they got to the fourth floor, people were already awake and moving toward one of the apartments. The men behind Shay stared in surprise.

"There was only supposed to be two apartments with people up here," said one of them.

Shay didn't comment because rubbing in the fact that they had been so very wrong wasn't the important thing right now.

"C'mon, keep moving," she said, to the people who had stopped to gawk at them.

The one apartment that had a functioning fire escape was packed with people waiting to get out of the building. By now, the smoke was thick and Shay knew that the fire was spreading.

"Alpha team to Beta, what happened down there?" she asked into the radio.

There was no answer and she asked again.

"Alpha team to Beta!"

"Alpha, where are you?" Chris' voice crackled over the line.

"We are evacuating the fourth floor via the fire escape on the east side of the building."

"Negative, get out of here on the double, there's word of the vigilante in the area."

She looked at her fellow officers, who had begun to move toward the window in spite of the fact that civilians were still waiting to get out. When they met her gaze, both of them stopped and stepped away. Whether or not they decided to help, Shay wouldn't abandon these people.

"Once the civilians are safe we will be at street level," she replied.

Chris started to swear at her and she turned her radio off.

"You're either really brave or really stupid," one of the officers said.

"Or both," the other said.

Shay grinned at them.

"What are your names?"

"Jason Lester."

"Mark Smith."

"Okay, Smith and Lester, you're following my orders, got it? So neither of you are in trouble, I am. Either of you have a problem with getting them to safety first or with me taking charge, say it now."

They shook their heads and she smiled at them.

"Okay, get these people down that fire escape, I'm going to check the other apartments."

She ran out and didn't wait for niceties as she barged into every apartment to check that they were clear. It was in the last one where she found a man passed out on his bedroom floor reeking of rye whiskey. He was just thin enough for her move and when she did he mumbled something at her. She reached up and grabbed the mostly empty bottle of whiskey on his bedside table and dumped it over his head.

He howled and shook, especially when he saw her. The man ran out of his apartment in nothing but his boxers and a thin under shirt. The moment he hit the landing and saw the smoke, he froze.

"C'mon, it's a fire, don't just stand there!"

He stumbled forward and Shay took his arm, pulling him into the apartment.

Lester grabbed the man and carried him over the edge of the windowsill, as Shay let out a deep cough. The smoke had gotten bad enough that just a bit of exertion made her chest feel like someone had filled her lungs with cotton.

"Go, I'm right behind you," she said to Smith.

He nodded and she followed hot on his heels. Smoke billowed out of the windows on the front of the building and when Shay's feet hit the cement she could see the garish light of flames licking the building.

People milled around across the street, clutching their loved ones and any belongings they had managed to grab before getting out. Chris stood a few feet away talking to his task force. The moment she saw his smug face the control on her anger snapped. When his men ran to go do whatever he'd instructed them, Shay marched up to him and stood toe to toe, not caring that the man towered above her.

"What the hell happened?" she asked.

"What does it look like, someone had explosive—."

"Bullshit! This is exactly what you wanted, this kind of destruction to draw the vigilante out. Well? Where is she? Did your plan work?"

Chris' jaw tightened and he leaned down until their faces were inches apart.

"Now you listen to me, you little bitch. I don't know who you screwed to get on this team, but I'll be damned if I'm going to let some uppity piece of ass criticize me."

"Wow, how original. I've *never* been accused of sleeping with someone to move up in my career. You come up with that all on your own or did you read it somewhere?"

His eyes bulged and he opened his mouth to likely let loose a tirade when he was cut off by blood curdling screams coming from the building.

"Someone is still in there!" cried one of the residents.

"Did you clear the other floors?" Shay asked.

"There wasn't time," Chris said through clenched teeth.

Shay swore and turned to Lester.

"Radio for fire and paramedics. I'm going in to see if I can help get anyone out."

"You don't have gear for that," Smith said.

"And you don't have the authority to order a call for anything," Chris fumed. "This is exactly what we need to—"

"Lester, call it in. Smith, try to make sure these people stay back."

"Yes ma'am," Lester said, shooting Chris a glare that could melt steel.

Smith strode toward the crowd, trying to get them off the street so the fire engines and paramedics didn't run them over. Just as she stepped off the curb, a vice like grip seized her upper arm. She turned to look into Chris' furious eyes.

"I'll have you fired for this. Fisk told you to obey me!"

She ripped her arm out of his grasp.

"You go right ahead and tell him."

And with that she ran across the street. Without stopping to think, she burst through the broken down front door. The fire was above her but spreading fast and the smoke was thick, stinging her eyes and lungs. The first floor had no apartments, so she climbed to the second and was met with flames everywhere.

"Hello? Is anyone here?" she called, coughing and doing her best to stay away from the heat.

Another scream and the pounding of a door to her right had Shay running half blind toward the sound. She was met with a solid door that looked new, and pounded on it.

"Help us!"

Shay coughed as she tried to kick the door down but it held fast. The rifle she'd been issued had remained strapped to her back this whole time. She had hoped she wouldn't have to use it, but now it was going to be the only way to get these people out.

"I'll..hold on! I'll get you…out! Just stand back!"

Hoping that the people inside heard her, Shay let loose a stream of bullets where the door knob and dead bolt were holding the door closed. The door may have been thick and new, but it was no match for the large rounds in her gun.

The frame and door gave in seconds and Shay was able to kick it the rest of the way open. Three terrified pairs of eyes met her and she helped them over the splintered wood of their door and out into a hallway that was now consumed by flames.

"We're trapped!" one of the woman cried.

Shay looked around, frantic as she tried to see a way that wasn't completely blocked by the fire. As she stepped forward, flames burst in front of her, the heat licking her hand. The pain was distant in her mind as primal fear took over. She was going to die in this inferno.

No I'm not! I'm not going to die because of a man like Chris!

She forced her mind to stop spinning and looked around once more when she spied the apartment they'd just come from. The flames were close, but they hadn't consumed the space yet. They might be able to get a few precious minutes of safety while Shay figured something out.

"Your apartment," Shay said, the words punctuated by more coughing, "get back in...we might be able to wait for the...fire department."

As they made their way back toward the apartment, the floor boards in front of them gave out, one of the women nearly falling through. Shay grabbed onto the woman's nightgown and pulled her back from a fiery death as the flames began to catch on her pants. Shay's mind scrambled for another way out but there wasn't one.

The women huddled together, sobbing and coughing as the reality of their death closed in on them. Shay was finding it hard to breath, and her vision was going fuzzy when a pair of feet appeared in front of her. She looked up, somehow not surprised to see the blazing eyes of Fahrenheit staring back at her.

"No," she gasped, "you have to...get out of here!"

"I was thinking the same thing about you," Fahrenheit said.

As the shocked women looked on, the vigilante lifted her arms and the flames that were licking at their skin retreated and wrapped themselves around her. Within seconds, Fahrenheit had absorbed enough of the fire that there was now a clear path for them to escape.

"I can't hold it for long," she said, her voice strained. "Go."

Shay waved at the women cowering behind her to move. They stumbled down the charred stairs, holding one another and looking back as if they couldn't believe that they'd just seen.

"Thank you," Shay said, staring in wonder at the woman before bolting after the survivors.

Shay burst out of the building, gasping for air, her legs shaky. Large hands seized her under the arms and pulled her away from the building just as the fire engines screeched to a halt.

"Are you alright?" Lester asked.

She coughed in response, her lungs seizing and burning.

By now, the residents of the other buildings had fled their homes either to keep themselves safe or see what the ruckus was all about. The street was clogged with people and the task force wasn't able to keep them all contained.

Shay looked around, grateful that the fire department was here but wondering where in the world the paramedics were.

Chris better not have called them off.

Shay was about to ask Lester about it, but then the telltale lights and siren of the medics careened around the corner.

"C'mon, you need some medical attention," he said.

She started to shake her head and he picked her up.

"You want to walk or be carried?"

She pushed against his chest and croaked out, "Jerk."

He gave her a little grin and escorted her to the nearest paramedic.

As she sat on the sidewalk, oxygen mask on her face, Shay looked at the building. The flames were starting to be controlled by the fire department, but the surrounding buildings weren't out of danger yet. As some of the flames started to reach toward the other buildings, Shay saw them retreat back toward the tenement.

Oh god, she's still in there. If Chris sees…

Looking around she noticed that everyone was too busy helping the residents to notice her. Ripping the oxygen mask off, Shay tried to run toward the alley to see if she could get a message to Fahrenheit, though with the way her lungs still hurt it was impossible to get enough air to truly run.

She didn't know why it was so vital, why she was willing to risk her life and career to make sure the woman got away. The only thing that was clear to Shay was that everything was more complicated than she first thought.

The flames began to dissipate faster than they should have and Shay knew it would only be a matter of time before Chris and his Beta team noticed.

"Fahrenheit?" she croaked, her voice raspy from the smoke and heat. "Are you here?"

Like an apparition, Fahrenheit stepped through the smoke, her orange and white suit barely smudged with soot. Shay was taken aback to see that the sparks that danced over the vigilante's skin, the way her eyes glowed like the dying embers of a campfire, the strength and confidence in the way she stood there. She was dangerously beautiful and Shay found herself inexplicably pulled toward her.

"You need medical attention," Fahrenheit said.

Shay frowned. There was something familiar about that voice…

She shook the thought loose, there were more important matters.

"You have to get out of here. They did this to draw you out."

"Well, it worked."

"Yeah, but…please, go. I don't want them to have any justification for this sort of thing in the future."

Fahrenheit held her gaze and took a step toward her. The smoke still obscured her features, but Shay was able to see the curve of her jaw and nose, and once again felt a tingle of recognition. The vigilante looked as if she wanted to say something and then snapped her mouth shut, gliding back into the shadows and smoke once again.

"Take care of yourself, officer."

And she was gone.

CHAPTER TWENTY-ONE

T ina, along with Rick and one of her body guards, surveyed the damage to the tenement. The building was one of many she had tried to buy from the slum lords who lived in high rises downtown. Now, looking at the burned out husk, seeing the faces of the devastated residents, Tina felt a hot stab of anger and guilt in her heart.

"How did this happen?" she asked the building manager.

He shook his balding head, clothes still covered in soot. Tina knew he was a decent man, all things considered. He never cheated anyone, tried to get things fixed with the little resources the landlord gave him. He even let people slide on rent when they needed to.

When he looked up at her with empty, exhausted eyes and shook his head in bewilderment, Tina knew that he was just as confused as everyone else about what caused the building to go up in flames.

"Some of the residents said they saw Fahrenheit," he whispered the name like it was a holy word.

Tina glanced over at where Colleen and Wanda were handing out hot meals to the homeless former residents and shook her head.

"The vigilante wouldn't do that."

"No ma'am but…well, there was also some police here. They were evacuating people, said there was danger and then a few minutes later, the fire started. People are saying that it was to catch Fahrenheit, but she was too crafty for 'em. Any way…I know I don't have proof but…"

"Yes?"

"I think the police set the fire, let some people get trapped inside so she'd come."

Tina's eyes narrowed as she stared at the building. If that was true, then the task force had just escalated this to a degree Tina was not ready for.

I have trouble keeping the police from ruining High Tide when I'm not fighting a war with another boss. This has to end, and soon.

"Thank you for your honesty," she said, patting the man on the shoulder. "You should get some food and rest."

He took a few steps away and then turned back to her, tears glistening in his eyes.

"You know ma'am, if not for Fahrenheit, my wife and daughters would be dead. She saved them, along with a few others that were having trouble getting out. And she kept the flames from spreading to the other buildings. This would've been a lot worse if not for her. I'll forever be grateful to her for that."

"As will I."

He nodded and got in line for some breakfast.

The smell of fire still hung in the air, and scattered about were tendrils of smoke curling from the rubble. Tina had already called the man who owned the building, making him an offer that he immediately took. She would rebuild and offer the residents first pick of the new apartments, but that would take time.

"Check with the building managers of the other tenements around here," she said to Rick. "Tell them I have people in need of housing and that we will be paying their rent for the next two months. And be clear that no one is to be evicted to make room."

Rick nodded as she looked at the people huddled in groups on the sidewalk. So many children, so many people who were barely scraping by to begin with and now they didn't even have the little they'd managed to accumulate.

Tina felt anger start to throb through her body, blood rushing in her ears. Hers wasn't the first black neighborhood to be terrorized or viewed as expendable. But that didn't make it any less infuriating.

How many more places will they tear down just because they can? I thought I could build this place up but look at what's happening before I've even gotten started. Plenty of other vigilantes are operating in Metro City, I've seen the reports, buried on page twelve if they're printed at all. But those are white ones, so they're not a threat.

Tina didn't realize her hands were curled into tight fists until Rick's fingers wrapped around her hand. She looked up and saw the way his lips pressed together, how hard his gaze had become and realized he was feeling the same as she was.

"I thought that I could protect all of this...I could bring so much life back into High Tide," her whispered voice had an edge of bitterness to it. "But I don't know now. What's the answer? A club opening?"

"Maybe. Maybe not. The club was meant to give them a place to be proud of. That's still important."

She shook her head and then stopped, as another thought hit her.

It could be important in another way. Maybe as a trap?

The theater had been so much a part of her dream of the future for so long, that the thought of building it up only so she could trap Von and Mr. Price made her furious enough to resist the idea. There had to be another way.

"We'll get there," she said, her voice firm, quiet. "Come hell or high water, we will."

"Some days…I gotta admit, it's hard to believe that."

She nodded and that was all. There was nothing else to say.

The last plate of eggs and bacon was handed out, and the truck was halfway loaded up when Tina made her way over to Colleen. She hadn't slept all night, the attack by Andrew and the fire perpetrated on the innocent people around her were certainly part of it. But the thing that spun in an endless loop in her mind, stirring the embers of fury was the memory of Shay, leg on fire, suffocating as she tried to get the family out of the building.

Afterward, alone in her apartment, Colleen had a chance to wonder at the blinding fear she'd felt at the thought of losing this woman she was just starting to know. She wasn't willing to go so far as to say that she loved Shay, that felt ridiculous. But the vigilante couldn't deny that in a very short amount of time, Shay had become one of the most important people in the world to her.

The more this all spun in her mind, and as she looked into the faces of the families around her, the more Colleen wanted to set all of Von's buildings on fire and watch in gleeful delight as his aspirations floated away as ash on the wind. She wanted to pummel her brother as bad as she also wanted to spirit him away and dig out that splinter of hurt that drove him to believe he was only good for destructive deeds. And she wanted to hug Shay, to feel her warm curves pressed against her own, to get lost in her kisses and know that she was safe.

There's no way Shay is going to let this go, not after losing Walter like this. She'll dive right in and I'll find her with a shard of ice through her chest.

The box of plastic forks she was packing away started to smoke in her hands and Colleen drew the heat back into her veins. She had to calm down otherwise she would go supernova right here.

And I should really save that for that son of a bitch Von.

The thought brought sparks falling from her finger tips that she immediately snuffed out.

"I need to talk with you," Tina said, startling Colleen out of her thoughts of vengeance.

She took another deep breath and walked with her mother far enough away from the crowd that they wouldn't be heard.

"You know who did this I assume?" Tina asked, her voice tinged with fury.

"Yes."

"And the dead cop last night? The one with the ice through his chest. Were you there, as well?"

Colleen nodded, the memory of Walter dying fresh before her eyes.

"We have to get this under control," Tina continued. "And for starters, we need to neuter Von."

"By taking Andrew away from him."

Tina hesitated and Colleen's stomach dropped. She knew what her mother was going to say.

"I won't kill him," Colleen said before her mother could utter the words.

"I'm not asking you to. I…I don't want you to."

Colleen's jaw dropped.

"Well, don't look so surprised," Tina snapped. "I'm not a monster. I want him out of here, away from Von at the very least but I need to know if that's possible, especially after last night."

"I don't know. He's convinced that he has to do this and I don't know why."

"Do you think you can get him to tell you?"

Colleen paused, considering it. Andrew certainly hated her less than Tina but would that be enough?

He spared me…he could've tried harder to kill me and he didn't. That's something.

"I think so," she finally answered, "but it's not going to be easy. I don't think he's going to go willingly."

Tina's brow furrowed at that, her gaze becoming distant and Colleen knew her mother was plotting.

"Get him to talk to you," Tina said, "feel him out and see if there's anything we can use to get him away from Von."

"Alright. What are you going to do?"

"I have a club to open."

Colleen stared at her mother, sure she must've heard her wrong. Standing here in front of the burned rubble of one tenement, the now homeless families crowded on the street, knowing that Andrew was killing people because of some insane belief that he had to, Colleen had hoped that Tina would look past her own plans and do what was right.

"In the midst of all this, it's still about you, isn't it?" she said, her voice hard.

"What, no? How can you say that?"

"How can you think of opening that club in the middle of this? How can that be your aim? Do you even care what is happening to Andrew, besides how it affects your grand plans, that is?"

"Of course, I care. It's always been about you and Andrew, about our family and doing what was best for it and High Tide."

"I never wanted any of this, you did."

Tina's jaw dropped, a laugh of disbelief escaping her lips.

"I never wanted this war with Von, this destruction!"

"Not the war, but the power, the prestige."

"And what *do* you want Colleen? Do you want to be the hero, the one above it all? The one worshiped by the masses? Or just some bystander?"

Colleen opened her mouth and stopped, unable to come up with a response because the truth was that she didn't know what she wanted. She used to say that the title of 'hero' was something she didn't desire, and that might still be true. But she also felt that she was the only one that could protect High Tide.

Is that true though? Or do I just want it to be?

"You don't know, do you?" Tina pressed. "That's be-cause you won't just grab onto something, take a leap of faith. No, you have to know every single angle, know exactly how it's going to go before you do it."

"Yes, mother, you're the picture of spontaneity, aren't you?" the sarcasm dripped from her lips. "You who never do anything without a dozen back up plans. I may not know what I want, but at least I care if I hurt people, I don't act at the expense of others."

Tina leaned forward so that Colleen could see the cold fury in her eyes. She wanted to take a step back, but held herself firmly in place.

"You may think I don't care about you and Andrew, but it's for you that I'm doing this. For you and everyone else here. If we retreat every time we're threatened, we will never build anything lasting. I refuse to give in."

Colleen shook her head.

"Keep telling yourself that Tina, maybe it'll make you feel better when everything around you has burned to the damn ground and you're all alone."

With that, Colleen turned on her heel and walked away. In the end, it really didn't matter why Tina wanted to help Andrew, as long as he was saved. But the truth was it still grated on Colleen that her mother couldn't do something selfless for once.

And if she's going through with the club opening then I've got to make sure things don't go to hell or we'll have a massacre of Metro City's best and brightest on our hands. And boy, won't the cops and the press just love that. High Tide club opening kills Metro City's favorite white people.

She ran a hand over her face, feeling the full impact of her sleepless night and the ever growing burden on her shoulders.

A wave of whispers rose up from the people around her. Colleen looked up in time to see a patrol car pull up, and the one person she wanted to see step out.

Shay knew it was probably the last place she'd be welcome, considering who had started the fire, but she couldn't stay away. She had to look them all in the eye, had to apologize for what she'd participated in and try to make it better, even though there was no way she could.

The moment she stepped out of the patrol car, her left calf reminded her that she had a first degree burn and that she should be taking it easy. She limped a few steps from the car and stopped, suddenly aware that she had no idea how to begin.

That's when her eyes fell on the one person she realized she needed to see in that moment.

Colleen wrapped her arms around Shay in front of everyone. What they might see as a hug between friends in the aftermath of something terrible, Shay knew to be something more. The way Colleen clung to her, the tears shining on her cheeks when she pulled away, it all said that Colleen needed her in a way that went beyond simple friendship. And Shay could not deny that she felt the exact same way.

"Did anyone die?" Shay whispered when Colleen let her go.

"No, but there were plenty of injuries and it's going to take at least a year before Tina can rebuild the place."

Shay nodded, looking at the smoldering ruins. The memory of the flames licking her skin, the screams of so many innocent people and Chris' smug smile all ran through her mind.

"Hey," Colleen said, her fingers warm on Shay's wrist, "let it go. You did what you could."

"It wasn't enough. I couldn't stop them and so many people were hurt."

"But you saved people, too. Residents would have died if not for you."

"And if not for the task force I was on, people wouldn't be without homes today."

"If it makes you feel any better, Tina is determined to rebuild better apartments for them. It's a small consolation but…"

"It's something."

They both stood there, staring at the building until Shay shook herself and looked away.

"Have you been to work yet today?" Colleen asked, her voice hesitant.

"No, though I'm sure there's a firm reprimand waiting for me."

Colleen nodded, biting her bottom lip. She wouldn't meet Shay's eyes, which made Shay suspicious.

"What's wrong?"

"Nothing," Colleen said a little too quickly, "I'm just worried for you, that's all. It's…everything is so…"

"Yeah, it is."

Shay let her fingers intertwine with Colleen's, their hands hidden by their bodies and the squad car. The small contact was a comfort to Shay's heart and a sudden rush of desire for more flooded her.

"I know that things are gloomy at best right now," she said, voice low so only Colleen could hear, "but can I see you tomorrow night?"

Colleen's lips curved up into that slight smile that Shay was starting to treasure.

"Absolutely. Eight o'clock, my place?"

"Yes."

Their eyes met and for a split second, Shay wished they were alone so she could capture that beautiful face between her hands and kiss Colleen senseless.

"I should go," Colleen let go of Shay's hand. "And you need to go to the precinct."

"Yeah…though I really don't want to."

"Call me later if you need to talk."

Shay nodded, though there was something about the way Colleen said it that made her think that she knew something that Shay didn't.

Driving back through High Tide, Shay saw every fearful look leveled at her and cringed. After last night especially, there was no way she could blame them.

Shay took her time parking the car and walking into the precinct. There was no way the captain was going to let her stay on the task force, not after blatantly disobeying Chris. Though she didn't regret her decision, she did feel grief that this one moment would cost her the chance at a detective's badge.

Though maybe I could ask the captain to reinstate Walter and we could be back on the beat...I guess that wouldn't be so bad.

When she stepped through the door, however, Shay was stopped in her tracks by the grim smiles the dispatchers gave her. Had word traveled that fast? Then she noticed the tears in their eyes and how one was wiping her nose with a hankie. The hair on Shay's arm stood on end.

"We're so sorry, Officer Reynolds," one said. "Let us know if you need anything."

She stared at them in confusion as dread washed over her.

"Oh, lord," said another one, "you don't know."

"Know what?" she managed to ask.

"Oh, honey," said the one with the hankie, "it's Walter, he's—"

She didn't give her a chance to finish before bolting into the main room of the precinct. A dozen faces turned to look at her, and then away. A look at Walter's old chair and the black band around it sent Shay reeling. She grabbed the door frame to steady herself.

"Reynolds...Shay, I'm so sorry," Fisk said. "Walter was a pain in the ass but he was also a good cop. He's going to be missed."

"H-How?"

Fisk hesitated, jaw tightening.

"A large shard of ice, right through the chest."

Blood roared in her ears and Shay felt a cry build in the back of her throat.

"Captain is talking with the commissioner now," Fisk continued, "and I've already been planning on how to get the bastard."

"I want in," she croaked through clenched teeth.

"Shay—"

"If this is about last night, you know as well as I do that what Chris did wasn't right so don't give me the excuse that standing up to him means I'm out. I saved his ass and you know it. I was Walter's partner and I deserve to help get the piece of shit that killed him!"

Fisk exhaled through his nose, eyes narrowed as he chewed on what Shay had said. Finally, he nodded.

"I'll talk to the captain. And for what it's worth, I agree with you, about everything."

"It's not worth much if you want the honest to god truth because I think you knew what Chris was going to do, but we can talk about that later."

Fisk opened his mouth to retort something but was cut off by the captain coming out of his office and yelling for everyone to shut up and listen.

The room went silent, except for the hum of the dispatchers taking calls in the next room.

"I just got off the phone with the commissioner," he said, the grim set to his face making Shay nervous, "and although the task force has been working admirably to catch the vigilantes in High Tide, after last night the commissioner feels that we need help to prevent any further loss of property or life."

"Shit," Fisk murmured next to her, "here it comes."

Shay's entire body went tense in the moment it took the captain to spit out the thing they'd all been dreading.

"As of today, the task force will answer to Agent Ward from The Bulwark. Fisk, get everything you've got together and be ready to brief the agent whenever he decides to grace us with his presence. As for the rest of you…we will meet at Paddy's tonight after shifts to toast Officer Lyle. And Reynolds, I need to speak with you. That's all."

Everyone was still as Shay made the long walk toward his office. Instead of the sneers and curious stares she was used to, the officers around her nodded, or gave her a sad salute as she passed.

Gee, if I knew that all it took to gain a modicum of respect was to lose my partner…

She couldn't even finish the thought. Bile and anger clogged her mind and throat.

"Take a seat," Captain Hill said gently, flopping down into his chair. "I'm sorry about Walter. We may have had our disagreements, but…he was a good officer."

Hill took a sip from an antacid bottle and cringed as he swallowed. There were deep shadows under his eyes and his minimal hair looked like he'd been pulling on it.

How long has it been since he slept…maybe not since letting Walter go…he did say there were dirty cops here, and the way the captain is acting it looks like something more than just the loss of an officer is going on.

"Did he call you before…well, before he died?" Hill asked.

And that sealed it for Shay. The captain was digging for information and Walter's corpse was barely cold.

He's worried…no, afraid. So, he knows who did it and why…

Her hands shook and blood, once again rushed to her ears, but Shay reigned it all in, bit by bit.

"No, sir," she managed.

He nodded and lit a cigarette.

"He didn't have any family, just a few ex-wives that told me politely where I could stick my…well, they didn't seem to care about his demise. I hate to ask, but would you go to his house and see if he took home any files or things that might give a clue as to what happened?"

If he's asking me to do it he thinks I'm clueless, or it's a test. Either way, I need to know and I'll play the game if it gets me to Walter's killer.

"Of course, sir, I'll go today."

"Good, thank you. I'll see you at Paddy's, I assume you'll be there."

"Of course."

The captain nodded and took a long drag from his cigarette.

"Sir, about The Bulwark—"

"Federal sons of—I can't believe the commissioner is doing this," Hill clutched his stomach and winced. "Damn ulcer. Don't work too hard Reynolds or you'll turn out like me."

"Yes, sir. When should I report to Agent Ward?"

He frowned at her as if he didn't understand what she was saying.

"I'm still on the task force."

"Oh…yeah, that. Uh…well, after you've taken a few days—"

"I'm fine sir, and I want to catch who did this. It was a shard of ice through the chest, that means one of the powered individuals."

"How did you know that? We haven't even released it to the press yet," then his face hardened and he swore. "Fisk, damn it I told him—"

"I had a right to know. Walter was my partner. So, when do I report to Agent Ward?"

The captain took another drag of his cigarette and blew the smoke across the table at her. Shay didn't even flinch as she held his gaze. She was not going to be kept out of this.

"Tomorrow," he said finally. "I need you looking through Walter's apartment today."

"Yes, sir," she got up from her seat, not waiting to be dismissed.

"Reynolds, keep your nose clean. If you pull with Agent Ward what you did with Chris last night, you'll be in records until you retire."

She nodded. Might as well let him think she was going to be compliant.

Shay didn't even look at her fellow officers as she walked out. She didn't want their pity, their words of condolence. It would only temper the anger burning in her and she needed that to fuel everything that came next.

It turned out that Walter lived a short distance from the precinct in a building that had seen better days but wasn't quite a slum yet. When she opened the door to his basement apartment, the place was a complete disaster. She drew her weapon and scanned the dimly lit living room.

The TV had been smashed in and parts taken out, couch stuffing had been flung everywhere and the carpet had been sliced up. Shay stepped gingerly over the threshold, body tense and sense alert for the smallest sound or movement. Stepping further into the apartment, she looked into the tiny kitchen and cringed at the mess. Plates smashed, food stuff spilled over every surface, even the pipes from under the sink had been taken apart.

Whoever this was, they were desperate to find what Walter was hiding.

The bedroom and bathroom were similarly tossed, the mattress shredded and every hiding place imaginable exposed.

Shay had the sinking feeling that if Walter had been hiding anything here that it must've been found.

She was about to turn and leave when something caught her eye. Under the remnants of his mattress, a photograph album barely showed. The book was old, the spine broken either from age or mistreatment at the hands of whoever tossed the place.

There was an old photo of Walter and a beautiful woman in a wedding dress followed by smiling faces of the couple, sunny afternoons and the picture of a chubby baby.

Walter said he didn't have family…

A few pages of happy family photos and then there was a newspaper article and a program for a funeral. Shay opened it with care, the paper old and yellowing. Inside were two female names with the last name Lyle. Tears stung her eyes as she read the newspaper article.

They died in a car crash…poor Walter.

She was about to close the album when something strange poked out from under the funeral program. Using her fingernail to carefully pry it away from the album page, Shay saw a small slip of paper with a bank's name, a safe deposit box number and the word "spaghetti", which could only be a code word to get into the box.

"But where's the key?" she said to herself, looking around the train wreck of an apartment. "If there was one around here, then they probably found it…unless it was hidden someplace they wouldn't look."

She thought of Walter, of the things he said, forcing her memory to comb through every syllable. Then it hit her like a pail of cold water.

"He wore a chain around his neck! What if he had the key on him? He must've known that this would happen one day, that's why he hid this in the album, he wouldn't have kept the key and this in the same place, he was too smart for that. But how do I get the key?"

She ran a hand over her face and felt the elation drain out of her, replaced by fatigue. Captain Hill wanted her to find something because he was involved in whatever got Walter killed, Shay was almost certain of it. Asking about a key would raise suspicion.

"Unless I can get a peek at the report from the officer that found him...a key might've made it into the list of items found with the body, unless Hill or someone else got to it first. Then there's the vigilantes...where do they fit in? He had a CI relationship with Fahrenheit but what about the other one? Did it go sour?"

She sighed and slumped down onto the floor of his apartment.

"Walter, why couldn't you just tell me more?"

The grief she'd been holding at bay with a wall of anger began to seep through as tears burned in her eyes. Shay realized that she'd honestly been waiting for the old man to walk through the door any minute and berate her for not staying away.

When her eyes fell on the funeral program, the full knowledge that he was never coming back, that she'd never hear that raspy voice again, never share a cup of bitter coffee and give him grief, hit her like Mack truck. She gasped and gulped as sobs tore their way up her throat. She held it back at first, then a scream of rage fueled despair erupted from her and she pounded the floor with her fists.

"God damn you, Walter! If you'd just let me help you then maybe you'd still be alive!"

Before she knew it, the grief turned to rage for last night, for the people who were victimized by the task force, for the racist words she had to tolerate day after day. If she could have, Shay knew that flames would've erupted from her finger tips and engulfed the room around her.

But she didn't possess that power. So, she kicked the refuse of Walter's life, sending it flying across the room. With a scream, Shay overturned the mattress, the side table and lamp. Sweat trickled down her spine and she just barely stopped herself from punching the wall.

By the time she was done, she felt a little lighter, a little cleaner. A purpose was before her and she couldn't achieve it if she let herself get lost in her emotions.

Shay roughly wiped the tears away and bent down to pick up the piece of paper she'd dropped. Her gaze fell on a picture of Walter and his wife in a broken frame on the ground and she let a few more tears fall onto the shattered glass.

"I'll find who did this. And I'll make them pay. I promise."

CHAPTER TWENTY-TWO

A ndrew pounded the punching bag with fists of ice, droplets of frost falling from his bare skin. Colleen's horrified expression, and the question she'd asked him spun like a storm in his mind. Nothing he did could help him get away from it.

I'm a monster…she thinks I'm a monster.
The sight of his spear of ice slicing through the officer's body flashed through his mind and Andrew winced. The memory was so vivid he half expected to see blood on the floor at his feet.

Instead, it was sand that spilled into a small pile from the rips he'd created on the punching bag.

"Damn it," he said, reaching up to replace it when two small knives flew through the air and lodged in the ruined surface of the bag.

A prickle of unease crawled down his spine but Andrew didn't even turn around.

"Hello, Maiden," he said, having no idea what her real name was. "Here for a little work out?"

He set the punching bag in a corner and turned around to find a knife hovering at his neck, the blade barely touching his cold skin. Maiden's eyes shone with manic glee behind her mask and Andrew knew that if he could remove it, he'd see a wide grin on her face.

"To what do I owe this?" he asked. "You bored or just looking to get your ass kicked?"

She shrugged and Andrew took the opportunity to hit her in the back with a block of ice. She pitched forward and the knife fell at his feet. Andrew pulled on the moisture in the air and blasted her with frost. She spun out of the path of the onslaught and tossed two knives at him in one smooth motion. Andrew dodge one, but the other sliced his side and he grunted in pain.

The knives were sharpened so that they could slice through a person as cleanly as silk. The gash may have looked small, but Andrew knew it was deep enough. If Maiden was here to kill him for letting Colleen go free, he wouldn't be so easy to hit again.

Andrew coated the floor with a sheet of ice and encased Maiden's feet and primary throwing arm in a cast so she couldn't move it. She pulled at her frozen limbs, giving Andrew the chance to bring the ice up to the rest of her body, forming a frozen sarcophagus around her.

"Well," he said, walking up to her. "That was bracing, thanks."

Pride goes before the fall, and Andrew knew it when he turned his back on the frozen psychopath only to feel a hot slice of pain in his shoulder.

He cried out as he pulled the knife free, turning just in time to see the arsenal of iron headed his way. Andrew threw himself to the floor as the knives lodged into the wooden post behind him.

"Sore loser, huh?"

Andrew gathered all the moisture he could to himself, the blood on his body freezing, as he became covered in a sparkling layer of frost.

"Let's see you do anything after I freeze your heart, you—"

"That will be enough," Mr. Price's soft, lethal voice cut through the battle.

Andrew could feel the cold blooded bastard behind him, and knew that Price would skin him alive if he didn't obey. Still, Andrew didn't relinquish his power immediately.

"Sub Zero, you will obey me."

Fury lanced through him. Mr. Price's leash on Andrew's life had started chaffing long ago, now it was a red hot sore spot. But if Andrew had learned one thing, it was patience. If he played the game well, if he held on long enough, one day he'd see Price's blood at the end of his ice.

"Thaw her now."

Andrew withdrew the ice from Maiden as slowly as he could so it would hurt more. Mr. Price knew it, but made no comment. If Maiden had been sloppy enough to become encased in ice, she'd have to deal with the pain of it.

Maiden collapsed forward once the last of the ice was gone, curling in on herself and shivering violently.

"Now that the two of you have gotten your sparring session out of the way," Mr., Price said tossing them both towels, "I require your presence upstairs."

Andrew hated turning his back on the woman, even though she would never dare disobey Mr. Price. He chilled his body enough to slow the flow of blood from his wounds and bit down on the pain every time he moved.

Show no weakness. Show no fear. Show no grief.

By the time they stood in front of Price's desk, Maiden's shivering had lessened, though her clothes hung on her thin frame in a wet, misshapen lump. Her mask was wet and Andre saw her reach under it to wipe moisture away. He grinned, knowing that she was ten times more uncomfortable than he was.

"Now, children, I don't mind you testing one another, but next time, don't try and kill. I still have need of you both."

They both nodded.

"The police commissioner has decided to give way to the government agency called The Bulwark to hunt Fahrenheit and you, Sub Zero. You must be careful not to be caught."

Andrew swallowed. The Bulwark was spoken of in hushed tones even in the hellish labs he'd been imprisoned in. Though they had sounded like the kind of scary stories parents told their children to keep them in line, Andrew had seen the agency's handiwork up close on one of his first missions. The powered people they'd captured were hollowed out, crazed husks of human beings that had to be put down like dogs.

I wouldn't wish that on my worst enemy.
He glanced over at Maiden for a second.

Okay, maybe I would.
"What does this change?" he asked.

"Nothing. If anything, this is an advantage."

"How?"

"Your sister won't be able to resist saving you if she thinks you're in danger, no matter how angry she is at you. I want you to drive her into the arms of those idiots. If she kills them or gets captured, either outcome works in our favor. In the meantime, we must prepare for the final phase of our plan."

"And what is that?"

Mr. Price held his gaze, a tiny, serpentine smile on his face.

"Want to check my work, make sure I'm leaving a neighborhood to have dominion over?"

"Something like that."

"When it's time for you to know, you will. Now stitch yourself up," his gaze flitted to Maiden. "And dry off, I've got work for you."

He waved his thin fingers at them and they walked out of the office. As the door clicked shut behind them, Maiden nodded her damp head to him, the mask glistening.

"You saved her for a fate worse than death. Do you hate her that much?" she whispered in a haunting, child-like voice.

Andrew watched her walk up the stairs, his stomach roiling as he realized that today wasn't a sparring session. It was an assassination attempt.

She knows that I let Colleen go. Does that mean that Price does too or is Maiden keeping that to herself?

It was a question Andrew knew he wouldn't have the answer to until it was too late.

CHAPTER TWENTY-THREE

A war raged in Shay's mind as she walked up the stairs to Colleen's apartment. She wanted to lose herself in the company of the tall, enigmatic woman, to forget Walter, and The Bulwark for just a few, glorious hours. And she felt horribly guilty about it.

Paddy's had been tense and miserable the night before. Usually people share stories of fallen officers, and their partner would give a tearful toast. But the only stories anyone really knew about Walter were the cases he'd gone out on a limb to solve, and that just didn't seem right, all things considered.

When it came time for Shay to speak, she couldn't get any words past the knot in her throat and ended up simply asking everyone to raise their glass and remember him.

The only good part was when Fisk found her sitting alone and didn't say a word, just sat down and helped her finish a bottle of Walter's favorite whiskey.

Which is why I've had a raging headache all damn day. Or was Agent Ward the cause? The bastard.

Ward brought two others with him and they holed up all day picking over every file and report that even had a hint of something to do with vigilantes. When Shay suggested that they look into the northern precinct, who was starting to report on other vigilante activity, Ward had chuckled and handed her his coffee cup.

"Aren't we ambitious? Two sugars and no cream, thanks, love."

Shay had conveniently forgotten to bring the cup back.

Now here she was, in a pair of faded cotton shorts and blouse, head and heart aching, about to knock on Colleen's door and all she could think of was how she should be out hunting down the ice powered vigilante that had murdered her partner.

Walter would want me to be happy…he'd tell me to do this, I know he would, I just—

The door opened before she'd had the chance to knock, revealing a tired looking Colleen. Shay had intended to say something witty, something that wouldn't bring up memories of dead partners and tenement fires. But the second she opened her mouth, all of the emotions she'd been pushing away broke free of their prison, and she burst into tears.

Warm arms encircled her and Shay leaned into Colleen's body, letting her be the strength that held Shay up.

"I'm so sorry," Colleen whispered, her voice thick with emotion. "We don't have to do anything tonight. It's really okay."

"No," Shay said, pulling away and dabbing her eyes with shaking fingertips. "I know it sounds terrible, but I just need to forget for a few hours."

"No, it doesn't sound terrible. It sounds completely understandable. I'll raid the kitchen downstairs. We might have some rocky road in the freezer. We can sit on the floor, eat junk food, tell bad jokes and just…"

Shay gave her a shaky smile, her fingers curling around Colleen's.

"And what?"

Colleen bit her bottom lip and looked down.

"I didn't mean...I'm not trying to take advantage of you."

Shay was surprised to find herself chuckling and tipped Colleen's chin up with one of her fingers. She could smell the spicy perfume and hair oil that Colleen used, see the sheen of her moisturizer and wondered why she never saw the hints of orange in her brown eyes before. Suddenly, the very thing that Shay needed became crystal clear. It wasn't junk food, or alcohol. It was this woman in front of her.

They'd shared a lot at this point, each other's fears and memories of childhood. But the one threshold that would confirm everything hadn't been crossed and Shay knew it was now or never.

As she hesitated, Colleen's breath brushed against her skin, quick but not fearful, and full of the kind of tension that came from longing.

"I'm going to kiss you now," Shay said, her lips hovering so near Colleen's that she brushed against them just from speaking.

"Oh god, yes."

Shay didn't care if someone walked up the stairs; the heat in those words drove all caution to the wind. She pressed her lips to Colleen's, her hand cupping the taller woman's cheek.

Colleen opened her mouth to taste Shay with slow, languid strokes of her tongue, her hands firmly gripping Shay's ample hips. Each kiss was like a balm to Shay's aching soul, as if Colleen were drawing out all the fear and grief. The pressure of their lips increased, their bodies pressed against each other and Shay felt her thighs light up with heat that shot straight between her legs. She wanted more. More of Colleen's lips, more of her body.

Shay's hands slid up along Colleen's bare arms, reveling in the feel of her soft skin under her fingertips. The taller woman shuddered, letting out a gasp just before pulling Shay into the apartment. Without bothering to let go of one another, Colleen kicked the door closed and circled Shay in a tight embrace, like being pulled in from the cold night and into a warm, safe retreat. Shay never wanted to leave.

Her fingers slid under Colleen's shirt and up to her perfectly rounded breasts. Finding her nipples taut, Shay pinched them ever so slightly and Colleen groaned deep in her throat. Shay began to kiss her way up Colleen's long neck, pinching and caressing as she did when Colleen suddenly pulled away, leaving Shay feeling like the sun had gone behind the clouds.

"Wait," Colleen said, breathless and eyes shining. "You…you're grieving, vulnerable and I-I can't take advantage of you."

"You're not."

"But—"

"If you don't want to, then that's one thing. I won't be offended; we can go raid the kitchen downstairs. But, if you want me like I want you," Shay pulled her shirt over her head, then unclasped her bra, throwing both to the floor and grinning at the way Colleen's gaze turned hot while she took in Shay's bare chest, "then I'm all yours."

Shay could almost feel Colleen's eyes as they traveled down her body, the tall woman standing before her with an expression full to the brim of hungry desire. It was agony standing there, her body thrumming with passion, waiting for Colleen to touch her.

Finally, Colleen reached out and ran her fingers up Shay's arm, to her shoulder and then down her chest in a slow, feather light touch that left a trail of pin pricks on her skin. When Colleen began letting her lips follow the path of her fingers, Shay buried her hand in Colleen's hair, letting out a gasp of pleasure when her lips began to work on her breasts.

Their short journey to the bed left a trail of clothes, tossed away with passionate sighs and giggles. By the time they tumbled onto the bed, the grief that had haunted Shay was a distant pain in the back of her head. The only thing she was aware of was Colleen – her hands and mouth on her skin, leaving trails of pleasure and heat in their wake.

Colleen lay under the thin sheet, and stared at Shay as she slept, curled up next to the vigilante like the most beautiful surprise of her life. Even though outside her window, the world was falling apart, Colleen couldn't help indulging in this tiny pocket of peace she had found herself in tonight.

She'd imagined what it would be like with Shay many times, but the reality was so much more intimate, so much more overwhelming in the best kind of way. Colleen had always held back a part of herself, even with Karen. She was never able to let go and simply trust anyone. Tonight was different. Colleen couldn't help but reveal herself completely to the woman. It was the first time Colleen understood how joyful sex with someone could be, and she hungered for more of that connection, being known and knowing someone so deeply.

Even still, I didn't tell her everything, did I?

Guilt stabbed at her mind and Colleen tried to push it away without success. She shifted, putting her arm over Shay in an attempt to become too distracted to give her worries any room to play. The smaller woman's eyes fluttered open and the moment she saw Colleen, a sleepy grin lit up her face.

Colleen returned the same grin, brushing her fingers over Shay's cheek.

"I'm sorry I woke you," she whispered.

"It's okay, I probably shouldn't spend the night anyway," she snuggled in closer to Colleen and sighed with contentment. "Even if I want to."

Colleen drew small circles on Shay's back with her finger tips, lazy, light movements that made goose flesh rise on her skin.

"Mmmm...how do you do that?" Shay asked.

"What?" Colleen's stomach dropped as she realized what had happened.

In her relaxed state of mind, she'd let out a tiny bit of heat into her fingers without thinking about it.

"It's like...little zings of heat," Shay said, looking up at her.

Colleen knew that this would be the time to tell her, a perfect opening after they'd shared something so intense and pure. She opened her mouth to tell her the secret that weighed her down so much when Walter's dying words hit her like a slap across the face.

He told me to keep her safe. If she knows who I am, she's going to want to know who killed Walter and then what? If I don't tell her, I'll lose her. If I do and she goes after Andrew...

An image of Shay with ice through her chest made her heart kick behind her ribs. She had to keep this a secret, just a little longer. When everything had settled down, then she could come clean and Shay would be safe, she'd understand.

I hope.

Colleen swallowed down the lump in her throat and gave her lover a shaky smile.

"Static electricity, maybe?"

"Maybe. Whatever it is, I like it."

Colleen held her tighter. This one good thing in her life was more fragile than anything she'd ever held. Colleen knew better than most that it was the good things that had a tendency to blow away like ash on the wind.

"Hey," Shay said, leaning back to look Colleen in the eye. "What's wrong?"

"It's just…everything. High Tide, what's happening it's all so…"

"Yeah, I know. It weighs me down, too."

For a while they just laid there, holding one another. Outside, sirens wailed, some far away, others too close for comfort. Shay planted little kisses on Colleen's collar bone just before snuggling in closer and sighing.

"You can stay if you want," Colleen whispered into Shay's hair.

"I can't…I wish I could but…I can't."

Too soon, Shay pulled away and sat up, shoulders sagging.

"I should go. There might be some word from the task force or…I don't know. It's all so mixed up, Colleen. I don't know if I'm doing the right thing trying to hunt down the vigilantes, and then one of them kills Walter and I'm so angry," her voice broke and she shook her head. "He trusted one of them, the one they call Fahrenheit."

Colleen went still, heart thumping in her chest.

"How do you know that?" she asked.

"I caught him talking to her…and then she saved my life the other night, along with some of the residents. She stopped the fire from spreading. Those aren't the actions of a criminal. But then, the other one kills Walter, and I read the report of the crime scene today, there were scorch marks at the scene. So, was Fahrenheit there to help or hurt? Who was she fighting? Walter or this other one? I just wish I could ask her, could know what she knew and then maybe I could piece this together."

Colleen wanted to soothe her fears and answer her questions so badly that her chest ached with it. But she couldn't, not without revealing everything.

And maybe she wouldn't reject me…but she would want to work with me. No, I promised Walter and I won't have Shay's blood on my hands. I can't let anyone else have a target on their back because of me. I'll fix this myself.

She sat up and wrapped Shay in her arms, doing the little she could to help her feel better.

"It's all going to work out. I promise."

"How?"

"I don't know, but I believe it will."

Shay looked up at her and smiled.

"You're pretty amazing, you know that? And I'm not just talking about in bed."

Heat rushed into Colleen's face and she bit her bottom lip.

"You're not so bad yourself."

"And you are adorable when you get embarrassed!"

Shay kissed her, slow and soft.

"I have to go, but can I see you again? Maybe tonight, if I don't have to work?"

Colleen nodded.

"I'd like that."

She slipped into a soft, thin robe as Shay quickly dressed and smoothed her hair.

"Call me tomorrow. I don't think Wanda will give you any of my messages."

"No, probably not."

With one last kiss, Colleen closed the door and tried to convince herself that this beautiful relationship wasn't doomed to fail.

CHAPTER
TWENTY-FOUR

S hay stared at the crime scene report for what felt like the thousandth time. The list of belongings was small and a key wasn't listed among them. She'd dissected Walter's wallet, examining every scrap of paper, every card and making her own notes about each. There were half a dozen phone numbers, and all but one of them were either disconnected or the people on the other end claimed they were clueless as to who she was talking about. The number she was about to call had been buried deep in the wallet on a faded slip of paper torn out of the phone book.

It rang so long that Shay was about to hang up when a gruff voice answered.

"St. Nic's boxing gym, who's this?"

"Uh, hello, my name is Shay Reynolds and I'm—"

"Not interested."

"Wait! I'm calling about Walter Lyle. Did you know him?"

The man on the other end paused and she heard a door closing before he spoke again, his voice measured and suspicious.

"Who's asking?"

"I'm his partner...former partner and I need some help."

"Why call me?"

"Because I believe he was looking into something that got him killed and I wanted to know if you were one of his contacts, if you could give me some insight."

"Christ...he's dead?"

"Yes."

"I guess the bastards got him, then."

Shay's skin prickled at the words, every sense snapping into focus.

"Who?"

"Listen, I'm sure you're just trying to help but—"

"I'll get myself killed? It's too dangerous? Yeah, I've heard all that before, but obviously I don't give a damn. Walter didn't deserve this, and I want justice for him."

"You'll be waiting a while. I tried to tell him that no one stands up to these people and survives. I wish he'd listened."

"Give me a name, just a place to start."

He sighed, a deep, throaty sound.

"I'm sorry. I don't want any more blood on my hands. Good luck."

The line went dead and Shay slammed the receiver down.

"Damn it!"

"Rough day, Reynolds?" Fisk asked, leaning one hip against her desk.

"What do you want?"

"Whoa, don't take it out on me. Not when I've got some good news for you."

"And what is that?"

"Chris was transferred to a different precinct this morning, he's off the task force. I also requested that you stay on and suggested that you would be the best consultant to those federal idiots. You're welcome."

He grinned down at her like he'd just laid the world at her feet.

It was the exact wrong thing to do right after her first good lead had shot her down.

"Thanks, that's just great," she snapped, jumping to her feet.

"Hey," he stepped in front of her, brows drawn over his eyes in confusion, "I thought you'd be happy."

"Happy to work with federal agents who could care less about High Tide, who think I'm the coffee fetching girl? You despise them, would you want to be stuck working with them instead of out there catching the person that killed your partner?"

Fisk stepped closer to her, eyes intense on her face.

"This is how you catch the guy, Reynolds. They have the ability to do things we can't and stay above scrutiny for it. You want justice? I just handed you the perfect way to get it."

Shay set her jaw.

"Begging your pardon, Detective Fisk, but you didn't *hand* me anything. I earned it."

He opened his mouth to respond but Agent Ward shouted for her from what used to be the task force's planning room.

"Can you come in here, darlin'? We need a consult."

Shay shot a look at Fisk that made him actually take a step back and marched toward the room. She didn't realize that Fisk was hot on her heels until Ward chuckled and held up his hand.

"Protective of your little friend? We don't really need you in here."

"Well sir, I'm the head of the task force, Reynolds is one of my officers, so I'm coming in anyway."

Ward gave Fisk an appraising stare and then nodded as if he were being quite the magnanimous superior. A bolt of satisfaction shot through Shay and she had to bite down on a grin.

How do you like it, Fisk?

As Fisk walked past the agent he stopped and turned toward him with a cold glare.

"Oh, and if you need coffee, fetch your own. She's not your secretary."

Ward chuckled.

"Sensitive, are we? I didn't realize I was being disrespectful." Though Ward was grinning, his eyes were bright with anger when he turned to Shay. "My apologies Officer, it won't happen again."

She gave him a nod and turned to the table in the center of the room. It was covered in a large map of High Tide, the map she had marked for the task force.

"You took this from my desk?" she asked before she could stop herself.

"You weren't here and Fisk mentioned how you'd figured out this pattern. You don't mind do you? After all, you have more reason to want to catch these freaks than any of us in this room."

It was an exceptionally low blow to use Walter's death like this. Her body tensed and she could hear her pulse pounding in her ears as she tried to reign it all in. Blowing up would solve nothing, and would only confirm that she didn't belong here, that she was too volatile to do the job.

"No, I don't mind," she muttered.

"Excellent," Ward said, the oily smile planted firmly on his square face. "We know that you attempted to draw the terrorist out by creating a fire amongst the people she cares about. You were there, did you see any evidence that it worked?"

Shay swallowed as her mind tried to create the right answer. The vigilante had earned her respect that night, but what she felt now was much more like a primal need to protect her, no matter what.

"No sir, there was no evidence that the vigilante was there."

I'll be damned if I call her a terrorist.

Ward's gaze pinned Shay to the spot and she wanted so badly to look away. It was as if the man were trying to dig through her mind and find the memory of that night. On an instinct, Shay thought of something, anything else. Her old pair of running shoes, the way her floor creaked when no one was there, how her mother kept calling her morning, noon and night.

"Still, it seems suspicious that the fire remained contained to the one building. Almost as if someone were controlling it."

Shay shrugged.

"I was grateful that more homes weren't destroyed. The mechanics of it didn't interest me."

"Maybe they should."

"Maybe."

That feeling returned and Shay dug her fingernails into her palm to keep her mind here in the present.

Finally, Ward looked away, a muscle in his jaw tensing.

"Let's move on to next steps. Obviously, this one cares about the people, I think your former team mate was correct in his assessment, though his execution was a bit sloppy. We need to round up anyone who's had any documented contact with the terrorist. From the largest to the smallest. Bring them in, let them stew, hell, book 'em on some small charge and let's see what she does."

Shay's jaw dropped, her gaze pivoting to Fisk, who stood with an equally shocked expression.

"You're talking about bringing in almost a hundred people," he said, "and for what? That's harassment, I can't do that."

Ward smiled.

"Well, I can. If you and Officer Reynolds don't have the stomach for this, then I suggest you leave."

"No," Shay burst out. "I'm not going to abandon those people to you and your ham fisted agents."

"Reynolds—" Fisk said, his voice filled to the brim with warning.

"Ham fisted?" Ward said at the same time.

"They've been brutalized enough this summer just because they happen to live in the neighborhood that the vigilante patrols. If you're going to cause further trauma, then I think someone should be there to advocate on their behalf."

Shay lifted her chin, back straight, daring Ward to disagree. Instead, he laughed.

"Officer, we are not the enemy here! Of course, you should be there to speak on their behalf."

"I should?" her voice became hesitant as she waited for the other shoe to drop.

"Yes. I think having someone there like them would go a long way towards getting them to open up," Ward turned to Fisk and nodded. "I can see why you insisted on her being on the team. She's quite clever actually. What a unique find for the precinct."

The pencil she held in her hand snapped at the words, chest heaving with quick breaths that threatened to erupt into words she would definitely regret later.

"I need...excuse me for a moment," she said, rushing out the door.

She was half way to the bathroom when Fisk called her name and ran up behind her.

"I'm sorry," he said, "I thought I'd be helping, I had no idea—"

"Save it. I'm glad you did, even though I want to punch the bastard in the face."

"That makes two of us."

"Just promise me you'll help me protect those people. I know I can't stop him from doing this but...they're innocent."

"Of course I will."

She started for the bathroom again, then looked over her shoulder at the confused furrow of his brow and sighed.

Sure you will. Until it interferes with your promotion or impressing them or until you think I'm being over dramatic. Sure you will, Fisk.

"I need to use the restroom," she said. "You planning on camping out and waiting for me?"

Fisk opened his mouth and snapped it shut, shaking his head.

"I'll see you back in there."

She waited until he was back in the room before leaving through the door at the end of the hallway. It let out into a long, wide side alley where delivery trucks usually pulled up. The hot air hit her square in the face, thick and stinking of exhaust from the street. Shay paced, letting loose a stream of swear words punctuated by grunts of anger.

If only I knew how Walter contacted Fahrenheit, I could meet with her, gauge what kind of person she is and warn her. Instead I'm stuck working with men that see innocent people as pawns.

She let out a grunt and kicked the nearby trash can, the contents spilling out in a pungent heap.

"You're the cop trying to catch the vigilantes, right?" asked a voice behind her.

Shay spun around, fist raised and at the ready.

The thin woman in the hat and dark clothes put out her hands, face down cast as if she were trying to hide.

"I just have information."

"What kind of information? And how do you know me?"

"I saw you a couple of times, with that guy that got killed, the cop?"

"Why won't you look at me?"

The young woman hesitated, and glanced up just enough for Shay to glimpse a vicious patchwork of scars on her pale face.

"I'm sorry," Shay said, lowering her fist in shock. "Go on."

"I-I saw who killed him and I think I know where he's going to be."

Suspicion slithered down Shay's spine, her instincts whispering that this was just too good to be true.

But if I can bring something else to the table, maybe the people of High Tide won't be used as bait.

"Alright, tell me."

"He hangs out at a couple of different locations in both High Tide and Devil's Own. The Sweet Spot is one of his regular haunts."

"Anywhere else?"

The woman gave her a few more addresses but emphasized that the candy shop was the place she'd seen him most.

"Thank you. Why are you telling me all this?" Shay asked.

The woman shrugged, long blond hair sliding out of her hat to veil her face.

"It wasn't right, what happened to your partner. He was always nice to-to girls like me."

Realization hit Shay and she nodded. Walter had often been seen buying hookers a cup of coffee or ordering them to go get some dinner instead of arresting them. She teared up thinking that she might be talking to one of the women he'd helped with his kindness.

"Here," she said, digging a five out of her wallet, "get yourself something to eat."

The woman took it without a word and skulked away.

Shay turned over the information the woman had given her, wondering why the ice vigilante would be at a candy shop so often, when she heard the garbage can she'd kicked move on the filthy concrete. When she looked over at it, the can was standing up right, the lid securely fastened.

That's...who could've—

Shay ran up and down the alley, searching for...who? Another powered person, a vagrant with an environmental conscious? But the only person there was her.

"Reynolds, you coming back or what?" Fisk shouted from the hallway.

She jumped, heart pounding and ran to the garbage can. With quick movements she examined the area around it, looking for any place someone could hide or for a string attached to the can. There was nothing and she was left staring in confusion at the thing, her mind desperate to have an answer that made sense.

"Reynolds!"

"Yeah, yeah, I'm coming," she said, taking one final glance before walking back into the hall.

Fisk frowned at her, arms crossed.

"What's going on?"

"Wh-what?"

"You look like you've seen a ghost. What's that?" he gestured to the slip of paper she held in her hand.

She told him about the mysterious woman and what she'd said, leaving out the part about the garbage can. The last thing she needed was Fisk thinking she was going crazy.

"This is a good lead, better than the plan Ward is fixated on," Fisk said.

"I agree, but I don't think there's a way to talk him out of it."

Fisk paused, eye brows drawing together as he turned the problem over in his mind.

"What if we went?"

She stared at him, positive she wasn't understanding.

Fisk must've seen the disbelief on her face because he gave her a little smile.

"You're a good cop, and I think together we might be able to not only solve Walter's murder, but catch this vigilante at the same time."

"You don't want someone else? Someone more…qualified?" she asked, her voice hardening on the last word.

"And who would that be? I've read your file. I've seen your work. You and I, we're the best cops here."

Shay waited for the backhanded compliment and when it didn't come she couldn't help a shocked laugh shooting out of her mouth.

"I never thought I'd see the day."

Fisk had the good graces to wear an embarrassed smile and nodded

"I know, and…I'm sorry about that. What do you say?"

Shay bit the inside of her cheek, mulling it over. Fear of what Ward and his men would do stuck to her mind like a burr on a sock, but she also knew that if she and Fisk caught the vigilante that killed Walter, that could give the captain what he needed to kick the agents out of the precinct.

"Alright," she finally. "Let's do it."

CHAPTER TWENTY-FIVE

C olleen's senses were on high alert as she patrolled her usual area around High Tide. She hadn't seen very many cops tonight, a sign that something had changed. And, considering recent events, probably not for the better.

With everything that had happened, Colleen opted to start patrolling from the roof tops. Plenty of buildings were close enough that she was able to simply jump and make it to the next. But, a few were too far apart so Colleen decided to try out something she'd been working on. Now, as she stood on the edge of one of the buildings, staring across at the next roof top, pulse thrumming in her ears, the vigilante wondered if she shouldn't just climb down to street level, after all.

"I can do this...I can do this...Oh my god, I don't know if I can do this!"

After Haven, Colleen's powers had increased quite a lot, and even though she didn't have a lot of time to explore what that meant, she'd stumbled upon a new ability a few days ago and had been trying to practice as much as possible.

Stepping away from the ledge, Colleen stood in the middle of the roof and concentrated as she pointed her palms down. Twin streams of fire shot out of her hands, strong and intense. It launched her into the air several feet until she extinguished them. She'd mastered short bursts so far, but it was the longer ones that would potentially take her from roof to roof that she hadn't tested yet.

"Okay, see, you can do this. You just need to get a hold of yourself," she said, shaking out her hands. "If Marco can swing on a stupid cable line I can do this."

It was now or never.

With a deep breath, Colleen ran and leapt off the edge of the roof. Her stomach dropped as she began to fall and she threw her hands out, flames shooting out once more. The action propelled her up in a short burst, just enough for her to grab onto the edge of the next roof and pull herself over.

Once her feet landed safely on the roof, Colleen flopped down onto her back, her breaths fast as what she'd just done hit her.

Panic welled up in her throat at how close she'd come to falling onto the concrete, followed swiftly by elation.

She'd done it! She'd flown!

Colleen let loose a victorious laugh and jumped to her feet.

"Not bad, needs work but seriously not bad!"

She was about to practice the burst a little more, to see if she could go longer and get herself completely over the ledge of the next rooftop, when an unmarked van pulled up to the apartment building across the street. Men in riot gear poured out of the vehicle and broke down the door of the building. Immediately following, Colleen heard shouts, voices and more than a few sounds of gunfire. Her muscles tensed, ready for a fight when she saw the men forcing people out of the building and into the waiting vehicle. Most were in whatever they had on for bed, others looked like they had just gotten home from swing shifts. Some were crying, while others did their best to just do what they were being ordered to.

What is going on? Is the task force doing mass arrests now?

There were only five men and while they were holding large rifles, Colleen was sure she could get the jump on them.

After torching a building , god only knows what they'll do to these people. The trick is going to be not hurting any of the civilians.

She scanned the street where the van was parked and saw the perfect distraction.

A beat up old car that had been tagged with graffiti sat several feet up the street from the van. It might have belonged to someone, but Colleen doubted it since it hadn't moved in over a month.

Taking a deep breath, she threw four fireballs at the abandoned car. Instantly, the flames caught on the paint and upholstery, causing some of the residents to shout and point. Two men stayed behind to keep loading people in the van, but the other three went to investigate. When they were close enough to the car, Colleen dragged the flames down and surrounded the men with them. They gave a shout of panic, firing their weapons in all directions. The people outside of the van screamed and ran for cover, a few making it back into the building.

Colleen grit her teeth at the carelessness of it and bolted down the fire escape.

"Pick on someone your own size," she said, running across the street, straight for the men.

One of them ran up to her from behind the van, leveling his gun at her. Colleen flung a fireball at him, letting it singe his pants.

Usually, that was enough for an officer to flee, as was the cage of fire she was quickly constructing around the other men. But this time, the officer didn't miss a beat. Instead, he fired the gun straight at her.

Colleen flung herself to the left, and felt the graze of something sharp against her skin. And then she felt a terrifyingly familiar cold sensation seep through the wound.

"No," she whispered, as the green residue glistened on the cut.

She knew who these men were now, panic clouding her mind in the wake of the realization.

The Bulwark were in High Tide.

The fire she'd surrounded the men with was dissipating as the solution did its work, her powers already being affected. Colleen had experienced what a full injection could do, and knew that she wouldn't stand a chance against them if that man got off another shot.

She forced her mind to work even as her chest felt heavy with fear. Lobbing one fireball after another at the man with the gun, as well as the others who were escaping her disappearing flames, Colleen took off at a full sprint.

Behind her, all hell was breaking loose as the residents began to fight back and flee from the van. She could hear the shouts of the agents, the slap of their boots following her as she ducked down the nearest alley way and jumped up onto a chain link fence. Once over, she was running for everything she was worth down the street.

The screech of tires pierced the night, a van careening onto the street behind her.

Colleen threw herself down another narrow alley way and pulled down a fire escape. The van over shot her and she heard them turning around. It was only a matter of time before agents poured out of the van and shot her full of the green solution.

To throw the men off, Colleen skipped the fire escape. She continued down the alley and leapt over the five foot wall at the end. If she could be sure that she had full access to her powers, Colleen would have tried out her new skill of flying. But as it was, she knew that her powers had to be conserved. On the other side of the wall was a struggling garden and a woman standing outside enjoying a cigarette that she promptly dropped when she saw Colleen.

"Holy shit it's—"

"Shh! You never saw me."

"Right, come on then."

The woman opened her back door and waved Colleen through.

"Alright, one second."

To lead the agents away from the woman's house, Colleen laid down a thin line of fire from the yard, over the woman's fence and onto the street. Then she ran into the small house, the woman behind her.

"Down the hall, the second door, it's a bedroom. The closet has a trap door in the floor and hidey hole, don't ask questions and for the love of god, don't let any sparks fall or we'll all be higher than a kite."

That's when the smell of the cigarette the woman had been smoking hit Colleen and she couldn't help a grin.

Does everyone in High Tide have secret compartments for things? Or is it just my good luck?

The hole was barely big enough for her to crouch in with the door closed but it would do until the agents had searched this area.

Which will hopefully be quick.

The earthy smell of pot mixed with the faintest hint of mothballs and leather created a very odd, heady aroma that made Colleen a little sick to her stomach.

Soon, voices filtered to her, muffled and deep, then the tramp of heavy boots. Sweat broke out all over her body, dripping down her back and side, her stomach churning with the fear of discovery.

Minutes felt like hours until the boots left the bedroom and the voices disappeared. Once it was quiet, though, the woman didn't come get her. As Colleen began to worry that the woman might be too high to remember the vigilante hiding in the hole, the door above opened and the woman's smiling face peered down.

"Now *that* is how you stick it to the man!"

Colleen chuckled in spite everything and climbed out. The skin around where the dart of green solution had grazed her was numb and a little swollen. And while her powers were still accessible, Colleen could feel the difference, like a light bulb someone had thrown a scarf over, not gone but dimmer.

"I think they've moved on," the woman said, lighting a new cigarette and taking deep pull from it.

She held it out to Colleen, who shook her head.

"I don't think that's a great idea right now, but thanks."

"Suit yourself. You wanna stick around for a while? I made some chocolate cake."

"No, thanks, I don't want to put you in anymore danger. Thank you for hiding me."

The woman grinned.

"Any time Fahrenheit."

Though she'd meant what she said and knew that the safest thing to do was get back to her apartment, the last thing Colleen wanted to do was step out into the night and chance running into those men.

There has to be two teams, there's no way they could've mobilized that fast after the residents caused so much trouble. That means…they could be patrolling anywhere.

She took a deep breath and decided on the direct route to Wanda's, which, thankfully, was only a few blocks away.

The roof tops weren't an option since she couldn't fly between them right now, so she stuck to the shadows. Still, every sound, every bit of movement made her heart jump into her throat. Once she almost charbroiled an alley cat, that hissed at her and took off. When she was a block away from home, a bum digging through a garbage can startled her so bad that she did lob a fireball at him and immediately recalled it when he let out a high pitched wail.

Normally, she would've stuck around and apologized, tried to get the guy some food. But Colleen was so scared that he might have alerted The Bulwark agents, she took off into the night and didn't stop until she had climbed the fire escape and scrambled into her apartment.

Even then, she paced in terror, ripping the suit from her body and throwing it into her closet. Every muscle in her body trembled, her breathing ragged and tears made hot tracks down her cheeks.

Maybe a shower…nice cold shower…

She was halfway to the shower when her foot landed on something cold and damp. She looked down to see a sodden comic book, tiny bits of ice falling from it when she picked it up. Andrew wanted to meet.

"But not tonight…I can't."

She tossed the comic onto her one good chair and practically ran into the bathroom.

The moment the spray hit her skin, a sob flew out of her mouth, surprising Colleen with its strength. Soon, she was crying in earnest, the terror of the night leaching out of her body, swirling down the drain with the dirt on her skin.

She was just toweling off when someone knocked on her door. Her heart stopped, body frozen to the spot.

Was it them? Were they here to just question a resident or to capture Fahrenheit?

"Colleen? It's Shay. Are you home?"

Her shoulders relaxed and she ran to the door, wrapped in nothing but a big fluffy towel.

The moment the door opened, Colleen crushed her lips to Shay's, who returned the kiss with fervor.

They didn't speak for a whole, glorious hour.

CHAPTER TWENTY-SIX

The next night, Colleen paced back and forth in the candy shop, every muscle in her body flooded with heat and adrenaline. Sparks fell from her finger tips and fizzed out before hitting the ground.

The black vans were out again, and while Colleen managed to stop one group from rounding up citizens last night, another group had been successful. Over a dozen people had been taken to the precinct last night, for no other reason than the fact that Fahrenheit had saved them. One of the taken hadn't come home yet and no one knew why, though Colleen could guess. If they'd exhibited any kind of powers, or too much sympathy toward Fahrenheit, that would be enough for the agents to hold them longer.

Word spread fast in the neighborhood, and tonight a lot of residents were too scared to be out of their houses, afraid that just by showing their faces they'd be dragged downtown. And while Colleen wanted to burst with fury at what was happening, she was also terrified of The Bulwark agents.

I barely escaped the last time I faced down some of them, and that was with Karen's help. It's just me now.

Shame welled up and Colleen ran a hand over her face to try and wipe it away. She'd never backed down from helping the people here, until now.

The air took on a sudden chill and Colleen formed a fireball in the palm of her hand, pivoting around to see her brother standing at the back of the store, his face glistening with frost.

"It's dangerous out there right now, you should be hiding," he said.

"You should be, too."

"Yeah well, I'm a sucker for clandestine meetings."

Colleen couldn't help a snort that turned into a buried sob.

"Why did you do it?"

It wasn't the question at the top of her mind, she didn't even know she was going to ask it until the words were out of her mouth, then Colleen realized it was the only question she wanted the answer to.

Andrew let out a heavy breath that puffed into a small cloud in front of him.

"It's complicated."

"No, it really isn't. You killed a man in cold blood, why?"

"It doesn't matter now."

She took a step toward him, jaw dropping.

"Of course it matters! What you did was—"

"Monstrous? The act of a terrible person?"

"Not you."

"Oh, really? Do you have any idea what I've done to stay alive, to earn this chance at freedom? How do you know that they didn't turn me into the kind of man who wouldn't blink at slaughtering someone like that? How do you know anything about me anymore?"

It was a fair question, one that she'd honestly asked herself many times. But when she was tempted to give in and admit that her brother had become something unrecognizable, Colleen would remember that he still loved her and Tina. There was something still there, buried under all the ice he put around his heart.

"I just do," she answered. "I believe you're still the man I knew, somewhere in there. And that's why I can't understand why in the hell you'd do that!"

Andrew's gaze flicked up, cold and hard as an ice berg.

"You, that's why."

"Me?"

"That warehouse you knocked over, the officers you hurt? That had consequences, and one of them is that my boss got twitchy. He figured out we had a mole feeding information to a cop. Just so happens that one of our informants in the precinct pointed the finger at Walter and the rest is history."

The guilt already swirling in her gut grew, threatening to spill over into her throat. She swallowed it down and concentrated on the fire in her veins, the people she'd helped.

"Don't try to pass off what you did onto me," she finally said. "You had a choice."

"No I—"

"Yes, you did! You could have reached out to me, you could've asked us for help. But instead, you think you have to do this all by yourself."

"I was doing just fine until the two of you decided to finally step up. Too little too late, by the way."

"Oh yeah, you've got this great plan! You want to force me to leave. And not just me, Tina as well. You're being an asshole. And it's a stupid plan, by the way."

"Why? Because it didn't come from you?"

"No, because there's no way in hell we could abandon this place, or you!"

They stared at each other, chests heaving in anger. Finally, Andrew looked away, his bottom lip out just a little as he stewed. The sight made Colleen have to bite back a sudden smile. Her brother needed to admit responsibility for what he'd done, but he was also in a terrible mess that he couldn't get out of on his own.

He needs my help. And he's going to get it whether he wants it or not.

She walked up to him and bumped his hip with hers. He shoved her back, not hard but enough to move her a little.

"I didn't want to kill him," Andrew whispered after a beat. "I really didn't, Col."

She nodded, relief flooding her, though she didn't show it.

"Okay, I believe you but…Andrew, you're not alone. Please let me help you."

He let out a long exhale through his nose.

"You're not going to stop."

"Nope."

He exhaled again and nodded.

"I'm the mole."

She almost choked, eyes wide and jaw dropping.

"I told you at the beginning," Andrew continued, "there is a lot more going on than you know. I had everything under control, I had a plan and you just couldn't leave well enough alone."

"I put you in danger."

"Sure as shit did."

"I'm sorry."

"I had a hard choice to make," he whispered, voice heavy. "I didn't want to kill Walter, he was a good man and an important part of my plan. But, it was that or the whole thing falls apart and I couldn't let that happen."

"So, what now? Tell me how to help you. We want the same things."

Andrew chuckled, a sad, empty sound.

"We do, but you can't help me Col. I made a deal with the devil, and I can't get out of it yet."

"Jason James?"

He took a step back at the name, eyes wide in shock. "How—?"

"Long story and I don't have proof that would stand up in court, but I know it's him."

"Not him specifically but the men under him, yeah. They won't let me go, not until I'm dead or I bring them down. So you see, I've got to play the long game, even if that means killing a man like Walter."

Colleen's mind chewed Andrew's words. She couldn't stand by and let her brother be a prisoner like this, not while breath was left in her body. There had to be something she could do.

And then it hit her.

"What if they thought you were dead?"

His eyes slid to her, narrow and suspicious.

"Hear me out," she said. "If we could make them think you'd died in a fight or in some kind of public way, then we could go away for a while, hide and come back when the heat had passed."

"We?"

"You really think I'm going to let you go by yourself? I...I owe you after Lumis."

"No Col, you don't."

His hand closed over hers, cold as ice against her heat infused skin.

"I want to help you, even if you don't think I owe you. Please, Andrew."

"And sacrifice High Tide, our home, to Von?"

She sighed through her nose, knowing he was right. Neither of them could leave while their home was threatened.

But what if we could kill two birds with one stone?

She grinned at him as beautiful plan took form, opening her mouth to spill it out like so much golden treasure when they both heard the back door open and close.

Andrew's gaze swung behind him and back to her.

"Did you get me here to trap me?"

She frowned.

"You dropped off the comic at my apartment."

The air went from chilled to positively freezing in an instant and Colleen pushed more heat into her body, sparks falling from her skin to sizzle into steam around her as they both realized that someone had lured them to the shop.

"No killing," she whispered.

Andrew snorted.

"Sure thing, sis."

"I'm serious."

"Fine."

They stood back to back, with Andrew facing the back and Colleen the front. She wondered if The Bulwark had somehow figured out their signal, if they were surrounding the building as she stood there, waiting like some prey caught in a trap.

"Metro City police, hands up!" said a male voice from the back of the store.

Andrew shot a blast of ice from his hands as a gun shot went off, breaking one of the glass candy containers to her right.

The front door of the shop burst open and, in the doorway, stood a painfully familiar figure.

"Hands up, now!" Shay screamed, gun leveled at Colleen.

She froze mid toss of a fireball, Shay's eyes widening as she took in the scene of Fahrenheit standing back to back with the ice wielding vigilante that had murdered her partner.

Colleen saw the moment this betrayal snapped into place for Shay, and cringed.

"Officer, please stop. It's not what you think!"

"Extinguish the fire now!"

"Enough of this," Andrew said, flooding Shay in white.

"No!" Colleen screamed, jumping in front of her brother's blast.

Shay fell to the ice covered floor, shivering as Colleen stood there, water dripping off of her.

"I was just going to stun her," Andrew spat, a squeal of tires punctuated his words and they both looked up to see a black van careening toward the shop. "Time to go."

He pulled on her arm, but Colleen wouldn't budge, her heart squeezing in her chest as she looked down into Shay's bitter gaze.

"I'm sorry," Colleen whispered, taking off after her brother.

Men began to pour out of the van as Colleen and Andrew bolted from the building. Shouts chased them as they ran down the street, dodging the bullets so carelessly shot at them.

Andrew pulled her down a side alley. There was a chain link fence at the end and Colleen blasted a hole through it with her heat. Andrew pulled her to the right and around a corner. They flattened themselves against the building, straining to hear the men pursuing them.

"We should split up," Andrew said.

"Alright, but we're not finished."

He didn't answer, just pressed her hand with his and ran down the street, white flurries in his wake.

I hope to god he's able to get away.

Shouts behind her made Colleen's blood run cold and she took off in the opposite direction of her brother.

CHAPTER TWENTY-SEVEN

T he blanket was soft around Shay's shoulders, the layer of frost slowly thawing from her body.

Everyone else is sweating but Fisk and I are still freezing an hour later…that man is far too powerful to be left loose.

"So, what the hell happened?" Ward asked Fisk, who was also attempting to defrost next to her.

Shay continued to shiver, remembering how they laid on the floor of the candy shop for a good half an hour as the agents pursued the vigilantes. Fisk had been frozen far more than Shay had thanks to Fahrenheit's intervention but it was still terrifying to be unable to move, left at the mercy of the ice powered vigilante if he returned.

She closed her eyes at the memory, shaking her head as she tried to make sense of it all. Wasn't Fahrenheit one of Walter's informants? Was she oblivious to the fact that the ice vigilante had killed Walter or were they working together to bring her partner down?

"Someone speak up, damn it!" Ward slammed his fist down on the meeting room table.

"What were you…doing there?" Shay asked through chattering teeth. "I thought our plan…was stupid."

Fisk cleared his throat next to her and cast a sheepish glance her way. Shay swore and wished she had the ability to punch him in his too perfect face.

"I didn't think it was good intel, there's a difference," Ward snapped. "But your partner over there signaled us when the terrorists showed up."

"So, that's why we waited so long to go in," Shay said, glaring at Fisk.

"I'm sorry R-Reynolds," Fisk said. "I thought...I thought it would work."

"By keeping me...in the dark?"

"You two can have your little lovers' spat another time," Ward said. "These two are smart and resourceful. We need a better trap. Especially since our civilian bait went underground somehow tonight."

"We did bring in four," said one agent from across the table.

"Oh four, well that solves everything! Anyone else have any other brilliant insights?"

Everyone ducked their head except for Shay who was in no mood to play humble. The man was worse than Chris ever was, and that was saying something.

"Well Reynolds, you're the only one who has the guts to look me in the eye after this fiasco," Ward continued, much to Shay's dismay. "Do you have anything of substance to add?"

Pure, unbridled defiance sprang loose inside of her and she raised her chin.

"Yes."

"Oh really? Well, out with it."

Damn, it! I don't, not really.

Her mind rifled through information and memories, tossing aside everything that came up. She was just about to admit defeat, when it hit her.

"Well, there's a big event in two days…in High Tide. The woman Von has been fighting with, she's having a theater opening. Von might show and—"

"And so will his lapdog. Well, I guess sometimes people like you can show surprising intelligence."

What the hell?!

She opened her mouth to lay into the man when Fisk's hand clamped down around her wrist. Shay's gaze swung over to him, burning hot and he shook his head. She could almost hear him say it: Ward wasn't worth it.

How the hell would you know, pretty boy?

But she bit her tongue just the same and sat back in her chair while Ward indulged himself in planning a raid on the theater opening.

It didn't occur to Shay until Ward was handing out assignments that she'd just sabotaged the most important night of the year for Colleen's mom.

Damn, she's going to kill me, especially if I have to cancel our date.

"Sir, this event is very exclusive," one of the agents said. "I'm not sure we can even get inside."

Shay saw her chance and raised her hand.

"I can, my friend invited me so I'm already going to be in there," she said.

"Fine. Reynolds, you're our inside eyes as far as guests go. Fisk, you pick six others and infiltrate the catering staff."

"Uh, that's going to be hard, sir."

Wards narrow eyed gaze swung to Shay, who just barely resisted the urge to shrink.

"And why is that?"

"Because Tina Knight is only hiring from within the community. Your men will stick out like sore thumbs."

Ward hissed out a stream of swear words.

"We'll figure something out, sir," Fisk said, once the tirade had stopped.

"Damn right you will!"

Ward continued planning the raid, Shay half listening as her thoughts were carried back to the candy shop and the sight of Fahrenheit chummy with the ice powered vigilante.

Why? Why was she there, why was she talking with him instead of bringing him to justice?

Only one answer made sense and for some reason it hit Shay right in the face: Fahrenheit was working with the man that killed Walter.

"We can't thank you enough for this, Mrs. Knight," said the older man, his face haggard with fatigue and worry.

"Of course, I'm happy to help you and anyone else, make sure you spread the word," Tina said, ignoring the headache throbbing behind her eyes.

"I sure will."

She gave him a smile as one of her bodyguards escorted him and his family into one of her cars. The moment they drove away, Tina slumped against the door jam and rubbed her temples.

"How many is that?" she asked Rick.

"Twenty-five tonight," he said, "but I think we'll have more tomorrow."

She sighed and walked into the living room, plopping down on the couch the moment she was near it. Rick thrust a glass of bourbon into her hand and sat next to her. For a while they were silent, her head on his shoulder. Tina wanted to rest, to let her mind unwind, but it was like a dog with a bone when it came to solving problems. Especially ones as big as this.

Her phone rang off the hook all day with people terrified of being taken to the station. Tina organized her meager forces into action just before sun down and gathered as many as she could into her townhouse and one of her spare homes. Knowing it was all she could do was frustrating at best, and now her mind tried to come up with a better solution even as sleep began to drag at her consciousness.

A hard knock at the door had Tina launch upright, mind alert for any new threat.

Rick swore under his breath and got up to answer it. When the door opened, and she heard Colleen's voice, Tina's heart gave a jagged beat in her chest.

Something's wrong, I can tell by the tone of her voice. And if she's coming to me...

"What happened?" she asked.

Colleen made sure the drapes were closed and tore off her mask, pacing as it dangled from her fingers.

"I saw Andrew tonight," she said, proceeding to launch into a recount of her conversation with her brother.

With each word, hope began to bloom in Tina's chest, even as her mind attempted to temper it.

"He can be saved, he just needs help," Colleen finished. "And I have an idea how to make that happen."

"I'm all ears," Tina said.

Colleen hesitated.

"I'm not sure you're going to like it."

"Why don't you say it and let me decide that for myself?"

"Alright then. I think we can both agree that the opening of the theater is a prime target for Von to hit. It's public and would make for a spectacle in his favor. It would also be a very public way for Andrew to appear to die."

The words hung in the air as Tina stared at her daughter. Since the fire at the tenement, this very thing had been spinning in the back of her mind. The idea that what she'd dreamed of for so long could be the answer to ending all this - if only she was willing to sacrifice it. She'd hoped it wouldn't come to this but after tonight, seeing the faces of the innocent people who were being terrorized for no other reason than knowing her daughter and knowing that there was a real way she could save her son, Tina knew it was time to put the dream on the pyre, and light it up.

My baby and my home, needs me.

"Alright," she said, her voice rough.

Colleen stared as if she couldn't quite believe what she was hearing. When Tina didn't say anything else, Colleen leaned forward, brow furrowed.

"Did you just agree with me about this?"

"Yes."

"Okay, maybe I'm more tired than I thought—"

"He's my son," Tina said, "and he needs my help. You're right about the theater opening. I am holding on to it, because…well the reason doesn't matter. But what does it serve if I have that place but you and Andrew aren't here to enjoy it with me?"

Colleen gaped at her mother and Tina exhaled in frustration.

"Really Colleen, is it so hard to believe that I would do this?"

"I-I'm sorry it's just…thank you."

That Colleen was truly this surprised hit Tina like a bullet in the heart. She turned away, not willing to show the pain in her eyes.

"You're welcome," she managed. "Now, I'm tired, can we plan this out tomorrow?"

"Of course, yes."

"It's dangerous out there for you, why don't you stay here for the night? There are some clothes in the guest room."

Colleen hesitated and Tina could see her daughter's mind working behind her eyes.

Searching for an alternative motive likely.

"Alright," Colleen finally said.

Tina was too emotional to trust her voice so she just nodded and followed Rick up the stairs.

Without a word, she pulled him into her room and laid her head on his chest when the door closed, leaning her weight onto him. His strong hands ran up and down her back, his broad body warm and firm as she pressed into him.

"What you did tonight," he pressed a kiss to the top of her head, "you're an amazing woman Tina Knight."

She wanted to argue with him, and she also wanted to agree but no words came to her. The last few weeks had seen her oldest friendship go up in smoke, the near loss of her life, her neighborhood terrorized by the police and federal agents, and now the sacrifice of her precious theater to save her son.

"I'm so tired," she murmured.

Rick scooped her up, pulled the covers back and laid her with exquisite gentleness on the bed. His lips were achingly soft when he pressed them to hers just before turning to go.

"Stay, please?" she asked.

"You sure?"

Tina nodded.

When Rick slid into bed behind her, his arm circling around her, Tina finally let a few of her tears run, quiet and hot down her face. Tears for the men and women she'd seen tonight. Tears for her broken family. And tears for the dream she was going to smash to pieces.

Tina thought sleep would come swift and blissfully oblivious. Instead, she lay there with Colleen's words dancing in her mind. The possibility that she could save Andrew and have him with her was too wonderful to be shoved aside easily.

After an hour, she realized that there was no use just lying there, letting her mind run away with her when there was work to be done. She slipped out of bed, careful to not wake Rick and crept downstairs.

She was just about to open the door to her office, when a low light from the kitchen caught her eye. Cursing herself for not bringing her revolver with her, Tina crept down the hallway, peeking around the corner to get a look at the intruder.

Colleen's face came into view, the light of the fridge illuminating the bags under eyes and Tina let out a breath of relief.

"I thought you'd be in bed," she said.

Her daughter jumped, fire forming in her palm. When she saw it was Tina, she closed her fingers over the flames and extinguished them.

"I'm hungry and…I couldn't sleep."

Tina sighed and walked into the kitchen. Without another word, she and Colleen took out cold cuts, cheese and bread to make sandwiches. They worked in silence until they sat down at the small kitchen table with their midnight snack.

"Why aren't you asleep?" Colleen said around a mouthful of roast beef.

Tina chewed slowly, thinking about her response. She understood why Colleen doubted her all the time, and couldn't really blame her no matter how much it hurt.

But in this moment, she wanted her daughter to hear what was truly in her heart.

"I want our family back," she whispered, surprised at the emotion seeping through every syllable. "I thought...I thought I could have that by providing respectability, by making our name stand for something better than what your Grandfather made it. But I know that's not the path forward anymore. I have to change the plan if I'm going to save Andrew, if I'm going to give you a real chance at a life you deserve. And, because I'm used to being in control, my mind won't let me rest until I've figured out the new plan."

Colleen chewed the last of her sandwich, two little wrinkles appearing between her eye brows as she sat thinking. Tina took a sip of her milk and waited, out-wardly showing no sign of the nerves dive bombing in her stomach.

"Thank you, for doing this," Colleen said. "I know I should be more understanding about you and your life but...I'm still angry at you about all of it. You didn't do anything to protect us against Grandfather. You just let him, and then you stepped right into his shoes when he died, plotting and making deals that are part of why we're in this mess. You're doing the right thing now but I can't help wondering what your secret angle is, how it's going to benefit you in the end. And it makes me nervous."

Each word was like a knife straight at Tina's heart. She didn't begrudge Colleen her anger or hurt, hell she shared a great deal of it when it came to her own mother, god rest her. But after what she'd gone through, Tina had a different perspective on her mother and why she had done what she had.

I had hope that one day Colleen might be able to see the same thing but I don't think she ever will. Because unlike me, she held onto her moral compass.

"You were always stronger than me," Tina said, the words surprising her almost as much as they did Colleen. "You resisted your grandfather's influence, found a way to protect yourself. I never could and...it cost me so damn much."

She closed her eyes as her husband's face floated to the surface of her memories, so young and handsome, so gentle. He'd trusted her, had made the sacrifice a parent should in order to protect Andrew and Colleen. And what had she done with it?

I made the deal with my father to keep them all safe, but only really managed to make it easier on myself. No more. It's time I paid up. The only question is, what is the price going to be?

"Tina," Colleen said, interrupting her thoughts, "you should know that Andrew might resist this. He believes that he can't be free from Von. We might have to...force it a bit."

Tina stared at her daughter as the words sunk in. This wasn't what she needed right now.

"You're telling me that your brother didn't agree to anything?"

"He would have if we hadn't been interrupted by the cops, I'm sure of it!"

Tina sprang up from the table, and turned away. She had a solution to this, but it wasn't a good one and she didn't want Colleen to see that truth written all over her face.

Andrew trusts her, it seems, and probably doesn't trust me. I can use that but damned if it doesn't hurt like hell.

"What's wrong?" Colleen asked.

"I'm just surprised, that's all," Tina said, stifling the instinct that told her to be honest with Colleen. "This will make it all very difficult."

"I know but…trust me, he wants to get out of all this, I could see it."

Tina nodded.

"Why don't you go to bed, I'll be up for a few more hours, adjusting a few things for the opening now that we're doing this."

Colleen hesitated, and Tina could feel her gaze searching for what was really going on. She turned and gave her daughter a tired grin, hoping it was enough.

"Alright," Colleen finally said, her voice hesitant, "but don't think you have to do everything. I'm here, too."

She nodded.

"Of course."

Tina went to her office and shut the door. As she paced the room, the pieces of the plan she needed started falling in front of her and Tina's heart sped up at the sight of them. She scribbled notes, people to call, and arrangements to be made. As she did, other things popped up, and before she knew it, the way forward appeared before her, clear as day and ten times more frightening than anything Tina had attempted before. She wracked her brain, trying to find another way, but she knew there wasn't.

She poured herself a drink with shaking hands and downed it in one go.

It doesn't feel fair, but I know it is. This is the price I need to pay, the price of their freedom from me, from the whole damn thing.

It took the rest of the night to write the letters to Andrew, Colleen, and Rick. When she was finished, the birds outside her window started their early morning song in spite of how dark it still was, and though Tina still felt afraid, she also felt peaceful.

This was right. This would work.

And that was all that mattered.

CHAPTER TWENTY-EIGHT

The next two days passed in a haze of worry and nerves for Colleen. The plan seemed simple enough, but something about the way Tina avoided some of the specifics with excuses about last minute adjustments, made Colleen nervous, to say the least.

The Sweet Spot had become too dangerous to meet, so Colleen had left a note for Andrew instead, using the code they'd created as children to send secret messages to one another. She'd kept it simple, asking him to be at the theater opening, that she had found a way to get him out of all this. Whether or not he got the message, or would do as she asked, was up in the air, and it did nothing to calm her nerves as the night of the theater opening approached.

To distract herself, Colleen went over the plan again and again.

When Andrew showed up, she, as Fahrenheit, would pick a fight, cause panic and make everyone leave. Then she and Andrew would move the fight to the theater where they would pretend to kill each other, out of sight, and set the place on fire. Tina had procured two cadavers that would be Colleen and Andrew's body doubles once the fire was out. Colleen had no interest in knowing how her mother had gotten the bodies, and thankfully Tina hadn't offered.

They would escape through the bootleg tunnels and to safety where Colleen would say goodbye to her brother and Tina but remain in High Tide to watch over the place. By leaving Fahrenheit behind, The Bulwark wouldn't have a reason to stay.

That was the part Colleen wasn't at all sure about. Would Von really fold after this? Was it a big enough hit to his resources to lose Andrew? And would she be able to do anything to keep her home safe as Colleen instead of Fahrenheit?

A knock on her apartment door made her heart leap. The last two nights, she and Shay had spent every moment together, curled up in one another's arms, acting as if the entire world outside wasn't pulling itself apart. It had been selfish, indulgent and Colleen had savored every moment of it.

But now she had to try and convince Shay not to come to the opening tomorrow night while not revealing why and not hurting the feelings of the woman that had come to mean the world to her.

"I come bearing pizza," Shay said, when Colleen opened the door.

The smell of pepperoni and sausage made her mouth water.

Hard conversations are best on a full stomach, right?
With a couple of pilfered bottles of beer from the bar and chipped plates, the two of them sat on a worn rug and chatted about clothes, music, everything but Shay's job and Colleen's family.

But when the pizza box was empty, and the beer bottles rinsed, there really wasn't any reason left to avoid what had to be said. Colleen took a deep breath, and her stomach flipped.

I need a minute…just a minute to get my words straight.

"I need a minute in the bathroom," Colleen said, rushing toward the room and closing the door.

She turned on the faucet, letting the cold water run over her fingers, concentrating on the feel of it against her hot skin.

"Hey, did I leave my watch here last night?" Shay asked from the other side of the door.

"Uh…I don't know, check the bed side table."

Colleen threw some water on her face as she pulled herself together and then gasped in panic.

The bedside table! No…no, that's where I put Walter's key!

"Wait, don't look in the drawer!"

She threw open the door, face dripping with water and saw Shay standing there, Walter's chain, with the key on the end, dangling from her fingers.

For several seconds, Colleen couldn't speak. She could only stare at Shay's stricken expression.

"What are you doing with this?" she whispered.

"I…I can explain…I…Oh my god, I think I'm gonna be sick."

Shay's eyes snapped up to hers, fury boiling in their dark depths.

"Why do you have this, Colleen?"

The vigilante opened her mouth but no sound came out. This wasn't how tonight was supposed to go, Shay wasn't even supposed to find out she was Fahrenheit!

"Well?" Shay asked, walking slowly toward her. "Why?!"

"I…I'm…"

And then Shay stopped, eyes widening in horror.

"No, that's not possible," she said. "You're…you're Fahrenheit?"

Colleen couldn't speak, so she just nodded and created some fire in the palm of her hand. Shay stared at the dancing flames, tears forming in her eyes.

"Why didn't you tell me? Did you…did you help kill Walter?"

"No," she closed her hand over the heat. "I was working with him. I was there when it…he gave that to me to give to you."

"Then, why didn't you?"

"Because I couldn't figure out a way to do it without revealing who I was."

"You were afraid," Shay spat the last word out, tears falling down her face.

"Of course I was afraid! I didn't want to lose you, and I didn't want to be locked up."

"I wouldn't have locked you up!"

"And how was I supposed to know that?"

"Because you know me! You know that I have feelings for you, you know that I'm not a monster. And you also know how hard this has been, not understanding what happened, not having answers. But instead of having the guts to come clean and help me, you kept all of this from me!"

"I was trying to protect you!" Colleen cried. "Walter told me to protect you and I knew that the moment I gave that to you it would be all you could see. You'd rush out and put yourself in danger and I couldn't let you do that."

"Let me? You don't get a say in my life, in what I do or don't do, Colleen!"

"I'm not trying to control you, I'm afraid for you."

"And for yourself! You can make it about me, but you were really trying to protect you."

The words hit Colleen like a physical blow and she stumbled back.

"And the man that murdered Walter," Shay continued. "I saw the way you were with him the other night. You know him, you're on his side."

"He's my brother, of course I'm on his side! But that doesn't mean I agree with what he did."

Shay's jaw dropped.

"Your brother?"

"Yes, he was also one of Walter's informants but things went wrong, Andrew was about to be found out so he…he…"

"He killed my partner to save his own skin."

Colleen closed her eyes as the full impact of this fight started rolling over her. Shay had every right to be angry, but she wasn't even trying to understand where Colleen was coming from, that there was more than one side to this.

I have to try and make her understand, I can't lose her!

When Colleen opened her eyes, tears dropped from her lashes and she saw Shay walking to the door.

"No, wait, please don't go! Not like this."

Colleen ran to stop her but when she grabbed Shay's arm, the cop pulled herself out of Colleen's grasp.

"Don't touch me!"

"Please Shay, please let's talk a little more. I know we can work this out if you just let me explain."

Behind the fury in her eyes was grief and hurt, which oddly gave Colleen hope. If Shay truly hated her, she would only have hate in her eyes.

"After what we've shared, after how open I've been with you? How could you not trust me?" Shay said, her voice breaking.

It was a very good question and Colleen didn't have a good explanation for it. She opened her mouth to try but nothing came out.

"Goodbye, Colleen."

At first, Shay walked out of the apartment, slow and sluggish as if her limbs were fighting with her to move. But then, as Colleen watched, the cops back straightened and she bolted down the stairs, slamming the door at the bottom. The second she was gone, Colleen crumpled to the floor and sobbed.

CHAPTER TWENTY-NINE

S hay smoothed her hands over the short, dark green dress she bought for the opening of The Torch and Grier. When she'd first tried it on all she could think about was Colleen's reaction to seeing her in it, how she'd take it off of her later that night. Now, her mind was preoccupied with how Colleen would look at her when she showed up with Bulwark agents to arrest Fahrenheit.

To arrest Colleen. I'm helping these idiots take her down tonight…

She closed her eyes and tried to push away the nausea and headache that had plagued her since this morning.

After she left Colleen's last night, Shay didn't sleep a wink. Every time she closed her eyes, the only thing she could think about were all the times Colleen could have told her that she was Fahrenheit. Each time stung more and more until Shay felt like her whole body was one big bruise. When she could finally stop picturing every interaction with the woman she cared for, her mind jumped to all the questions Shay had no answers for.

Was it all fake, a way to get information?

Was she ever really on Walter's side or just playing him to protect her brother?

Would Colleen have ever told her the truth, or would she have simply dropped Shay when it all got to be too hard?

The web of questions was a torture Shay couldn't escape, not even now, awaiting her final briefing with The Bulwark before heading out for the opening.

The plan was fairly simple but Shay ran through it in her mind anyway, hoping to focus her energy where it needed to be: on the job, not on her girlfriend.

Ex…I think. Ugh! Alright, the plan…think of the plan.

After getting inside, she was to wait half an hour, so that enough people arrived to obscure a dozen unknown faces. She'd excuse herself to go to the restroom, but head to the stage door and let the agents inside. Then it was a matter of waiting for Sub Zero and Fahrenheit to show up, at which time, Shay was supposed to sneak out and let the agents do their job.

She looked over at the men talking a few feet away, their faces beaming. Excitement was palpable in the air as the Bulwark agents prepared to infiltrate the most prestigious event High Tide had seen in decades. The handpicked men were dressed in tuxedos that were specially designed to hide their protective vests and special guns, which were loaded with some kind of thick green solution in the darts.

Instead of starting the operation at the precinct, Agent Ward had secured an abandoned bakery one block away from the theater to act as a staging area. The agents not infiltrating the theater were on standby in case something went wrong, all of them pacing like caged animals in their tactical gear.

Why do I get the impression that they're all hoping it does go wrong?

The thought brought bile to the back of her throat as she realized just who would be squarely in the cross hairs of everything tonight and she rushed outside. The fresh air, though hot as hell, did help abate the temptation to puke up what little she had eaten today. Shay closed her eyes and took deep breaths to steady herself, trying to focus on the task at hand. But Colleen's face kept appearing and she ended up worrying about her safety.

There's no way to think about any of this without thinking of her, she's one of the damn targets!

And that, right there, was the major problem. Despite the lies, and the questions Shay still had, she didn't believe that Fahrenheit was the same kind of threat that Sub Zero was. Even if she hadn't known who was behind the mask, Shay wasn't sure she could justify taking the fire powered vigilante down with the ice wielding one.

But…what if I don't? What if I warn her, so she has time to escape.

Shay snorted.

She's been trying to protect her brother this whole time. Do I really think she's just going to walk out and let us have him?

Colleen's face swam up in her mind, clear and beautiful. So many memories in such a short amount of time, and not one of them gave Shay a reason to put her in the hands of someone like Agent Ward.

"I have to try," she whispered to herself. "I can't do nothing. Maybe…maybe I can use her feelings for me to…"

She cringed at the thought of manipulating Colleen like that, even as she clung to it as an option. Her feelings for the vigilante were stronger than Shay had thought if she was willing to go to such lengths to save her.

That realization did nothing to comfort her as she walked back into the room of abandoned bakery. On the contrary, it made everything ten times harder.

"Alright everyone, listen up!" Agent Ward said, a gleam of excitement in his eyes. "Our job isn't the safest, or the easiest, you all know that. But we are the only ones standing between the innocent people of this country and those who would destroy our way of life. You've all seen what these terrorists are capable of, some of you have lost loved ones to them."

Ward looked squarely at Shay, who hated him a little bit more for using her grief like this.

"So don't give them an inch! There will be collateral damage, but try to minimize it. And, whatever you do, don't let them escape! Good luck."

Shay grit her teeth and turned away, wishing she had a different place to wait for her time to arrive when Agent Ward walked up to her and held out a small gun to her.

"What's this for? I thought I was going in unarmed."

"I'm taking no chances," he answered. "It's loaded with one dart that will remove their powers. If you come in contact with one of them before we get in there, use it and stash the body."

She swallowed.

"It kills them?"

"No, but it will de-power and knock them out. Good luck, Officer."

And with that, he walked away, leaving Shay with a new possibility open to her.

If I shoot Colleen with this, I can get her out of there before anything happens. I can save her.

She stuffed it into her small handbag, and for the first time all day, Shay felt like she had a clear way forward.

The moment Andrew stepped into Mr. Price's study, he knew something was wrong.

Metal Maiden was loading up a bandolier with knives, half a dozen gunman were checking their weapons and Mr. Price was wearing a wide grin that looked ghoulish at best.

"You wanted to see me?" Andrew asked, eyes scanning the room.

"Yes, I have wonderful news. Tonight, you will get your inheritance."

Andrew's heart gave a hard lurch in his chest and he couldn't hide it.

"What?"

"I wanted it to be a surprise," the odious man continued. "Tonight is the opening of your mother's theater, and there will be no better time to kill her and capture your sister. The confused and terrified civilians will create the perfect chaos for you to get to both of them. And, we will destroy Tina's precious project in the process."

"Capturing Colleen was never part of the deal," Andrew's voice was hard, his hands clenching into frost covered fists.

"I thought you might want her by your side, after all you two are very close, aren't you?"

The sharpness of Mr. Price's tone wasn't lost on him. As he looked into his eyes, Andrew could see that Mr. Price knew far more than he had let on.

He knows I've been seeing her, knows that I never wanted them gone. This is his final test of loyalty and if I balk he'll have his psycho lap dog stab me in the back.

"She'll never agree," he said, trying desperately to find a way around this. "She will force us to destroy her and I doubt that's what the Big Boss wants."

Mr. Price's face tensed in spite of the smile that remained.

"I'm getting the impression that you aren't fully on board with things. Don't you want High Tide? Don't you want what is yours?"

Andrew's mind reeled as he floundered about for what to do next. There was no good option, no way out of this. He had to go along with it and look for an opportunity to save his sister and mother.

"Very well," Andrew said. "I'll make sure Colleen—"

"No," Mr. Price interrupted, "I want you to deal with your mother. Far be it for me to deny you such a final catharsis as destroying the woman who never appreciated you and killed your grandfather. Leave your sister to Metal Maiden."

Panic began to worm its way up Andrew's spine, but he clamped down on it, even as Metal Maiden's eyes shone behind her mask.

"I'll be gentle, I promise," she whispered.

Mr. Price chuckled.

"I certainly hope not, my dear. But, do leave enough of her alive for us to use. A power like hers doesn't come around very often."

That's all we are to them, our powers. We aren't people. I made my bed, I've got to live with that, but I won't let Colleen suffer like me.

He met Metal Maiden's stare and leveled a cold grin at her.

Between Colleen and me, we should be able to take this bitch out. And maybe...maybe Colleen's plan, whatever it is, will actually work. Maybe after tonight, we can all be free of this.

CHAPTER
THIRTY

T ina's hands shook as she took the envelope out of
her silver clutch. This was it, the end of the road
she'd paved with blood, tears and broken promises. She
thought she could make it all worth it, that she knew
how to rebuild everything. But the truth was like a piece
of jagged glass in her heart. The theater opening, going
straight, none of it was never going to make it all better.

But this will. It has to.

"You wanted to see me?" Rick said, walking into her
office.

She met his warm eyes and saw the love he had for her
shining out of them. It used to make her feel cherished,
special. Now it was like someone was twisting a knife
in her heart.

*So much wasted time. I could've…no, stop it! You're
stronger than this, don't let what-if's distract you.*

She walked from behind her desk, her black and silver sequined dress swishing with each step. Rick's eyes
flicked down her body, taking in the way the dress
hugged her curves. The envelope felt heavy in her hand
and she clutched it tight to keep from abandoning this
whole thing.

"You look nice," she said. "A tuxedo suits you."

"Just trying to look like I belong next to you," he replied, his voice heavy with desire.

"You've always belonged next to me."

The words shocked them both, it hadn't been what she planned on saying at all. But when they were out of her mouth, Tina realized that it was very true. Rick was her perfect match, the one who saw her and still loved her. It was a cruel irony to accept it tonight of all nights, when she had to let go of everything. But maybe, that's what she deserved.

"I need your help," she said.

"Anything."

"This won't be easy for you. In fact, I think you might hate me for it."

"Never. I could never hate you."

She gave him a sad smile and nodded.

"Even so, this is…"

He curled his fingers around her free hand and pressed.

"Ask me. I'm yours."

Tina looked up, their faces so close that she could see every scar he'd taken on her behalf, the flecks of gold in his light brown eyes. She wanted to kiss him, to let him lay her on the desk and take away all the fear and anguish that plagued her. But she had to be strong. They'd had many nights together, and though it didn't feel like they'd spent nearly enough time exploring one another's bodies and souls, at least it was something. Tina stepped away, putting some much needed distance between them, and handed Rick the envelope.

"These are instructions for later tonight," she said, schooling her voice and face into a very well practice hardness. "Colleen thinks that she's staying here to protect High Tide, That because no one knows she's

Fahrenheit, she can remain and watch over things. But Mr. Price is determined to have her, and this ruse won't keep her safe from him if she stays. So, when everything happens, I need you to get Colleen and Andrew out through the prohibition tunnels. There's a trap door in the large broom closet, that's the entrance, the key is in the envelope. It will let out in Rachel's root cellar. She will have keys to a car for you. She also has a small safe of mine that has money in it, the combination is written down. It will be enough to get you to the address written on the outside of one of the letters in that packet. There are also letters written for you and my children."

Rick looked from the thick envelope in his hand to her, a deep frown etched onto his face.

"Tina, what is this? What's going on?"

"I need you to swear to me, on the love you have for me, that you will take Andrew and Colleen and you will do everything I just said. And, afterward, everything that is laid out in there."

He studied her, eyes narrowed. Tina could see the exact moment when Rick figured out what was going to happen tonight.

"No," he said, moving to her. "You can't...I won't let this happen."

"You have to. Listen to me, please," she cupped his cheek, stopping his head from shaking. "You are the only one I can trust to get them to safety. I know what I'm asking of you and...I'm so sorry Rick. Truly. I just don't see another way."

"But why?" his voice broke on the words, twisting that pain in Tina's chest.

"Think about it. I'm the one Price wants, the one that is the true lynch pin of all this. If I'm gone, if I'm taken out of the equation and in the process Andrew and Colleen are spirited away, then everything is fixed.

Price will think they died, or if he doesn't, he'll have High Tide and that will be enough. They will be free to do whatever they want with their lives."

"Come with us. I'll go get them right now and we can leave, please don't make me do this!"

"Rick, stop. You know I'm right. If I run, and Mr. Price thinks the children are alive, we will never be safe. It has to be this way."

"I can't let you die," he broke then, his face crumbling.

"Yes, you can, because I need you to do this for me. Please?"

She let the fear and desperation seep into that last word, let all of the vulnerability that she'd hidden for decades spring free knowing that Rick would never be able to deny her anything once he heard it.

His jaw tightened under her hand, tears slid hot down his cheeks and she wiped one away with her thumb.

"I promise," his whisper was jagged.

Before she could thank him, Rick turned and practically ran from the room leaving Tina alone with what was before her.

As she stepped out of the taxi in front of the theater, garment bag awkward in her arms, Colleen sniffled and wiped an errant tear off her cheek. Since Shay left last night, she'd been alternately crying and furious. She could understand how Shay could be so angry, after all Colleen had lied to her on more than one occasion. But she was angry that Shay also couldn't seem to understand the position Colleen was in.

She tried calling, but the phone just rang and rang and after a while it didn't even do that anymore. All day, Colleen had tried to figure out how in the world she was going to fix this if Shay wouldn't even speak to her, and she came up with nothing. Now, there were much more pressing matters that needed her attention and all Colleen could think about was whether or not she'd be able to salvage this after everything had settled down.

Inside, the theater was buzzing with activity, as musicians set up for the band and catering staff carried cases of wine, food, and glasses to the bar. She narrowly avoided colliding with a man carefully balancing two bottles of champagne on a box of glass ware, then managed to collide with one of the sound men carrying a speaker toward the stage.

It was two hours before the doors would open and the theater buzzed with opening night energy, though it hadn't seen one of those in decades. Colleen felt her own butterflies, like dive bombing crows in her gut, and took a deep breath as she searched for Tina in the chaos.

When she finally spotted her, Tina looked like a bona fide queen in her sequined gown, hair swept up in a simple knot with diamond pins holding it in place. She said something to a delivery man and then scanned the room until her eyes fell on Colleen, who waved at her. Tina's smile was tense, nervous and Colleen's own nerves ramped up their activity in response. Next to Tina, Rick glowered at everyone, the rather relaxed demeanor he'd had the past week gone. That was when she noticed Rick's fingers tapping the back of his hand, which were clasped in front of him.

Rick is nervous...I don't think I've ever seen him truly nervous.

It was not a pleasant revelation to say the least.

"I'm here, now what?" Colleen said, unable to hide the grumpiness from her voice.

"Let's go upstairs to my office," Tina replied, her hand on Colleen's elbow. "I have something to show you that I think you'll like."

Rick followed them up the stairs but stayed just outside the door after Tina whispered something in his ear.

"Why did you insist on me coming so early? I could've gotten ready at my apartment," Colleen said, throwing the garment bag onto the office desk.

"Well, it just so happens that the new suit is finally ready, and I thought you might want to take a look, maybe wear it under your dress for when things get…interesting."

Colleen thought it was a waste to show her a new suit that she really wouldn't be able to wear after tonight, but swallowed the comment when she saw the excited gleam in her mother's eyes.

"I'll admit, I wasn't exactly sure how that was all going to play out, but wearing it under my dress? It's pretty short."

Tina gestured to another garment bag hanging from a hook by the closet.

"See for yourself."

Colleen unzipped the bag and let out a laugh of surprise as she took the suit in. It was the same color as her previous suit, except this one had a halter top and a matching skirt that Colleen suspected would hit her just above the knee.

"You expect me to fight in this? You do realize my legs will get scratched to hell, not to mention everyone seeing my underwear every time I bend over."

Tina's mouth twisted into a grin and she pulled the skirt up to reveal a pair of matching briefs.

"And you also have elbow length fingerless gloves if you would like to add that. The only thing I couldn't figure out were shoes but you can do that. There's also a duplicate of your original version made out of the same material as this one, which is lighter and breathes better. Or at least that's what your friend Marco told me."

Colleen spun around, heart jumping into her throat. "You spoke to Marco?"

"Yes. He told me to tell you to call more and that there's always a place for you in Jet City. I'll leave you to get ready."

There was a touch of bitterness in her mother's voice and Colleen understood why. She wanted Colleen to stay and make a life for herself here. And, if Colleen were being honest, she wanted that, too.

If everything goes well tonight, I might be able to do that. She smiled as she changed into the suit, in spite of the fact that counting on victory before anything had started was a fool's game.

When she slipped the red halter dress over her head, Colleen was surprised to find that the sequined collar of the dress hid that part of her suit perfectly and the skirt of her dress hung a few inches longer than the suit. It would be hard to make sure her dress didn't shift too much as she moved and reveal the skirt of her suit, but it was better than having to run away and change when the fighting started.

Colleen applied her makeup with extra care and fluffed her natural hair with a pick. When she was satisfied with the look she forced herself to smile, the face she would have to wear for the night's…festivities.

"We're almost ready to open the doors," Tina said, walking back inside the office. "The press is clogging up the entrance but a few of Metro City's finest are there keeping them away."

"Not too many though, correct? You waived off the additional security, right?"

"As we discussed, yes. I don't want a lot of collateral damage here tonight either."

The two women stared down at the floor, each suddenly lost in their worries for the night.

"You think he'll show?" Colleen asked after a moment.

"It's been unusually quiet where Von is concerned these last few days," Tina replied, voice tinged with a heaviness. "I think he's planning on making this a spectacle of victory. And I think your brother will be at the center of that."

"What's wrong?" Colleen asked.

"I wasn't going to tell you this but...I really am trying, Colleen. Trying to be better, to be what you both deserve, even if it's too late."

"It's not."

Tina gave her a weary smile.

"Thank you. I'm not sure I believe you but...thank you, nonetheless."

Colleen swallowed down the nerves that had formed a ball in the back of her throat and took a deep breath.

"What do you need to tell me?"

Tina reached into her silver clutch and pulled out a syringe filled with bright green solution. The solution that would take away the abilities of a powered person and leave them sick and weak.

Colleen stepped back as fear twisted in her gut.

"Wh-what are you doing with that?" she asked.

"I brought it here tonight because you said you weren't sure that Andrew would come willingly, even though he wanted out."

Understanding slammed into Colleen's mind and she felt sick.

"So you were going to inject him with that to take him down?"

"Yes."

"No, I won't let you do that to him."

"I don't want to. But if we have no other choice—"

"No! You have no idea what it's like when that poison gets in your blood. It's...It's torture."

"Colleen listen to me," her mother's voice hardened. "We are putting every single person out there at risk. Every one of them could die if this goes badly and you two come to blows. Even if you don't but the few cops that are here get involved, it could get out of hand too quickly for us to do anything. If this is as bad as you say, then Andrew will appear to be dead or dying. Then, you set fire to the theater, and the escape is assured."

Colleen shook her head, trying to ignore the sense her mother was making.

"We don't have time for this, listen to me!" Tina grabbed Colleen's arm and forced her to look Tina in the eyes. "If your brother refuses to come along, if he decides to continue to play his part, I will do it and it's going to be up to you to get him out of here. When you get him, you find Rick, do you understand? Rick knows what to do. The three of you leave, don't look back, don't stop. Just run."

At first, Colleen didn't understand what Tina was telling her. But then it sunk in and Colleen's eyes burned with tears.

"No," she shook her head, "no Momma, you can't—"

"I'm who they're here for," she said, tears shining in her own eyes. "I can get close to him because of that. It's…it's the right thing, baby."

Colleen threw her arms around her mother and held onto her as if she could stop everything from happening. Sobs shook her body as she mumbled "No" over and over again.

"Now, now," Tina said, pulling away and patting Colleen's face with a hankie. "Stop all this fuss. You're ruining your face and it's not going to change anything, is it?"

Colleen captured her mother's hand and squeezed it, but her mother slipped out of her grasp and squared her shoulders.

"It's time. Are you ready?"

No, I'm not ready! I'm not...not ready.

It felt like someone was pressing down on her shoulders, and Colleen's knees buckled. She grabbed onto a nearby chair to steady herself then looked into her mother's eyes. Tina was steely, back straight, gaze never wavering. If she could face tonight with such courage, then surely Colleen could, too?

The vigilante took several deep breaths, clenched her jaw and walked out the door.

CHAPTER
THIRTY-ONE

S hay's eyes took in every person from where she stood at the bar situated in the palatial lobby of the Torch and Grier. She was nursing the champagne she'd ordered, and tried to relax a little. She'd expected to run into Colleen right at the beginning, but so far she hadn't seen a sign of her.

The guests in attendance were a glittering procession of starlets and the old money crowd. Some seemed genuinely happy to see the historic building restored to its former glory. Others were unable to conceal the fact that they only there to be seen and discredit Tina Knight's hard work, even with their false smiles.

Shay glanced over her shoulder and saw Tina smiling with three members of the Metro City elite, their thinly veiled looks of judgment made Shay wonder how in the world the woman put up with them. She scanned the faces of the waiters making their way with careful steps around the growing crowd of people and felt her stomach flip. The Bulwark hadn't really counted on so many people being fashionably late, so Shay had been in the theater for well over thirty minutes by now. Each minute past her allotted time was one more chance to see Colleen, something that Shay desperately needed to do.

She reached into her handbag and felt the cool metal of the gun Ward had given her.

I'll dose Colleen, get her into a bathroom stall then let the agents in and circle back to get her and leave. I doubt any of them will miss me when everything goes down.

The flash bulb of a nearby camera went off and Shay flinched at the bright light. When her vision cleared, she could see a group of local celebrities posing for pictures and decided to move away from the spectacle.

She hadn't gone five steps when she nearly collided with a gorgeous, tall woman in a fiery red dress.

Colleen's lips parted as her wide eyes latched onto Shay's

"What are you doing here?" Colleen asked, her voice horrified.

Shay had rehearsed what she would say, the right words to use to ensure that Colleen wouldn't think too long or hard about the fact that, if Shay was truly furious, there's no way she would set foot in this theater tonight. But, now that she was face to face with Colleen, the words stuck in the back of her throat.

I'm about to manipulate and lie to her, just like she's done to me this whole time. Except, I'm going to drug her.

The gun felt heavy in her handbag as Colleen began to look around frantically.

"C'mon," she said, taking hold of Shay's elbow and moving her toward the ladies' room.

Wait…it couldn't be this easy, could it?

"Where are we going?" Shay asked.

"I need you to leave."

That's when Shay noticed that a small side door was on the way to the ladies' room and they were headed straight for it.

Oh no, no, no! This is going to ruin everything. I've got to get this out quick and get her sedated.

As they walked, Shay reached inside her purse and wrapped her hand around the gun. Just before they reached the door, Shay stopped walking.

"I'm not leaving yet."

"Shay, I don't know why you're here, but you have to leave!"

"Why, because we had a fight and suddenly I'm not welcome here?"

"No, because…" Colleen swore under her breath. "Because all hell is going to break loose here tonight and I don't want you anywhere near it."

Now it was Shay's turn to stare in shock and confusion.

How does she know that? Did I let it slip? Does she have another contact?

Colleen must have mistook Shay's gaping to mean that she was hurt because she sighed and put her warm hands on Shay's upper arms, face softening.

"Look, I'm sorry I'm being gruff. I…I'm actually happy to see you, but your timing really stinks."

"And why is that?"

Instead of Colleen answering, screams echoed from the other side of the lobby, snapping Shay's mind into focus.

Shit, did they decide to breach?

"Oh, no! Shit, no," Colleen said. "Shay, that's…I'll explain everything, but trust me when I say you have to go."

The air took on an unnatural chill and that's when Shay knew exactly who was here and why Colleen wanted her to leave.

Her face hardened as she turned toward Colleen and drew the gun from her purse.

"Shay, what the—"

"He's not going to get away this time."

And she fired.

Colleen braced for the bullet from Shay's gun, but it never came. Instead, a knife hit the dart filled with green solution, which burst against the wall next to her.

Shay was going to dose me with…

She wanted to ask why, to demand to know if Shay hated her that much, but there was no time. From the direction the knife had come, a woman was walking through the fray of goons attacking theater guests, a metal mask on her face.

"You need to go," Shay said.

"No."

"The Bulwark is going bust in, they've been waiting! You have to go!"

Colleen realized why Shay might have wanted to dose her then, but she couldn't take too much time with it. The woman with the metal face was advancing, her floating knives slicing into anyone that got in her way.

"Shoot another dart at her," Colleen said.

"It only had one."

"Damn it. Okay, last time I saw Tina she was in the theater, she has another syringe of the stuff. I'll hold her off until you come back with it."

"You trust me with it after—?"

"Not really but short of deep frying her I don't have a better plan!"

Shay nodded and took off toward the theater entrance. Colleen indulged in last look, hoping she makes it out of this alive. With one tiny spark, she set fire to her beautiful evening dress and slapped her mask on. The sudden change, though small, caused something to click in Colleen's brain and she no longer felt afraid or unsure.

She was Fahrenheit, she was powerful and she was about to kick this metal lady's ass.

Just as the woman got within range of Colleen's fireballs, loud, masculine shouts punctuated the screams of civilians. In a few minutes, the lobby would likely be overrun with Bulwark agents.

Better make this quick

Colleen shot two quick blasts of fire at the woman's feet, intending to singe her shoes and pants. But she moved with cat like reflexes, coming up on one knee and flung her hands out. Six knives flew at Colleen, who raised up a fiery shield just in time to soften the metal of the blades. They were no longer sharp, but they were traveling fast enough to hurt when they hit her chest.

Colleen gasped and bolted toward the metal woman, lobbing fireballs as fast as she could make them. The woman spun and dodged faster than Colleen had ever seen, the glint of projectiles streaming toward Colleen in her wake. She shifted her focus to intercept the knives and succeeded with all but one, which lodged itself in her upper arm.

She hissed and went to pull it free when the knife moved, digging itself deeper into her flesh. The pain exploded behind her eyes, driving her down to her knees.

"Pressure points," said the metal woman, stalking toward her. "So few people bother to learn them."

The knife pressed again and Colleen's mouth gaped in a silent, agonizing scream.

Other knives rose up in at the powered woman's command, all pointed at Colleen like a small army of very large silver hornets.

"I was told to bring you in alive, and you will be. But before then, I think it might be fun to see you bleed."

Another knife zoomed into her forearm and she screamed at the pain.

"Bulwark," she hissed at the woman. "They're...coming."

"Oh, I know," she said, her voice soft. "Don't you worry. I won't let them get you."

The knife in her forearm pressed and Colleen fell forward, holding herself up with the one arm that wasn't in excruciating pain.

The metal woman bent down close to Colleen's ear, the cool surface of her mask brushing against her cheek.

"I'm going to enjoy doing this to your brother later tonight, but I thought I'd practice a little on you first."

The words reached Colleen in the haze of agony she was in, strengthening her resolve so that she could think for the second it took to access her powers.

Everything turned bright, power coursing through her veins like molten earth and Colleen felt everything snap into focus. Just as knife in her forearm was about to dig in deeper into her body, Colleen flashed a burst of heat right at the mask covering the woman's face. She screeched, clutching at the metal, which had suddenly become misshapen, as if molding itself to her skin. Her cries were sharp and unearthly as she stumbled back, knives falling to the carpeted floor.

Colleen pulled the blades free, gasping at the last burst of pain. The metal bent in her grip and she dropped it to the floor as the woman used her powers to bend the metal mask off her face. When it peeled back, her skin was red and blistered, eyes full of murder settling on Colleen.

The sounds of gunfire, followed by a rush of cold air came from the far side of the lobby and Colleen knew that Andrew was fighting someone.

It's probably The Bulwark, I have to get to him now!

Colleen was about to turn to leave, when the woman raised her arms, spittle flying from her mouth as she used her powers on…

A groan sounded from above and Colleen looked up to see the huge crystal chandelier begin to shake as an invisible hand pulled it down from the frescoed ceiling.

The vigilante leapt out of the way just as the thing crashed to the floor, shards of glass falling over her, cutting her skin. There was no time to waste on pain, however. She could hear the metal start to shift behind her and knew that she had to get distance between herself and this woman. Colleen took off at a run toward the theater just as shouts and gunshots echoed behind her.

"Federal agents, put the chandelier—"

The words were cut off by the high pitched screams of the agents.

There was no time for Colleen to slow down and see what the woman did or if any of the agents survived it. She had to put up a barrier between her family and the others so they could get to safety.

I'm not supposed to set the fire the place until we're all together but we're just going to have to deal with it.

Pushing aside all the warning bells going off in her mind, Colleen raised up a wall of fire that stretched from floor to ceiling and from wall to wall. A sudden light headed sensation caused her to stumble against the wall and the fire almost got away from her but she took back control just in time. The blood loss combined with using her powers was starting to wear on her, but there wasn't time for passing out.

Push through it! Only a few more minutes and you'll be able to rest…

She'd never tied off something this big, but she had to buy everyone time. Gritting her teeth and ignoring the throbbing pain in her arm, Colleen barely managed to tie the wall of fire off and step way. They had very little time to get out of the theater before it broke free from the barriers she'd set around it. Hopefully, it would enough.

CHAPTER THIRTY-TWO

A ndrew knew that the only way to make sure every-one lived through this night was to get to Tina and Colleen as soon as possible. But the moment they burst into the theater, Metal Maiden had begun causing chaos, her blades slicing through patrons and staff alike. Within minutes, the red carpet was darker from the pools of blood left in her wake.

I hope to god Colleen can handle her while I get Tina out of here.

People were already fleeing the theater when he stalked through the doorway and down the center aisle.

"Out, all of you! This is between you and me!" he said, spying Tina up on the stage.

What is she doing there? Does she want to die?

His mother's bodyguard went to draw a gun from inside his jacket and Tina stopped him.

"What's wrong mother, afraid to fight me?" he sneered, hoping that if any of Mr. Price's men were aware of this exchange, it looked good.

"Enough of this, Andrew," Tina said when he'd gotten to the foot of the stage. "You don't want to hurt me, or anyone here. I know that, so you can stop pretending."

His stomach dropped even as he kept the grin on his face.

Colleen didn't tell him exactly how this was all supposed to work out. She'd only said that, when he arrived, go find Tina. There would be a fake fight and to make it look good, she'd set the theater on fire and then they'd sneak out. But was the fight supposed to be with Tina or Colleen?

Damn it, you couldn't have been a little more specific?

Three men in tuxedos brandishing large rifles burst into the theater and fired at him without saying a word. Andrew threw up an ice shield, the darts pinging against it and falling to the ground. He took a step back and swore under his breath. Andrew knew exactly who he was dealing with now.

"Rick, help him!" Tina said.

As Andrew encased one of the men in ice, Rick fired on another, getting him center mast. The man stumbled but didn't fall.

"They have protective gear on!" Andrew yelled, and wrapped a thick helmet of ice around the man's head, cutting off his oxygen.

While he clawed at the ice suffocating him, his one upright partner fired at Andrew in quick succession. One dart came close enough to graze Andrew's suit jacket, while the other lodged itself in the back of a nearby chair. Rick shot the agent in the knees and the man fell to the floor, keening in agony.

"Shut it you, goon!" Andrew yelled, throwing a coffin of ice around him.

The man with the ice around his face fell to the ground with a thud and Andrew ignored him. If they were going to come for him, they deserved everything they got.

Tina stared at Andrew as if she'd never seen him before, fear sharp in her gaze.

He chuckled genuinely at the expression and walked up onto the stage.

"What's the matter, do I shock you?"

"Yes," she answered.

"Because I killed them?"

"Because…I think you might actually like it."

Andrew's smile fell at those words and he glared at her.

"Of course I don't like it! What kind of monster do you think I am? Just because I'm not the gentle, weak sucker I was when Grandfather was in control, doesn't mean I became a killer."

"What *have* you become?"

Gunfire echoed from the lobby and they could hear yelling.

"You really want to have this conversation now?" he asked her.

She shook her head and stepped toward him.

"No, I guess not."

He saw the syringe out of the corner of his eye and jumped back. His hands shot out, instinct taking over as he froze her in place from her feet to the middle of her chest. Rick leveled his weapon at him and Andrew flung a heavy layer of frost onto the man, causing him to fall over, shivering.

Andrew's hands curled into fists, his entire body going rigid as Tina's betrayal sunk into him like a hot blade.

"How could you?" he screamed. "Do you have any idea what you almost did to me?"

"Andrew, I w-was trying t-to—"

"No! You can't be trusted, can you mother?!"

"Andrew…please!"

Another gun went off inside the theater. This time, it was a bullet that nearly hit Andrew, lodging itself in the wood of the stage inches from his feet. He created two knives of pure ice and looked out into the theater, expecting more agents or possibly police. Instead, he saw a lone woman, in a stylish green dress, pointing a police revolver right at him.

Shay didn't want to leave Colleen alone with the powered maniac. And she most certainly didn't want to go looking for Tina Knight, who she was now sure had been in on everything going on in High Tide the past few months.

But the logic of it was too sound. Shay was outmatched and Colleen wasn't.

She took off toward where Colleen had indicated, eyes alert for the slightest hint of trouble. When gooseflesh rose up on her arm from a sudden cold wind, she stopped in her tracks, heart pounding.

The ice vigilante, the one that had murdered her partner, was nearby. She drew the police issued gun out of her hand bag, grateful that she had thought to bring it, and tried to navigate her way through the panicked crowd. As best she could, Shay looked for anyone with the telltale sheen of ice on their skin when she came upon one of the doorways leading to the theater itself.

She peered inside and felt another chill run down her body as a tall black man shot ice at three Bulwark agents. The sight of all that power so easily thrown around caused a jolt of fear to root Shay to the spot.

Those men are trained to take down someone like him and he's acting like it's just another day at the office.

Shay wondered if she should try to approach this from a different angle when Colleen's brother suddenly turned his powers on Tina, half encasing her in ice.

Something shifted for her then as she looked at the terror written all over Tina Knight's face. Was Walter afraid like that when this man had killed him? Did he have a chance to beg for mercy?

Shay's body grew hot, her focus narrowing until she was only aware of the powered man who had mercilessly killed her partner. Vengeance whispered in her ear and Shay shut out all other thoughts that might temper it, running to the stage, gun at the ready. Without a second thought, Shay fired at the man, and missed.

"No!" Tina shouted.

Shay fired and missed again.

Damn it! Concentrate, Reynolds!

"He-he's my son!"

Before she could fire again, the man shot a stream of ice toward her. Shay dove to the side to avoid it. Coming up on her knees, and fired again, this time hitting his leg. He cried out and clutched the wound.

"No…p-please don't!" Tina pleaded.

Shay walked up the stairs to the stage, careful to not lose her footing on the slick surface. Sub Zero glared at her with eyes a startling blue white in appearance.

"You killed my partner," she said, leveling her gun at him. "You put ice through his chest, why?"

He swallowed and had the good grace to look at least a little guilty.

"I had to…to protect my sister."

That gave her pause and Shay hated herself for it.

"Walter would never have—"

"Not Walter, Mr. Price, the real person behind the name Von. He and someone in your precinct ordered it. If I didn't kill him, they would've killed Colleen. I would guess that you know why by now."

"There's nothing you could say that would excuse what you did!"

"I know."

"Andrew," Tina said, her voice weak, "please let me go."

Andrew plucked the syringe from her hand and threw it on the ground, breaking it. Only then did the ice recede from Tina's body and she slumped to the ground, shivering.

"Tina," said a man stumbling onto the stage, his skin coated in frost.

Tina and the man embraced behind Andrew, who had never taken his eyes off of Shay.

"Well?" he asked. "Are you going to do it? I certainly deserve it."

Shay raised her gun, hands shaking. She'd imagined this moment every day since Walter died. Imagined how satisfying it would be to catch this man and make him pay.

Her finger tightened on the trigger, but she didn't squeeze it. Something held her back and she began to cry from the fury of it all.

"C'mon officer, isn't this what you wanted? To kill the monster who shoved a spear of ice right through Walter's heart?"

"N-no, please don't!" Tina said, trying to crawl toward them. "It's me you want. This is a-all my fault."

The man with her tried to hold her back but she got out of his grasp and crawled in front of Andrew. Slowly, she was able to get to her feet, though she was shivering horribly. Shay no longer had a clean shot of Andrew, but she held her gun at the ready just the same.

"Out of the way, Tina!" he said, shoving her aside. "This is right, I deserve this."

"No, you don't."

Again the woman was in front of him, the stubborn set to her jaw very familiar to Shay, who still held the gun up, unable to lower it.

"Shay, stop!" said a painfully familiar voice.

Colleen careened through the theater, the ice in front of the stage melting in her wake. As she ran, steam rose with each step.

"You don't want to do this," Colleen said, putting her hand on Shay's. "You're better than all of us, this isn't the way."

"You don't get to tell me anything! You lied to me about who you were, and I trusted you!"

Tears glistened in Colleen's eyes.

"I know, and we can talk about it all later but right now, we have to get out of here. The Bulwark is here and my fire wall will only hold for another minute or so before it starts consuming this place. We have to go now."

"Leaving so soon?" said a raspy voice from the theater.

Shay's eyes swung to the woman clad all in black, her face a terrible red mass of burns.

"Maiden," Andrew said, eyes wide.

"The party is just getting started."

Behind her four men in riot gear ran in and fired at Andrew on the stage. He raised up an ice shield and stopped huge darts filled with green solution.

"How the hell did they get past my fire?" Colleen said.

"Does it matter? We have to get out of here," Andrew answered.

The agents raised their guns to fire again, but Maiden flicked her fingers and the men were impaled with dozens of knives and metal pieces from the chandelier, which Maiden had apparently brought with her into the theater.

"Now, where were we?"

Tina turned to Shay and said, "Get them out of here, now!"

Then she moved faster than someone who was half frozen should've been able to and stood in front of the ice barrier before anyone could stop her.

"I'm the one you want," she said, in a clear, firm voice. "You can take me, and let them go."

Maiden's face split into a terrible grin as more agents began running into the theater.

"Since you insist."

"No!" Andrew screamed and threw up a thick wall of ice.

The knives lodged deep inside of them, but they wouldn't stay there for long. But before the villain could pull them free, Andrew gave another yell and three spears of ice erupted from the floor, shooting up through Maiden's body. Her eyes widened in shock, mouth gaping open and shut like a fish on a hook. The knives hovered for another second then clattered to the stage as she slumped against the implements of her destruction.

The building was starting to groan from the destruction of the fire. Shay knew that time was not on their side but what were they to do? Go outside and have Ward arrest Colleen and her brother? Or stay here and die?

"The fire is spreading, I can smell the smoke," the man behind Andrew said. "We have to leave now."

"If you run, you'll never be able to come back," Shay said, pressure building in her chest as the full extent of that statement hit her. "And even if you don't, I know The Bulwark will hunt you down. You...you can't..."

Tina gave her a sad smile.

"Two bodies will be found in the flames, and everyone will think they're dead. This will be closed soon, if the truth isn't revealed. Though, I must admit my perfect plan isn't quite so air tight anymore."

Shay started coughing, and Colleen's worried eyes darted around at the increasingly smoky room.

"We don't have time for this. We need to leave."

"How?" Shay asked.

"We have a way. What about you?"

"I'll run interference, try to buy you some time," she answered with a cough.

"We gotta go now!" Andrew yelled.

Colleen's gaze was tortured, unsure as she looked between her family and Shay. Maybe it was the emotion of the night. Maybe it was realizing that absolutely nothing in this life was black or white but instead beautiful, complex shades of gray. But whatever the reason, Shay grabbed Colleen by the back of the neck and pulled her down for a hard kiss, trying to say everything she didn't have time for.

When she pulled away, Colleen gave her a little grin and Shay knew it would have to e enough.

"I'll find you," Colleen promised.'

"You better."

Smoke started to pour into the theater in dark, rolling clouds. Soon, it would be hard to breath, and if the flames didn't get them, then The Bulwark would. Shay's eyes hungrily memorized Colleen's face, her hands tracing her lips before turning to Andrew.

"You have to make it look like I fought you," she said to him.

"If I knock you out—"

"Through the shoulder, right here, and a punch across the face should do it."

Shay thought he'd hesitate, try to talk her out of it. Instead, without another word, Andrew drew back and landed a solid blow to her cheek followed by a brutal stab to her shoulder. She staggered and fell onto one knee, shocked by the sudden rush of pain even though she was expecting it.

Colleen helped her up and Shay pushed her away. "Go!"

Through the quickly building smoke, Shay took one last look at Colleen's retreating figure, her heart cracking with the fear that it might be the last time she ever saw the woman she'd come to love. Then she was bolting for the fire exit, tears coursing down her quickly bruising cheek.

CHAPTER THIRTY-THREE

S hay was putting the finishing touches on her final report about the 'Incident' as it was becoming known.

A full blown man hunt had taken place in the weeks following the fire at that destroyed the Torch and Grier. Ward was unconvinced that the two bodies found were the vigilantes Fahrenheit and Sub Zero. But after two months of draining the city's and Bulwark's resources on an operation that yielded less than nothing, Ward was finally removed not only from Metro City, but the Bulwark too.

Shay grinned at the memory of his furious yells, the way the vein in his forehead had throbbed like it was going to burst. To say that no one missed the arrogant bastard was an understatement.

After that, it was just a matter of finding the information that Walter had hidden about Von, or Mr. Price more accurately. It had taken longer than she would've liked to break that snakes hold on High Tide, but this week, they'd done it. Price had taken his own life rather than be brought to trial, but there were a dozen men under him that were currently either doing plea bargains or awaiting sentencing. Though Shay knew that Price had been a small fish compared to the man really pulling the strings, she had been proud to bring the son of a bitch to justice. It had broken 'Von's' hold on the criminal enterprises in High Tide, and it had made Walters sacrifice seem less empty. Shay knew the real work was just beginning. There was still the matter of bringing down the one that had set Mr. Price up in power in the first place, but this was a step toward that and she'd take the victory.

"Got plans tonight?" Fisk asked, leaning on her desk.

Shay shrugged. It had taken her a little while to trust Fisk completely as a partner, but it had turned out that while he was a bit of a flirt, Fisk was also a good detective and an excellent partner. She felt like his equal, even if sometimes he still reverted to the sexual politics that dictated that she might need protecting.

Of course it helps that I saved his ass more than once in the last few months.

"I'm pretty tired. Was thinking of ice cream and a bath."

"Oh c'mon! This is huge! We just closed one of the biggest cases in the precincts history. We have to celebrate."

"Not tonight," Shay said with a laugh. "Tomorrow, I promise. Drinks and steaks."

"Why detective, is this a date?" he asked with an eyebrow waggle.

Shay snorted.

"You wish."

He shook his head and sauntered off, likely to find someone else to drink with.

Shay grabbed her coat and walked outside to hail a cab. The winter still had the city firmly in it's grasp and the chill cut through her heavy wool coat like a knife.

The thought made her think of Andrew and Colleen, hoping they were safe.

Or Colleen anyway. Still not sure how I feel about her brother.

She hadn't heard a thing from them since the fire. Not a word that they were safe, or that they knew what had happened here. That their sacrifice had meant all the difference in saving High Tide. Shay wished she could hear Colleen's voice, to tell her that she understood the impossible situation she'd been in. That she didn't hold any of her secrets against her.

But Shay was starting to think that maybe she would have to live with hoping Colleen knew all those things. It was likely the fiery beauty had left the country altogether for all she knew. It would have been the smart move, the safe one. And Shay hated to admit that even with all the things that happened, High Tide may not ever be safe for Colleen.

She walked up the stairs to her apartment with heavy feet. They'd won, and the only person she wanted to celebrate with was presumed dead by everyone but her.

In the moment it took to hang up her coat, the hair on Shay's neck stood on end. Something wasn't right. She drew her service revolver and walked slowly out of the entry way and into the apartment. Spinning toward the living room with her gun drawn, Shay froze at the sight before her.

Standing in front of her small fireplace, natural hair fanned out around her head, with tears running down her cheeks was the woman Shay had just been thinking about.

"Hi," Colleen said, her voice breathy, unsure. "I hope you don't mind, I let myself in."

Shay's brain stopped working completely. Everything slowed and faded into the background except the beautiful woman in front of her. It wasn't until Colleen gently pushed the gun down that Shay even realized she was still pointing it at her.

"I should've called," Colleen said, "but I wasn't sure…that is, Tina wasn't sure I should even come back at all. But when I saw the news I couldn't help it. I had to see you."

"Where've you been?" Shay asked, her voice rough.

"All over. Up state, Jet City, though that got complicated fast. Lately, we've been in London laying low. Turns out Tina and Rick had quite the large savings."

Shay nodded and tried to think of what to say. All the times she'd imagined this moment, dreamed of it, cried over it, there had been a hundred different things she thought she'd say to Colleen.

I'm sorry.

I understand.

I love you.

"Stay," was the only one that came out.

And it was the one thing she really hadn't meant to say.

Colleen's eye widened, lips parting and then she looked down, her skin darkening with a flush.

"I'm sorry," Shay said, stepping away from her to try and clear her head. "I don't know…I mean, you might just be passing through. Ignore that."

"Do you really want me to?"

No, Shay really didn't. But she hadn't seen Colleen in six months, and before that they hadn't exactly been in a good place. How could she honestly demand that this woman stay? But that is what she wanted, that and so much more. So, instead of lying about her feelings, and instead of admitting them, she turned toward the small collection of liquor in her kitchen and poured them both a generous whiskey.

Colleen took it with a little uptick of her lips that made Shay want to kiss her so bad that she downed far too much of the amber liquor.

"You alright there?" Colleen asked, her voice playful.

"Shut up," Shay said with a smirk.

They stood there, everything that had been left unsaid sat between them and got heavier by the second. Both of them sipping from the glass, catching each others' eye and then looking away. Until Colleen gave a nervous laugh and shook her head.

"This is ridiculous," she said, setting her glass down on the coffee table. "I've missed you every second and here I am unable to say anything because I'm scared. And really, what have I got to lose?"

Shay stared at Colleen, unused to this woman being the one to take charge of things between them.

"I wanted to call," Colleen continued. "I wanted to write, to send you a carrier pigeon, anything to let you know I was alive and missing you. But I couldn't. It would've endangered the others and I . . . I'm sorry Shay."

Those last three words carried so much meaning in them. So much more than just 'sorry I didn't call'. It was sorry for the mountain of secrets Colleen had kept from Shay, the hurt and the lies. Shay had thought she needed that before, when the pain of Colleen's deception and leaving had still been raw and aching. Now though, things were clearer. Shay could see the ways Colleen had tried to help, the ways in which her hands were tied.

"You don't need to apologize," Shay said, setting her own glass down.

"Yes I do."

"No, you don't. I've had a lot of time to think about all of this, and I see now the tangled web we were both in. I see how it couldn't have ended up any other way."

"I could've told you who I really was."

"And I still would've been angry at you. Still would've demanded your brothers' head for what happened to Walter. You owe me nothing, Colleen. Not an apology, not…not loyalty. Not an explanation."

Colleen swallowed, fidgeted with the end of her turtle-neck and then took a deep breath.

"What if I want to give you loyalty though?"

Shay's heart lurched and then began to beat at a gallop. She knew what Colleen was really saying and hell yes, she wanted it. But…

"It's more complicated than that though, isn't it?"

Colleen nodded.

"Yeah. I can't ask you to leave all of this. And you won't ask me to come back."

"Because you can't."

"Well, I could, but Fahrenheit couldn't."

"Could you really do that though. Give up on using your powers to help people?"

"Well," she got a little grin on her face, "no. But I *can* give up being Fahrenheit."

What Colleen was saying burst on her brain and Shay gasped, eyes wide.

"A new identity."

"Yep. Of course, I'd have to use my powers differently, create a different persona and all that. Then there's also being a bit more careful, less showy if possible."

It hit Shay then and she laughed.

"You already planned to do this, haven't you?"

Colleen bit her bottom lip and Shay nearly groaned at the sight. Damn, how was this woman still so tempting after all these months?

"A friend in Jet City helped me realize that I had options. So yeah, I've been planning this for most of the time we've been gone. But I wanted to let you know that

I was back before I did anything. I didn't want you to be taken by surprise or anything."

Shay's heart sank a little.

So this wasn't to rekindle anything…

"Oh…yeah, that's…that's nice of you thank you."

Shay picked up her glass and focused on the little bit of whiskey left. On the way the carpet needed cleaning. The flames dancing in the fireplace. Anything but on how her heart was lurching from hope to heartbreak and back again. She had no idea what to do, what to say. Was this even the right time? Should she wait, see if they could really be together anymore? Were they too different now?

She was just about to suggest that maybe they should pick this up tomorrow, when Colleen's warm finger tilted Shay's face up. It was the first time they'd touched in six months, and Shay's breath stuttered out of her at the electricity that shot through her at the simple collision.

"I didn't just come back for that," Colleen whispered.

Shay made herself look in Colleen's eyes, needing to know, once and for all what was or wasn't there.

And when she did, a broken sob fell from her lips moments before Colleen's claimed hers. It was a kiss of apology, of relief, of salvation. Shay let the glass fall from her hand and dug her hands into Colleen's hair, pulling her closer, angling her head to take the kiss deeper. How had she been able to breath, to function all this time without the one person who could fill her heart like oxygen filled her lungs? Suddenly, there was color in the world again. There was fire and life coursing through her.

Colleen's hands were tight on Shay's hips and she spun the detective around until her back collided with the wall.

"I've missed you so much," Colleen said, pressing her forehead to Shay's. "I was only half alive without you."

"Me too," Shay's hands ghosted up over Colleen's shoulders, down her arms. "I meant it. I want you to stay. I don't know how it's all going to work out or if we're stupid for jumping back in and I don't care. I love you Colleen, I never stopped. I don't think I ever will."

Colleen's laugh was pure, undiluted joy moments before she crushed her lips to Shay's.

"I was really hoping you'd say that," the fire starter said. "I wasn't sure how I was going to walk out that door."

"And now you don't have to."

Colleen grinned, her fingers grazing Shay's throat.

"Why detective, are you asking me to stay the night?"

"You bet I am. Tonight, and every night after."

"I think I can manage that."

Afterword

Thank you for reading the Heroes of High Tide duology. Originally, it was going to be a trilogy but life had other ideas.

I decided to change the ending of the book to close out Colleen and Shay's story in a satisfying way since I had made the decision not to continue the series. It wasn't easy to walk away from these books, to decide not to finish the trilogy. But it was the right one for me, for my mental health and for my career. I hope you've enjoyed their story and that you have checked out the other Vigilante Universe books from the Rise of Heroes trilogy. If you have and you just gotta have more, you can find my romance novels under the name Trish Heinrich. The first series, Silver City Celestials does take place in this world, but in a modern era. It is paranormal romance, not superhero.